Noonday

ALSO BY PAT BARKER

Union Street
Blow Your House Down
Liza's England (*formerly* The Century's Daughter)
The Man Who Wasn't There

Regeneration
The Eye in the Door
The Ghost Road
(The Regeneration Trilogy)

Another World
Border Crossing
Double Vision
Life Class
Toby's Room

Noonday

 *A NOVEL*

Pat Barker

HAMISH HAMILTON
an imprint of Penguin Canada, a division of Penguin Random House Canada Limited

Penguin Canada, 320 Front Street West, Suite 1400, Toronto, Ontario M5V 3B6, Canada
Penguin Group (USA) LLC, 375 Hudson Street, New York, New York 10014, U.S.A.
Penguin Books Ltd, 80 Strand, London WC2R 0RL, England
Penguin Ireland, 25 St Stephen's Green, Dublin 2, Ireland (a division of Penguin Books Ltd)
Penguin Books Australia, 707 Collins Street, Melbourne, Victoria 3008, Australia
Penguin Books India, 11 Community Centre, Panchsheel Park, New Delhi – 110 017, India
Penguin Books New Zealand, 67 Apollo Drive, Rosedale, Auckland 0632, New Zealand
Penguin Books South Africa, 24 Sturdee Avenue, Rosebank, Johannesburg 2196, South Africa
Penguin Books Ltd, Registered Offices: 80 Strand, London WC2R 0RL, England

Published in Hamish Hamilton paperback by Penguin Canada, 2016
Simultaneously published in the United States by Doubleday, a division of Penguin Random
House LLC, New York
Originally published in hardcover in Great Britain by Hamish Hamilton, an imprint of
Penguin Random House, Ltd., London, in 2015

1 2 3 4 5 6 7 8 9 10 (BVG)

Manufactured in the U.S.A.

Book design by Maria Carella
Cover design by John Fontana
Cover photograph: Second great fire raid in London, Dec. 29, 1940, by Herbert Mason ©
Galerie Bilderwelt / Bridgeman Images

LIBRARY AND ARCHIVES CANADA CATALOGUING IN PUBLICATION
Barker, Pat, 1943-, author
Noonday / Pat Barker.

ISBN 978-0-14-319822-2 (paperback)

1. London (England)--History--Bombardment, 1940-1941--
Fiction. I. Title.

PR6052.A6495N66 2016   823'.914   C2015-906635-2

eBook ISBN 978-0-14-319823-9

www.penguinrandomhouse.ca

FOR FINN, NIAMH, GABE AND JESSIE

Noonday

※ *ONE*

Elinor was halfway up the drive when she sensed she was being watched. She stopped and scanned the upstairs windows—wide open in the heat as if the house were gasping for breath—but there was nobody looking down. Then, from the sycamore tree at the end of the garden, came a rustling of leaves. Oh, of course: *Kenny.* She was tempted to ignore him, but that seemed unkind, so she went across the lawn and peered up into the branches.

"Kenny?"

No reply. There was often no reply.

Kenny had arrived almost a year ago now, among the first batch of evacuees, and, although this area had since been reclassified—"neutral" rather than "safe"—here he remained. She felt his gaze heavy on the top of her head, like a hand, as she stood squinting up into the late-afternoon sunlight.

Kenny spent hours up there, not reading his comics, not building a tree house, not dropping conkers on people's heads—no, just watching. He had a red notebook in which he wrote down car numbers, the time people arrived, the time they left . . . Of course, you forgot what it was like to be his age: probably every visitor was a German spy. Oh, and he ate himself, that was the other thing. He was forever nibbling his fingernails, tearing at his cuticles, picking scabs off his knees and licking up the blood. Even pulling hair out of his head and sucking it. And, despite being a year at the village school, he hadn't made friends. But then, he was the sort of child who attracts bullying, she thought, guiltily conscious of her own failure to like him.

"Kenny? Isn't it time for tea?"

Then, with a great crash of leaves and branches, he dropped at her feet and stood looking up at her, scowling, for all the world like a small, sour, angry crab apple. "Where's Paul?"

"I'm afraid he couldn't come, he's busy."

"He's always busy."

"Well, yes, he's got a lot to do. Are you coming in now?"

Evidently that didn't deserve a reply. He turned his back on her and ran off through the arch into the kitchen garden.

TWO

Closing the front door quietly behind her, Elinor took a moment to absorb the silence.

Facing her, directly opposite the front door, where nobody could possibly miss it, was a portrait of her brother, Toby, in uniform. It had been painted, from photographs, several years after his death and was frankly not very good. Everybody else seemed to like it, or at least tolerate it, but Elinor thought it was a complete travesty. *Item: one standard-issue gallant young officer, Grim Reaper for the use of.* There was nothing of Toby there at all. Nigel Featherstone was the artist: and he was very well regarded; you saw his portraits of judges, masters of colleges, politicians and generals everywhere, but she'd never liked his work. Her own portrait of Toby was stronger—not good, she didn't claim that—but certainly better than this.

She resented not having been asked to paint this family portrait: his own sister, after all. And every visit to her sister's house began with her standing in front of it. When he was alive, Toby's presence had been the only thing that made weekends with the rest of her family bearable. Now, this portrait—that blank, lifeless face—was a reminder that she was going to have to face them alone.

She caught the creak of a leather armchair from the open

door on her left. *Oh, well, better get it over with.* She went into the room and found Tim, her brother-in-law, sitting by the open window. As soon as he saw her he stood up and let his newspaper slide, sighing, to the floor.

"Elinor." He pecked her proffered cheek. "Too early for a whisky?" Evidently it wasn't: there was a half-empty glass by his side. She opened her mouth to refuse but he'd already started to pour. "How was the train?"

"Crowded. Late."

"Aren't they all?"

When she'd first met Tim he might've been a neutered tomcat for all the interest he aroused in her. She'd thought him a nonentity, perhaps influenced in that—as in so much else—by Toby, who hadn't liked Tim, or perhaps hadn't found much in him to either like or dislike. And yet Tim had gone on to be a successful man; powerful, even. Something in Whitehall, in the War Office. Which was strange, because he'd never actually seen active service. It had never been clear to her what precisely Tim did, though when she expressed her bewilderment to Paul he'd laughed and said: "Do you really not know?"

She took a sip of whisky. "I saw some soldiers in the lane."

"Yes, they're building gun emplacements on the river."

"Just over there?"

He shrugged. "It's the obvious place."

How easily they'd all come to accept it: searchlights over the church at night, blacked-out houses, the never-ending *pop-pop* of guns on the marshes . . . Such an inconsequential sound: almost like a child's toy. The whisky was starting to fizz along her veins. Perhaps it hadn't been such a bad idea after all. "Where's Rachel?"

"Upstairs with your mother. Who's asleep, I think."

"I don't suppose Mrs. Murchison's around?"

"Why, do you particularly want to speak to her?"

"More thinking of avoiding her, actually."

He looked at his watch. "She generally takes a break about now. I expect she's in her room."

But she wasn't. She was crossing the hall with a firm, flatfooted step, her shoes making minuscule squeaks on the tiles. "Ah, Miss Brooke, I thought it must be you."

Always that barely perceptible emphasis on the "Miss." To be fair, she had some reason to be confused. Elinor and Paul had lived together for almost six years before they finally married, very quietly, in Madrid. None of Elinor's family had been invited to the wedding and she'd continued to use her own name professionally—and also, to some extent, socially—ever since. Clearly, Mrs. Murchison suspected she was not, in any proper sense, married at all.

"Will you be wanting tea?"

"I'll see what my sister says."

Elinor picked up her case and carried it upstairs to the spare room. This should have been Mrs. Murchison's job, but really the less she had to do with that woman the better. Queuing in the post office once, she'd heard Mrs. Murchison whisper to the woman beside her: "She's a Miss, you know." Elinor knew exactly what she meant. *Miss*-take. *Miss*ed out. Even, perhaps, *miss*-carriage? No, she was being paranoid: Mrs. Murchison couldn't possibly have known about that. Of course there'd always be people like her, people who regarded childless women as hardly women at all. "Fibroids"—Mr. O'Brien had announced a few years ago when Elinor's periods had gone haywire—"are the tears of a disappointed womb." Obnoxious little Irish leprechaun, twinkling at her over his steepled fingertips. She'd just gaped at him and then, unable to control herself, burst out laughing.

In the spare room she dumped her suitcase on the bed;

she'd unpack later. Quickly, she splashed her face and hands, examined herself in the glass, noting pallor, noting tiredness, but not minding too much, not today at any rate. Through the open window she heard Mrs. Murchison calling Kenny in to get washed in time for dinner.

Kenny had a lot to do with Elinor's dislike of Mrs. Murchison. Given the task of dealing with his nits, she'd simply shaved his head, without apparently finding it necessary to consult anybody else first. Elinor had gone into the kitchen the morning after he arrived and found him standing there, orange hair lying in coils around his feet. Thin, hollow-eyed, the strange, white, subtle egg shape of his head—he'd looked like a child in the ruins of Guernica or Wieluń. She'd completely lost her temper; she was angrier than she'd been for years. Rachel came running, then Mother, who was still, only a year ago, well enough to come downstairs. "Elinor." Mother laid a cool hand on her arm. "This isn't your house. And that isn't your child." Which was, undeniably, true. Not her house, not her child, not her responsibility.

Outside, in the garden, Mrs. Murchison was still calling: "Kenny? Kenny?"

Well, she could call till she was blue in the face; he wouldn't come in for her.

A murmur of voices drifted across the landing from her mother's room: so she must be awake. It couldn't be put off any longer, though even now Elinor stood outside the door for a full minute, taking slow, deliberate, deep breaths, before she pushed it open and went in.

A fug of illness rose to meet her: aging flesh in hot sheets, camphor poultices that did no good at all, a smell of feces and disinfectant from the commode in the far corner. Rachel was sitting on the other side of the bed, her back to the window, her face in shadow. Mother's nightdress was open at the front:

you could see her collarbone jutting out and the hollows in her throat. Her chest moved, not merely with every breath, but with every heartbeat. Looking at her, Elinor could almost believe she saw the dark, struggling muscle laboring away inside its cage of bone. Mother's eyes were closed, but as Elinor approached the bed, the lids flickered open, though not completely. They stopped halfway, as if already weighted down by pennies. "Oh, Elinor." Her voice was slurred. "It's you."

Wrong person. "Hello, Mother." She bent and kissed the hollow cheek.

She was about to sit down, but then she saw Rachel mouthing at her. "Outside."

Elinor slipped quietly out onto the landing and a few seconds later Rachel joined her. The sisters kissed, Rachel's dry lips barely making contact with Elinor's cheek. They'd never been close. Toby, the middle child, had come between them in every sense. Looking back on her early childhood, Elinor realized that even then she and Rachel had been rivals for Toby; and Elinor had won. An empty victory, it seemed, so many years after his death.

"Has the doctor been?" she asked.

"This morning, yes. He comes every morning."

"What does he say?"

"You mean how long has she got? No, of course he didn't say. They never do, do they? I don't think they know. She'll hang on till Alex gets back—and then I think it might be very quick."

"When's he coming?"

"He's hoping they'll let him out tomorrow. But it depends on the consultant, of course."

Mother had always used her grandson, Alex, as a substitute for Toby. Was "used" a bit harsh? No, she didn't think so.

"I expect you'd like some tea?" Rachel said.

"Well, yes, but hadn't one of us better sit with her?"

"No, it's all right, I'll get Nurse Wiggins. Oh, you don't know about her, do you? She's our new addition." A fractional hesitation. "Very competent."

"You don't like her."

"We-ell, you know . . ." Rachel gave a theatrical shudder. "She *hovers*."

"You need the help, you're worn out."

"Wasn't my idea, it was Tim's."

"Well, good for him."

Rachel glanced back into their mother's bedroom. "Ah, she's nodded off again; I thought she might. I'll just nip up and get the Wiggins."

Tim had retreated to his study, so Elinor went into the drawing room to wait for Rachel. The farmhouse, which had been shabby, even dilapidated, when Rachel first fell in love with it, was now beautifully furnished. Oriental rugs, antique furniture—good paintings too. Nothing of hers, though. She had three in the Tate; none here.

Rachel came in carrying a tray, which she put down on a small table near the window. Out of the corner of her eye, Elinor noticed Kenny scaling along the wall, trying to avoid being seen from the kitchen window. "I see Kenny's still here?"

"Oh, don't talk to me about Kenny; I'm beginning to think he's a fixture. His mother was supposed to come and get him last Saturday. Poor little devil was sitting at the end of the drive all day. Suitcase packed, everything—and she didn't show up. And he never says anything, you know, never cries." She pulled a face. "Just wets the bed."

"He's still doing that?"

"Every night. I mean, I know you don't like Mrs. Murchison, but really, the extra work ..." She hesitated. "I don't suppose you could go and see her, could you? His mother?"

Not your house. Not your child.

"I'm actually quite busy at the moment."

"Busy?"

"Painting."

"Oh, yes. Painting."

That was only just not a sneer. The silence gathered. Elinor reminded herself of how tired Rachel must be, how disproportionately the burden of their mother's illness fell on her. "You know, if you liked, you could have an early night; I'll sit with her."

"No, there's no need. Nurse Wiggins does the nights."

So why am I here?

"Would you mind if I phoned Paul tonight?"

"Phone him now if you like."

"No, he'll be working, I'll leave it till after dinner."

"How is he?"

"A bit up and down. Kenny was disappointed he hadn't come. I think I'm a very poor substitute."

"Now that is something you could do. Make sure he turns up for dinner washed and reasonably tidy. He won't do anything for Mrs. Murchison and I just don't have the time."

Kenny. Somehow, whenever she was here, the responsibility for making Kenny behave got passed on to her. Still, it was the least she could do. So after Rachel had gone back upstairs, Elinor went into the garden, first to the sycamore tree and then into the kitchen garden, where he'd built himself a den behind the shed. No luck there either. The night nursery was the next most likely place.

As she climbed the stairs, Elinor was remembering her

first sight of Kenny, almost a year ago, the day the children arrived. A busload of them, carrying suitcases, paper parcels and gas masks, with luggage labels fastened to their clothes.

She and Rachel had arrived late at the church hall. It was rather like a jumble sale, all the good stuff disappearing fast, except that here the stuff was children. Pretty little blond-haired girls were popular and not always with the obvious people. You could see why the Misses Richards might want one, but Michael Ryan, who'd lived alone at Church Farm ever since his parents died and seemed barely able to look after himself, let alone a child, why was he so keen? Big, strapping lads, strong enough for farm work, they were snapped up. Older girls went quickly too. A twelve-year-old, provided she was clean and tidy—and not too slow on the uptake—was virtually a free housemaid. And then there were the children nobody wanted: families of four or five brothers and sisters. They'd have to be split up, of course. In fact, it was happening already. Some of the smaller children were wide-eyed with shock and grief.

Then she saw him. Pale, thin, his face slum-white, disfigured by freckles, orange hair, coppery-brown eyes. His trousers were too short, his sleeves too: he had unusually knobbly wrist bones. And a rather long, thin neck. For some reason, that made him seem vulnerable, like an unfledged bird, though closer to—she'd begun to walk towards him now—she revised her impression. Yes, he looked like a chick, but the chick of some predatory bird: an eagle or a falcon. Not an attractive child, but even so, he should've been picked by now—he was the right age for farm work.

And then she saw the lice. She'd never seen anybody with a head that lousy. His hair was moving. Made desperate by their overcrowded conditions, lice had started taking short cuts across his forehead. She was about to speak to him—though she had no idea what to say—when Rachel came up behind her.

"They want me to take three. *Three.* How on earth am I supposed to manage three?"

"What about him?"

Rachel peered at the boy. She was short-sighted and too vain to wear glasses. "Well, at least there's only one of him . . . Yes, all right, I'll see what she says."

Rachel went off to speak to the billeting officer, Miss Beatrice Marsh, who regularly made a mess of the church flower-arranging roster. They seemed to be having an extremely animated discussion. The boy showed no interest in the outcome. His gas-mask case was on a long string: Elinor noticed a sore patch on the side of his knee where the case had chafed against the skin. He had placed a battered brown suitcase between his legs and was gripping it tight, so at least he'd have something, a change of clothes, a favorite toy. But he'd lost his luggage label.

"Which school are you with?"

He shook his head.

You did it on purpose, she thought. *You threw it away.* Not that there was anything sinister in that. There were many reasons why a child might choose to slip off the end of one school crocodile and attach himself to a different one entirely. A teacher he didn't like, a gang of bigger boys bullying in the playground . . . Whatever the reason, he'd arrived in the village with no name, no history. Something about that appealed to Elinor. Bundled up, parceled off . . . and in the middle of it all, the chaos, the confusion, he'd taken off his label and thrown it away.

Only of course it couldn't go on like that. He had to give

Rachel his name, his address, because he wanted his mother to be able to find him. He wanted her a good deal more than she appeared to want him.

Elinor tapped on the nursery door. Kenny was playing with his toy soldiers—Alex's, originally, now his—hundreds of tiny gray and khaki figures spread across a vast battlefield, many of them lying on their backs, already wounded or killed. He looked up from the game, but didn't smile or speak.

"It's dinnertime. Have you washed your hands?"

He shook his head.

"Well, will you go and do it now, please?"

Still silent, he got up and left. Now and then it was brought home to her that Kenny hardly spoke—except, oddly enough, to Paul. And in the past year he'd scarcely grown at all. She looked round the chaotic room, decided to leave the toy soldiers undisturbed, but knelt to close the dolls' house.

Officially, Kenny despised the house and the dolls—wouldn't have been seen dead playing with them—and yet whenever she came into the room the dolls were in different positions and the furniture had been rearranged. She both loved and hated this house, which had once been hers. Her eighth-birthday present. She could still remember the mixture of delight and uneasiness she'd felt when the wrapping paper fell away and she saw that the dolls weren't just ordinary dolls: they were Father and Mother and Rachel and Toby and her. And the toy house was an exact copy of the house they lived in, right down to the piano in the drawing room and the pattern of wallpaper on the bedroom walls. It had always had pride of place in her bedroom, but she hadn't played with it much. She picked up the Toby doll, held it between her thumb and forefinger, and felt a pang of grief so intense it squeezed her heart. She remained kneeling there, on the cold lino, waiting for the pain to pass, then laid the little figure on its bed.

Rachel came in. "Ken——" She stopped when she saw Elinor. "Still playing with dolls?"

"I never did, if you remember."

"No, you didn't, did you? You were always out with Toby. I think I played with that more than you did."

Elinor went on putting the dolls to bed. One moment, she was looking through a tiny window, the next, she saw her own face peering in: huge, piggy nostrils, open-pored, grotesque. Then, immediately, she was back in the nursery, looking down at the last doll in her hand: Mother.

"Are you all right?" Rachel asked.

"Fine."

"Only you've gone quite pale."

"No, I'm fine." She fastened the front of the house and stood up. "Kenny's getting washed; at least I think he is. What about Mother, is she awake?"

"No, and anyway the Wiggins is there. Come on, I need a drink."

As they were going downstairs the telephone in the hall started to ring, and Rachel went to answer it. When she came into the drawing room a few minutes later, she was glowing with excitement. "That was Alex; he's coming home tomorrow. I'll go and tell Tim."

Left alone, Elinor thought: *Yes, good news.* But she couldn't stop thinking about her mother lying upstairs, dying, but clinging onto life so she could see Alex again, one last time. This was what they'd all been waiting for: Alex's arrival; the end.

※ *THREE*

Alex arrived the following afternoon, straight out of hospital with the smell of it still on his skin. Elinor witnessed his meeting with his father. Tim stuck out his hand and then, realizing too late that Alex was unable to take it, blushed from the neck up and let the hand drop. She sensed a great tension in Alex: something coiled up hard and tight. His face softened when Rachel came into the room, but otherwise he seemed merely impatient, anxious to get this visit over and move on.

Thinking he would like time alone with his parents, Elinor fetched a drawing pad from her room and went into the garden. She sat under the birch tree, her back pressed hard against its scaly bark, staring up through the branches at yet another flawlessly blue sky. The aeroplanes were active today, little, glinting, silver minnows darting here and there. Earlier, she'd started trying to draw a cabbage and it was sitting on a low stone wall, waiting for her, yellower and flabbier than she remembered. She gazed at it without enthusiasm, then forced herself to begin. *Draw something every single day,* Professor Tonks used to say. *Doesn't matter what it is: just draw.*

All the upstairs windows were open. Behind that one on the far left her mother lay dying, attended, at the moment, by Nurse Wiggins, a great, galumphing, raw-boned creature with a jolly, professional laugh and downy, peach-perfect skin. Her laugh, so obviously designed to keep fear and pain at bay, grated on Elinor. And yes, she did *hover*. But she was good at her job, you had to give her that, though her presence added to the tension in the house. Rachel, in particular, seemed to find it difficult to relax.

Elinor held the drawing at arm's length. Not good. Cabbages are shocking if you get them right, especially those thick-veined outer leaves: positively scrotal. Only she couldn't draw them like that, not here, surrounded by her family. She was unconsciously censoring herself, and it wasn't just what she drew, either. It was what she let herself see. This was one of the reasons she'd left home early, and refused, even after Toby's death, to go back. Her mother needed care and company: it had been obvious to everybody that Elinor, the then unmarried daughter, should stay at home and provide it.

Obvious to everybody except Elinor, who'd refused, and gone on refusing. It was Rachel, in the end, who'd found their mother a cottage within walking distance of her own home.

> *The caterpillar on the leaf*
> *Repeats to thee thy mother's grief.*

What the hell was that about? It was true, though. She'd have liked to do the drawing that would be the equivalent of those lines.

Voices from an upstairs window: Rachel and Alex. She'd be taking him up to his room. Elinor looked at the brown lawn, the wilting shrubs and flowers; everything seemed to be suspended. Was that the war? Possibly. Even the roses, this summer, looked as if they were expecting to be bombed. But no, it was more than that: closer. *She* was waiting: for something to happen or, more likely, for something to be said; but though Mother's thick, white tongue came out at intervals to moisten her cracked lips she stayed silent, drifting in and out of sleep.

Elinor glanced up, caught by some movement other than the ceaseless circling of aeroplanes in the sky, and there was Alex, in a white shirt with the sleeves rolled up, coming towards her over the lawn. "Aunt Elinor, I thought I'd find you here."

Flattering as always, implying he'd been looking especially for her. Alex was a devil with women, though his affairs never lasted long. It was the chase that interested Alex; the girls, once caught, quickly bored him. He bent down to kiss her, briefly cutting off the light.

Elinor was extremely fond of Alex, but wary of him too. He was tall, broad-shouldered and, despite his convalescent state, exuded virility. Beside him, she felt like a spindle-shanked elderly virgin, while knowing of course that she was nothing of the sort, but perhaps that's what middle age does to you? Makes you—women, perhaps, particularly—vulnerable to the perceptions other people have of you? She thought Alex might see her like that. He flirted with her rather as he might have done with a schoolgirl too young to be considered a possible conquest.

He sat cross-legged on the grass beside her, squinting through his spread fingers at the sky. More and more planes, great clusters of them, like midges over a stagnant pond.

"Been busy all day," she said.

"Yes, it's certainly hotting up. No raids though?"

"Not here. There was one near the coast, Rachel says, a few days ago. Thirteen people killed."

He was looking at the window of his grandmother's

room. "Strange, isn't it, how private life just goes on? People get married, have babies. *Die.* And all the time . . ."

"I find I alternate," she said. "You know, I'll have days when I think about nothing except the war and how terrible it is and are we going to be invaded . . . and then suddenly, for no reason—nothing's changed—it all disappears. And I think: Well, we're still here. We're still the same people we've always been."

"Oh, I don't know about that."

Something in his voice made her turn to look at him. She saw lines around his eyes and mouth that hadn't been there before. Suddenly, he did actually look like Toby; Toby as he'd been when he'd first come home on leave. So much had been made of Alex's resemblance to Toby, especially by her mother, but also by Rachel, that Elinor had always resisted seeing it. Alex was different, she told herself: brash, coarser. But now she saw how alike they really were, and it stopped her breath.

"How's the, er . . . ?" *Wound,* she meant.

He held out his arm. Suntanned skin, the tan fading a little now, after the long weeks in hospital. A dusting of blond hairs. "Not a lot to see, really. I got it in the elbow. The funny bone. Oh my God it was hilarious—and apparently there's some damage to the nerves." His fingers were curled over, the tips almost touching the palm. "I haven't got a lot of sensation here. Or here."

"So you're out of it, then?"

"Not if I can help it." He was flexing his hand as he spoke. "Though I don't know what I can do."

"Is it painful?"

"Can be."

Voices floated over the lawn towards them. Somewhere in the house a door opened and closed.

"Have you been in to see her?"

"Not yet. The nurse is in there doing something so I thought I'd leave it a bit. God, it's hot."

"I think I know where there's some lemonade."

And that, Elinor thought, crossing the lawn, was an appropriately maiden-auntish thing to say.

Outside the kitchen door, she paused to listen, but Mrs. Murchison was having her post-lunch break, so she opened the door and walked in. A porcelain sink, with two buckets underneath, a range that had to be black-leaded every morning, and a long table, scarred with overlapping rings where hot plates and saucepans had been put down. Above the table, a rack with bunches of dried herbs, ready for the winter, though at the moment there were still masses of thyme, parsley, sage, rosemary and bay in the kitchen garden—and hundreds of bees feasting on them.

The pantry opened off the kitchen. The lemonade jug sat on the top shelf underneath the one tiny window, its muslin cover weighed down by blue beads. She picked up the jug and two glasses and returned to Alex.

"Auntie Elinor, you're an angel."

This was going from bad to worse: aunt*ie*, now. He got up and dragged a small iron table closer. They were in deep shade: the shadow of a branch fell across Elinor's bare ankle so sharply it suggested amputation. The lemonade was cloudy, but relatively cold and sweet. Almost immediately wasps started hovering, drawn away from the easy pickings of windfall apples in the long grass of the orchard.

Elinor didn't feel like talking and evidently Alex felt the same, but there was no awkwardness in their silence. It was born of heat and exhaustion, and, on his side, recent illness and possibly pain. He kept batting wasps away. "Don't," she said. "It only makes them worse." *Why couldn't men leave things alone?* After a while she left him to it, leaned back against the tree and closed her eyes.

There were so many insect sounds—the hum of bees, the whirring of gnats, the petulant buzz of wasps—that at first she didn't notice one particular drone growing louder. A shadow swept across her closed lids. Opening her eyes, she saw a huge plane above the house, black, or at least it looked black against the sun. "Is it one of ours?" she asked. She knew it wasn't—the German crosses on its wings were very clear—only her brain refused to accept what her eyes saw. The plane banked steeply; at first she thought it was going away, but it circled and came back again, this time much lower. She got up to run to the house, but Alex caught her arm. *"No."* He pulled her back into the shadow of the tree. "Better not cross the lawn." She felt sick. There was a popping sound, curiously unimpressive, like a child bursting paper bags or balloons. Alex dragged her to the ground, facedown, and lay on top of her. "Don't clench your teeth." *What?* Pale faces appeared at the kitchen door. "Stay there!" Alex shouted, waving them back. He knew about this, they didn't, so automatically they obeyed. The plane veered away in the direction of the coast, falling, always falling, until it dipped below the level of a hill. The pressure on the back of her neck eased. She saw a ladybird, an inch away from her eyes, on the top of a grass stalk, waving its front legs, as if it didn't understand why the stalk had come to an end and there was only air. Now more planes were circling overhead—two? Three? She was afraid to look. "Ours," Alex said, letting go of her arm. She saw red marks where his fingers had been. *That'll bruise.* Slowly, she began to breathe more deeply, to direct weak, foolish smiles at the faces in the kitchen doorway: Rachel, Tim, Mrs. Murchison, Joan Wiggins. Everybody must've rushed down when they heard the engine directly overhead. Beyond the hill, a column of black smoke was rising. The British planes circled, then banked steeply and headed towards London. Alex helped her to her feet and she wobbled on boneless legs into the house.

"Jerry right enough." Tim gave a little cough, reclaiming status from his son. Then, abruptly, he turned on Rachel, his face contorted with anger. "What on earth possessed you?"

Elinor realized Rachel must've tried to run across the lawn to get to her son. Tim sounded so angry, but Alex was angry too: both of them, angry with the women because they hadn't been able to protect them. But then, gradually, everybody started to calm down. Mrs. Murchison put the kettle on for tea. "Oh, I think we can do better than that," Tim said, and went to fetch the whisky.

Mrs. Murchison turned to Nurse Wiggins. "You'll have a cup, Joan?"

"No, I'll be getting back."

In the turmoil of the last few minutes, the dying woman had been completely forgotten. Only now, conscience-stricken, Rachel remembered and ran upstairs.

※ *FOUR*

Elinor heard her mother wanting to know what was going on. She sounded wide awake, no doubt wrenched into full consciousness by the roar of the plane. A second later, there were footsteps on the landing and Rachel appeared, leaning over the bannisters. "You can come up now."

She was speaking to Alex, who grimaced and put down his glass. Elinor smiled, tried to look encouraging. She wondered what it was like to be Alex, to have seen so many men his own age and even younger killed, and then to come back into this other world, where an old woman dying in her own bed, surrounded by people who loved her, was treated as a tragedy. *They never really come back*, she thought, looking at Alex, thinking of Toby. Wondering if the same might not be true of Paul.

"You too, Elinor."

She didn't want to go; she thought Alex would want time alone with his grandmother—they'd been so close—but evidently Rachel thought otherwise. For whatever reason, she'd decided the whole family should all be there together.

Alex was sitting with his back to the door when she entered the room, his left hand resting on his grandmother's wrinkled arm, her dead-white skin and his brown hand shock-ingly contrasted against the pale blue coverlet. It imprinted itself on her mind, that image; she knew she would always remember it. Mother was smiling, though she could only smile with one side of her face; the other was twisted into a permanent droop or sneer. And she was struggling to speak.

"It's all right, Gran." Alex obviously meant don't bother, don't try to speak, but the old woman's mouth worked and worked at the words that wouldn't come. Then: "Toby," she said. "I knew you'd come."

Elinor saw Alex flinch. Rachel, who was standing on the other side of the bed, leaned forward as if to protect her son. Too late for that, Elinor thought. You should have been doing that years ago.

Shortly afterwards, Mother drifted off to sleep again. She seemed contented; happy, even. They listened to her breathing, waiting, and perhaps—some of them—longing, for a change in the rhythm, but, though the gaps between one breath and the next seemed sometimes impossibly long, her chest still rose and fell with the same remorseless regularity. This might go on for days.

I can't bear it, Elinor thought. And then: *Don't be stupid, of course you can.*

In the end the prolonged silence became too revealing. "I'll get Nurse Wiggins," Elinor said. She didn't know what Nurse Wiggins could do, but she felt the family atmosphere needed diluting. She ran quickly upstairs and tapped on the door at the end of the corridor. Nurse Wiggins appeared, bleary-eyed from lack of sleep, all that fresh, jolly hardness gone. "Yes, of course I'll come." She stifled a yawn, then yawned again. Moist, pink, catlike interior; huge tonsils.

Beginning to relax slightly, Elinor went first to her own room to splash her face with tepid water—no water was really cold this summer—was tempted to lie down for half an hour, but decided she ought to go downstairs. When she reached the bottom step she saw Alex and Rachel standing under Toby's portrait in the hall. Something about their attitude suggested the talk was private, so she retreated a few steps and settled down to wait.

Rachel was saying in a low, urgent voice, "You will stay, won't you?"

"Tonight? Yes."

"Only one night? I hoped you . . ."

"Yes?"

"Well, I hoped you'd stay till the end."

"Don't you think I've done enough?"

"You've only been here a couple of hours."

"I don't mean *now.*"

"Look, it'll only be a day or two. If that."

"I've got things to do in town."

"Can't they wait?"

"I've got a life."

"She loved you more than anybody."

"Me?"

He jerked his head at the portrait, then walked out into the garden, the front door banging shut behind him. Rachel stood for a moment, looking after him, and then, head down, crossed the hall into the drawing room.

Elinor lingered on the stairs for a minute, then went to stand where they'd been standing. *Killed in action,* she read, looking at the plaque, and even that wasn't true. She was remembering an incident when Alex had been five or six years old. He'd come running in from the garden, had stopped under the portrait, and pulled his sweater over his head. "Christ, it's hot!" She remembered him saying it, she'd thought it so funny at the time, his chubby red face struggling out of the neck hole, first one ear, then the other, almost as if the sweater were giving birth to him. Then, suddenly, he stopped, one arm still in the sleeve, and stared at the portrait. "It wasn't my fault!" Yelling, right at the top of his voice. Then, freeing his arm, he threw the sweater at the painting. There'd been something disturbing about the little boy shouting at the painted face of a man he couldn't remember. She'd wanted to . . . intervene, protect him somehow—but from what? *It wasn't my fault.* She hadn't known what it meant, then, and she wasn't sure she knew now. Of course, it might have been a reference to some childish game he was in the middle of, perhaps he'd been accused of breaking the rules, something like that, but no, it had been very definitely directed at the portrait. At Toby. So what was it? A repudiation of the grief that hung over the house like a pall of black smoke and wouldn't go away? A refusal to feel guilt—and how guilty they all felt, then and now. Especially now, when another generation of young men was dying. *We dropped the catch,* she thought. *Our generation.* Wondering why she'd suddenly strayed into cricket: the memory of Alex's white sweater, perhaps. *And Alex's generation is paying the price.*

She looked across the hall and saw him still standing there, the angry little boy. And then he turned and ran out into the garden, where the dazzling light swallowed him, like the skin on a sunlit sea.

Crossing the hall, she was about to follow that flitting shadow into the garden, when she stopped, for there, pacing up and down the lawn, smoking furiously, was the adult Alex. As she watched, he turned towards the house and stared straight at her. She raised a hand to wave, then realized that he couldn't see her. From where he stood, the hall would be in darkness.

She couldn't imagine what he felt, now the old woman who'd loved him and used him as a substitute for her dead son was herself dying. Loss? Relief? Or did he perhaps no longer care much either way? His face really had aged; she'd noticed it earlier, but it struck her again, now, with renewed force. When he was talking, the play of expression on his face softened the lines around his eyes and mouth, but now, in repose, they looked as if they'd been scored in with a knife. She remembered the identical transformation in Toby; how, suddenly, from being two years older, he was five, ten, fifteen years older. Out of reach.

As Alex was. He was his own man now. The war that had taken so much away from him, had given him that, at least.

FIVE

Elinor woke early from confused dreams of Paul. She'd telephoned twice the previous night, had listened to the phone ring in their empty house, walked in memory through the familiar rooms, seeing the dented cushions, hearing the affronted silence. What on earth could he be doing? He couldn't be on duty every night, but he certainly wasn't at home. Working late in his studio, she guessed, perhaps even sleeping there—he did that sometimes when she was away from home—but there was no telephone in the studio so she had no way of contacting him.

Throwing back the bedclothes, she went to the window and looked out, feeling the morning air cool on her sleep-swollen face. Five or six jackdaws were strutting across the lawn—little storm troopers—rapacious beaks jab-jabbing at the soil in search of worms. Drops of dew glinted in the grass. It was still only half light.

Something had woken her. She listened. Footsteps on the landing? No, no, it was much too early for anybody to be about. But then, the front door opened and Alex came out, carrying a suitcase, followed by Tim. She looked down at the tops of their heads, Alex's thick blond hair, Tim's pink scalp showing through carefully combed mouse-brown. They got into the car, moving heavily, not speaking, gray shapes in the gray light. Doors clunked, the engine coughed and choked before settling down to a steady hum, spinning wheels scattered gravel and away they went. She wondered if her mother was awake to hear it, and whether if she heard it she'd realize that Alex had gone.

BY LATE AFTERNOON the heat had become intolerable. Taking a break from the sickroom, Elinor went into the garden and watered the plants. Unlike Rachel—and their mother too, for that matter—she was no gardener, but watering was one job she did enjoy. She took off her shoes and let her white London feet explore the crumbly, moist soil. By the time she'd finished, all the paths were shining wet, and yet, even before she'd coiled the hose and restored it to its place by the tap, they were starting to dry. Steam rising from them, here and there.

Before dinner she went back to her mother's room, to the sour smell from the commode that no amount of bleach seemed able to remove. *And so it ends.* She'd been thinking things like that all day: vague, trite little phrases, trying to nudge herself into feeling the appropriate emotions, and never quite succeeding. The truth was that, like Rachel, she was too tired to feel anything very much. During the evening, Nurse Wiggins took over for a few hours; the sisters sat on the terrace in the breathy, moth-haunted darkness, smoking and talking—about nothing very much. Everything was subsumed in waiting.

Elinor was going to sit with their mother for the first half of the night. Neither of the sisters wanted her to be with a stranger when she died. At bedtime they went upstairs together, but outside their mother's door, Rachel lingered. "You will wake me, won't you?"

"Of course I will. Go on now, shoo. *Shoo*."

Sitting beside the bed, Elinor read for an hour, taking nothing in, listening to her mother's uneven breaths. Without realizing, she started to match her own breathing to her mother's, becoming in the process slightly light-headed. After a while, she gave up pretending to read and switched off the lamp. At least, now, she could open the blackout curtains and lean out of the window into the hot, still night.

Even flowers and grass no longer smelled fresh; it was as if everything had been singed. Searchlights fingered the underbelly of clouds, coming together sometimes to form a pyramid of light over the church tower. They seemed, in their constant, quivering, hypersensitive movement, to be living things, like the antennae on a moth.

A rustle behind her. Quickly, she pulled the blackout curtains across and groped her way back to her chair.

"Is that you, Elinor?"

"Yes." Elinor put her hand over her mother's eyes to shield them before switching on the lamp. "Would you like me to call Rachel?"

"No, let her sleep."

Another breath. And another. After each dragging pause, the skeletal chest expanded again. *Let go, just let go.* Elinor almost said it aloud, only she was too ashamed, knowing it was her own deliverance she was pleading for.

The old woman looked around the room, bewildered. "I thought Toby was here."

"When?"

"Just now."

"That was Alex, Mother. Yesterday."

"*No*, just now." The old woman's eyes focused on the empty space beyond the foot of the bed. "He was standing just there."

She's wandering, Elinor thought, resisting the temptation to turn round and check there was nobody there. But then her mother surprised her by turning towards her a gaze that was sharp, alert, even slightly malicious: a glimpse of the woman she'd once been. The thick, white tongue came out and moistened her cracked lips. Elinor bent forward to hear.

"I knew."

Humor her. "What did you know?"

"You and Toby." Her chest rattled—she might even have been trying to laugh. "Bed creaking, night after night, you must've thought I was stupid, I knew whose room it was coming from."

Elinor daren't acknowledge that she'd heard, still less that she'd understood. Instead, she asked, "Would you like some water?"

A reluctant nod. Elinor held the glass to her lips and watched the wasted throat working as she drank. After a while she waved it away. "Did you really think I didn't know?"

"We used to play, that's all."

"Play."

Elinor dabbed her mother's mouth with a folded handkerchief and settled the gray head back onto the pillow. She said, brightly, "Alex is coming again at the weekend."

"Alex?"

So Alex had stopped existing, which seemed rather hard on Alex, whose whole childhood had been warped by his supposed resemblance to Toby. How many other families were like this? The chair at the dining-room table that nobody ever sat in, the bedroom kept as it had always been: school books, toys . . . On the mantelpiece or the piano, photographs of a face that didn't age. Other people's lives molding themselves around the gap.

Another pause in her mother's breathing. Longer? "I'll get Rachel."

This time there was no protest. Blindly, Elinor stumbled across the landing and tapped on Rachel's door. After waiting a few moments, she pushed it open and peered into the darkness. That familiar married smell, male and female scents combined. "Rachel?"

A hump under the bedclothes heaved and muttered. Then Rachel, still half asleep, staggered to the door, struggling to get her arms into the sleeves of her wrap. "What's the matter? Is she worse?"

"No, I don't think so, she's awake, that's all. I thought you'd want to be there."

"Yes, of course. Oh God, I didn't think I'd get to sleep at all and I must've gone really deep."

Elinor continued along the landing to the bathroom.

"You are coming back?" Rachel sounded frightened.

"Yes, I just want to splash my face, I was starting to nod off in there."

In the bathroom, she stood for a moment with her back against the door, then went to the basin and turned on the cold water. Cupping her hands, she threw water over her face, neck, chest, before finally filling the bowl to the brim and pushing her head underneath the surface. Water slopped onto the floor, but no matter. She looked at her dripping face in the mirror, coils of wet hair stuck to her forehead, haunted eyes. Her nightdress was soaked. Her nipples showed through the white cotton like a second pair of eyes. *I look mad*, she thought.

Now, when it was too late, she wanted to argue. Once. It had happened *once*. It was all nonsense saying the bed creaked "night after night." As children, she and Toby had often crept along the passage to each other's rooms. The only way to stop them was to lock them in, and even then Toby had crawled along the ledge outside their bedrooms, careless of the forty-foot drop onto the terrace below. Only after his death had she looked down at that ledge and realized the risk he'd run. As a child, ten, eleven years old. Why? Why that need? It hadn't been sexual then, couldn't have been; he was too young. All that came later. And it happened *once*. Though, of course, saying you'd slept with your brother only once was a bit like saying you'd committed murder *only once*. It wasn't really much of an excuse.

Back in her bedroom, she changed into a fresh nightdress before going to the window and peering round the blinds. Searchlights illuminating steep cliffs and chasms of cloud. Then, as she strained to hear, there came that curiously unimpressive *pop-pop* from the marshes. A couple of weeks from now there might be German tanks parked on the village green—mid-September seemed to be everybody's best guess for the invasion—and yet here she was, remembering two children playing in the dark.

She needed Paul, not to talk to—she'd never told him about Toby, never told anybody—no, simply to have him here, his weight and warmth beside her in the bed. As for tonight . . . Well, she had to go back, see it through to the end, there was no choice. But on the landing she paused, still reluctant to go in. Through the half-open door, she saw a halo of soft light around the lamp, her sister's heavy shadow. *Not long now. Please God, not long.*

※ *SIX*

All the normal routines of the house had broken down, though food—mainly cold meats and salad—still appeared at mealtimes, laid out on the sideboard in the dining room. Elinor and Rachel ate—when they ate at all—in their mother's room. Paul, newly arrived from London, sat in solitary splendor at the dining-room table or, more often, took bread and cheese wrapped in a napkin and went out to sketch on the marshes. He'd responded to Elinor's plea for help; though, in fact, there was very little he could do, apart from just be there when she needed to talk. The only practical, useful thing he could do was spend time with Kenny, who seemed, for some extraordinary reason, to have become quite attached to him.

Returning late one afternoon from a sketching trip, he found Kenny loitering at the end of the drive. He'd been hoping for a visit from his mother, though nobody seemed to know whether he had any reason to expect one.

"Wishful thinking, I'm afraid," Rachel said. "I've no patience with the woman. I mean, I know she's probably having a hard time but then, frankly, so are we."

Paul found the sight of the boy mooching about at the end of the drive almost intolerable. The last bus had been and gone; she wouldn't be coming now—if she'd had any intention of coming at all. Kenny sometimes invented these visits because he wanted them so badly, though there had been times when she'd arranged to come and then just not shown up. "You all right, Kenny?" Paul asked, turning into the drive. He got a sort of smile in return, though he thought from the boy's swollen eyelids that he might have been crying. *Bloody woman.* He went into the house and poured himself a drink—Tim was still in London—but he couldn't settle so, in the end, he fetched a football from Kenny's room and they spent an hour in the lane behind the house kicking the ball around, using old coats he found in the under-stairs cupboard as goalposts. The sun sank lower in the sky, its blood-red smears widening to a flood, and still they played. Paul's shadow lengthened till it threatened to envelop Kenny, while, at the same time, the boy's shadow fled away.

They played until Paul was too tired to go on. "Come on, let's go and get something to eat." Kenny dragged his feet, complaining all the way, but then burst into the hall, eyes glowing, pupils dilated, looking like a little fox cub, with his thin, sharp face and orange hair. He even smelled strong and musky like a wild animal. Paul cut them each a slice of veal and ham pie and settled down to eat. Soon Kenny was yawning uncontrollably, tired out by the misery of his long wait as much as by the football; but at least he'd sleep. Ought to, anyway.

After Kenny had gone upstairs to bed, Paul got his sketchbook out and looked through the drawings he'd done that day, but after a while his eyes became so tired he switched off the lamp and simply sat in darkness, listening to the drone of planes. Somewhere close at hand an owl screeched.

Disturbed by the sight of Kenny loitering at the end of the drive, he'd started to remember going to the asylum to see his own mother, and how, by the end of four years, he'd known every stop on the journey, which always ended with him walking up a long gray corridor towards his mother, who stood waiting at the end. A fat woman in a hideous gray smock. He almost didn't recognize her, she'd put on so much weight. This strange woman, who felt different, looked different, even smelled different, who was always touching him, stroking his hair, fondling him . . . Now, when he didn't need it, when he was merely embarrassed by it. For the most part, he just stood there, putting up with it, but once, and he was almost sure it was the last visit, he just couldn't bear it any more and pushed her away. Really quite hard; she stumbled and might have fallen if his father hadn't caught her.

Had that rejection led directly to her suicide? It had happened not long afterwards. Did it seem to her that since her only child had turned against her there was nothing left worth living for?

No point in asking questions like that. He would never know the truth, and besides, he had, somehow or other, to forgive himself. After all, he'd been fourteen years old; not a child, admittedly, but certainly not a man. You have to learn not to be too hard on your own younger self. Most of the time he dealt with it by forgetting it. Only Kenny, his obvious misery, his separation from his mother, threatened to disinter these long-buried memories. But there was no point. Absolutely no point at all. Getting up, he poured himself a generous glass of whisky, selected a book at random from the shelves and threw himself onto the sofa to begin reading. He'd go back to the drawings later.

THAT NIGHT, the old woman sank into unconsciousness. There was no question, now, of taking turns in the sickroom; the sisters sat on either side of the bed, each of them holding one of their mother's hands, Rachel, pink and blurry with tears, Elinor, hard and white, defiantly unfeeling. The long hours passed. Mother gave no sign of knowing them. Once Elinor gripped her hand and said: "Squeeze if you're in pain." A slight, but unmistakable, pressure in return. So the doctor came to give morphine. And the wait went on. It was like watching a great liner begin to go down, lighted windows darkening one after another. Her breathing had changed; and then, in the last few minutes—only they didn't know they were the last—she started to vomit. They stared at the stains on the sheets. Elinor thought: *That's not vomit; it's shit.* A few minutes later, the death throes started. All her life, Elinor had believed death throes were some kind of poetic invention. Evidently not. The sisters held on to her, talking, trying to think of soothing things to say, until eventually she went slack.

"Is that it?" Rachel was still waiting for the next breath, but the old woman's chest didn't move. They looked at each other; the silence went on . . . "I think she's gone."

Rachel went to get Nurse Wiggins, who confirmed what by now they were both beginning to believe. In her deep, inviolable silence, their mother was still the dominant figure in the room. But then, Nurse Wiggins pushed the drooping head back—it had fallen forward so her chin was resting on her chest—and so her mouth fell open. Suddenly, she looked dead. Nurse Wiggins said she'd have to fasten up the jaw. And then there were sheets to be changed, the body to be washed . . .

The sisters sat together on the bed in Rachel's room while the nurse finished the laying-out. Rachel was twisting a handkerchief round and round in her fingers. "Why is it such a shock? It's not as if we weren't expecting it."

"Look, why don't you go back to bed and try to get some sleep? It's not as if you can do anything."

Before parting, they went back to their mother's room. She lay there, gray and remote, penny weights on her eyelids, her jaw bound up with a white cloth. Nurse Wiggins had put a posy of flowers between the clasped, brown-spotted hands. Immediately, Elinor wanted to snatch them away, it seemed so false somehow, but then Mother had always loved flowers. Rachel touched the cooling face and whispered, "Good-bye, Mum." Crying, she turned away.

Elinor went to her own room, also grieving, not for what she'd lost, but for what she'd never had, and never could have now. As she climbed into bed, Paul half woke and reached out to her, so she cried in his arms and let him soothe her to sleep.

When, a few hours later, she woke she heard her mother's voice say, as loud and clear as if she'd been in the same room: *I knew.* And from that moment, Elinor ceased to feel anything Rachel, or anybody else for that matter, would have recognized as grief.

The next day she hardly thought at all; she made telephone calls, sent telegrams, worked her way through her mother's address book, coming across the names of relatives and friends dimly remembered from childhood, but often finding, when she set out to contact them, that they'd died years ago. Her mother's eldest sister was so frail she might not be able to make it to the funeral, but her two younger sisters certainly would, along with various other relatives, nieces, nephews and cousins, and then of course there were the grandchildren. Gabriella, though heavily pregnant, had decided she would come. Rachel wanted to keep Mother at home till the funeral—it was the family tradition—but Tim, who'd arrived from London in the early afternoon, said: "No, not in this heat"—and the undertaker backed him up. So the sisters held on to each other in the drawing room, while the undertaker's men sweated and strained to negotiate the stairs.

A great deal had been achieved in a short time, only now there was emptiness. Mrs. Murchison was busy in the kitchen, preparing, for the first time in over a week, a proper sit-down dinner. She'd managed to get river trout for the main course, with potatoes and other vegetables from the garden, and she'd made an apple pie. "I don't know who she thinks is going to eat *that*," Elinor said, though Paul thought he might. And no doubt Kenny as well, if he chose to appear. He was being elusive, even by his own impressive standards. The last few days he'd simply raided the kitchen whenever Mrs. Murchison's back was turned and eaten whatever scraps of food he managed to find behind the garden shed or out on the marshes. He was becoming almost feral and nobody seemed to give a damn about it except Paul.

When dinner time came, Kenny was, predictably, missing.

"Paul, do you think you could find him?" Rachel asked.

"I thought I heard him come in just now."

"Well, he's not here."

Paul went first into the garden and looked up at the sycamore tree. Alex had used this tree as a refuge when he was a boy: the "safety tree" he used to call it. It interested Paul that Alex, with his privileged background, had felt the same need for a refuge from the adult world as Kenny did, who was so much more obviously disadvantaged. Oh, Paul didn't underestimate the psychological pressures on Alex. Nobody could grow up in Toby Brooke's shadow and not be distorted in some way; deformed, even. Paul's view of Alex was a good deal less favorable than either Rachel's or Elinor's.

"Kenny? Kenny? Dinnertime."

It was growing dark; he'd almost certainly have come in

PAT BARKER

by now. So Paul trailed to the top of the house, knocked on the nursery door and went in. Kenny was kneeling on the floor beside his bed, playing with toy soldiers. He'd laid them out, hundreds of them, khaki and gray, facing each other across no-man's-land: an appropriately mud-colored stretch of lino. The soldiers had belonged to Alex. As a child, he'd been obsessed with fighting the last war, convinced he could do a better job than the generals. *And who am I to argue?* Paul thought, persuading his stiff leg to bend. But really there was no time to get involved in this particular game. "Dinner-time, Kenny."

He didn't even look up. "Too hot."

"Apple pie? Custard?"

No answer. Paul picked up two of the little soldiers and laid them on the palm of his hand. Officers, wearing the dated uniform of the last war: tunics, peaked caps, breeches, puttees. He remembered the advice supposedly given to German snipers: *Look for the thin knees. Take out the chain of command.* They'd changed the uniform later, made it slightly more difficult to pick out the officers. He felt a sudden impulse to talk to somebody who'd been there; no, not even talk—just be with him. Share what there was to share, in silence. Nobody here he could do that with: certainly not Tim, who'd spent the last war behind a desk in Whitehall.

His silence caught the boy's attention. Kenny was adept at screening out nagging and shouting: he simply didn't hear it. Any more than he heard his own name being called. Attention means trouble, and trouble comes fast enough. But now, looking across the battlefield, Paul found those curious, copper-colored eyes fixed on him. Purple shadows underneath. He looked tired; tired of life. No child should look like that.

"Who's winning?" Paul asked, searching for a point of contact.

"Us."

"That's good."

"You won't tell them, will you?"

"Tell them what?"

"That I got the soldiers."

Paul was shocked. "Nobody minds, Kenny. You play with anything you like. It must be really boring, with nobody to play with. At least at school—"

"*School*'s boring. I hate it."

"What about it? What don't you like?"

"The way they pick on us."

"The other boys?"

"Yeah—and the teachers."

"Why do you think that is?"

"Dunno. I don't talk like them? And . . ." A sudden, painful, disfiguring blush. "Me hair."

"But it's all grown back."

"Doesn't stop 'em shouting, 'Baldy, don't sit by him, he's got nits.' "

"You haven't got nits."

"Doesn't stop 'em saying it."

"Perhaps if Auntie Rachel went down—"

"You joking? I'd really get me head kicked in then."

As he spoke he was scooping up handfuls of tiny khaki soldiers and dropping them into a wooden box. Heavy losses for one small square of lino. Perhaps they'd been defending a salient. Paul turned the two little figures over and over in the palm of his hand. Suddenly, he glanced up and saw the boy watching him.

"Were you in it?"

"The war?" Paul looked down at the battlefield. "Yes."

"Were you wounded?"

"Ye-es."

"Whereabouts?"

"Knee. Since you ask."

"Thought so, you got a limp, haven't you?" He hesitated, but only for a second. "Can I see?"

"There's nothing *to* see. And no, you can't."

"What was it like? Being wounded."

"Not very nice. Why do you want to know about that?"

"Just interested."

"But why are you?"

"I like hearing about people getting hurt."

Oh, do you indeed? "I was unconscious most of the time."

"Did you win a medal?"

"No."

"Why not?"

"I was never very brave."

The boy looked at him. "Bet you were."

"Bet I wasn't."

Kenny considered this, then unexpectedly laughed. "I'm going to be a soldier when I grow up."

"Well, if it goes on long enough you mightn't have much choice."

"Nah, won't last that long."

"We said that last time. Oh, unless we get invaded . . . Be over in no time then."

"Cheerful sod, aren't you?" Another handful went into the box. "Some people think we already have been." He glanced cautiously from side to side and whispered: *"Nuns."*

Oh, yes. Nuns on buses paying the fare with surprisingly masculine hands. "I shouldn't worry about that, Kenny. It's just a story. Newspapers'll print anything."

"You could kill one of them if you had a pitchfork."

"I suppose you could, though you'd need to make sure it wasn't a real nun first."

"S'easy, you just put your hand up his skirt and see if he's got a willy."

Mental note: Keep Kenny away from nuns. Suddenly tired of the whole business, Paul heaved himself to his feet. His stiff knee meant he had to get up like a toddler, pushing himself up with his hands, and he didn't like to be watched doing it. Looking down, he saw a neat parting in the orange hair revealing the dead white of the scalp, and felt a stab of pain, for the boy, for himself, for the whole bloody stupid business. "Come on, now. Dinnertime."

"I've got to wash me hands." He held them up as proof.

"All right, but *hurry up.*"

Paul went slowly downstairs. Crossing the hall, he stopped in front of Toby Brooke's portrait. Nigel Featherstone, no less. Now why on *earth* was he so successful? He'd never done anything that wasn't completely bland. Perhaps that was why. Who wants disturbing truths in the portrait of a loved one? Elinor's portrait of Toby, though not, in her own view, a complete success, was better than this. It caught something of the reality, the power, of that slim, voracious ghost.

Paul became aware of Kenny standing by his side. "Now he *was* brave." Toby, he knew from several accounts, had been a whole lot of things, but brave was certainly one. "See that?" Paul pointed to the canvas. "That's the MC, the Military Cross." He looked down at Kenny, who was staring intently at the medal. "Come on, they're all in there waiting. You must be hungry; I know I am."

Putting his hand on the boy's shoulder, he steered him towards the dining room.

Next day was a Saturday. At eleven o'clock, the vicar came to offer condolences and talk about hymns and readings. Then there were wreaths to be ordered, flowers for the church, cars to be booked—but how many cars? Rooms to be got ready for those who'd need to stay over. And they hadn't even started thinking about food and drink. By midafternoon, Rachel was exhausted. The rest would just have to wait, she said. "You forget how much work there is."

They decided to have tea on the lawn. All the leaves were limp, folded in on themselves in a desperate attempt to conserve moisture. There was a sweet, sickly smell of rotten apples lying in the grass. Drunken bees toppled from flower to flower.

"Where's Kenny?" Elinor said, resigned to another search.

He'd gone out early with a catapult, a slice of veal and ham pie wrapped in a table napkin, and a bottle of warm, flat lemonade. Nobody had seen him since.

Tim, Elinor and Paul perched on uncomfortable iron chairs and watched the shadows lengthen on the grass. Unmentioned by anybody, but dominating all their thoughts, was the stripped bed that had lately and for so many months held the dying woman. Mrs. Murchison carried out the tea-pot and plates of sandwiches but nobody felt able to start eating. Rachel was still indoors talking to Nurse Wiggins, who'd packed her suitcase and was preparing to depart. They were straining their ears for the sound of her car driving away, which somehow, they all felt, would mark the end of the whole long-drawn-out, miserable episode.

What a small part we play in other people's lives, Paul thought. *How quickly the water closes over us.* And almost immediately realized he didn't believe that at all. He'd been thinking about his mother a lot in the last few months, more than he'd done for years. He was haunted by images of her, some of actual events—the moment in the hospital, when he'd pushed her away—others imagined. Above all, he saw her walking across the mudflats to a tidal river, leaving a trail of footprints behind her. There were other markings too: rats' tails trailing across the mud, leaving lines and curves as indecipherable as the hieroglyphs on an ancient tomb, but carrying, he felt, some urgent hidden meaning, if only they could be understood. No, his mother was certainly not slipping away into oblivion; if anything, his relationship with her had gone on changing. He was older now than she'd ever been, and that realization brought with it a kind of tenderness, as if he were the adult now and she the child. Nothing to be gained by thinking like this. He closed his eyes and let his thoughts dissolve into the orange glow behind his lids.

When he opened them again, Kenny was walking towards him across the lawn.

"Thought so," Tim said, in that jocular, avuncular way of his. "Thought his belly would bring him back."

Kenny flicked a glance at him. Like most of Kenny's glances it seemed exclusively designed to establish that he was not about to be hit, and then he sat down, cross-legged, at Paul's feet. *Why me?* Paul thought, in equal measure flattered and exasperated. Above the creased shirt, the nape of the boy's neck stuck out—a dingy white, and far too thin for the size of his head. He reminded Paul of a baby blackbird: "gollies," they used to call them. The word brought back bird-nesting trips when he was a boy, Kenny's age or even younger, in the mythic golden summers before the last war.

At that moment they heard Nurse Wiggins's little car puttering away down the drive and Rachel appeared round the corner of the house, puffing her lips out in a pantomime of relief. "I thought she'd never go."

"She was all right," Tim said.

"Oh, I know *you* liked her," Rachel said.

Elinor shook her head. "She was all right, but it's never comfortable, is it, having strangers in your house."

"Servants are strangers," Tim said.

"Ye-es," Rachel said, "but you don't have to treat them as family. The trouble with Wiggins was she was here all the time."

Paul looked down at the top of Kenny's head, wondering how much of this he was taking in. He was such an obvious cuckoo in the nest himself, but fortunately he didn't seem to be listening.

Rachel and Elinor passed round plates of sandwiches. Tim said: "Shall I be Mother?" and poured the tea. Wasps kept up their priggish, bad-tempered whine around the jam and sugar bowls. One settled on Rachel's shoulder, causing a huge commotion until Tim picked up a napkin and flicked it away.

Elinor took another napkin and spread it over the gooseberry tart. "Trouble is they get sleepy. It's nearly always autumn when people get stung."

Rachel looked surprised. "It's not autumn."

"It's September," Paul said.

For a moment, Rachel looked completely bewildered, and

they understood how, for her, the whole summer had been swallowed up in her mother's dying. And immediately the shadows creeping towards them over the grass seemed longer and darker.

"Gooseberry tart," Rachel said. "Elinor, could you help Mrs. Murchison with the plates?"

The gooseberry tart, cut into huge slabs and drizzled with cream, was amazing: Mrs. Murchison had surpassed herself. The wasps certainly thought so. Paul was waiting for somebody to suggest they do the obvious common-sense thing and move indoors; he might have suggested it himself, only at that moment he heard a different kind of buzzing, and, almost simultaneously, the sirens set up their disconsolate wail.

Even then, the little group on the lawn was reluctant to move. Lethargy, caused by the emotional upheaval of the past few days, and the need, shared by everybody this summer, to make the most of every last glimmer of sunshine, kept them pinned to their chairs. Only Paul, who still, so many years after the last war, reacted rather differently from most people, jumped to his feet. Splaying his fingers, he peered through them at the sky. "My God, look at them."

A formation of bombers was coming towards them, fighter planes circling around them like gnats. Enemy fighter planes, there to protect the bombers from attack. Nobody moved; reluctant, even now, to take shelter from a threat they only half believed in. There'd been several raids in the last few months, but most of those on the coast; one or two on the outskirts of London. "Nuisance raids," the papers were calling them, though presumably they were more than a nuisance to the relatives of those who'd been killed.

Elinor was on her feet too now, shielding her eyes. "I don't think I've ever seen so many."

"They'll be heading for London," Tim said. "For the docks. I suppose I ought to think about getting back."

Rachel turned on him. "Why? What on earth can you do about it?"

It seemed impossible the planes should keep on coming, but come on they did. Kenny became tremendously excited and ran round and round the lawn pretending to be a Spitfire, which did rather underline the fact that there were no actual Spitfires in the air.

"Not much resistance, is there?" Elinor said.

"They're waiting." Tim didn't sound at all confident. "Being held in reserve."

"For what?"

Everybody knew something out of the ordinary was happening, but at the same time it seemed unreal, less threatening than the solitary plane that had flown low over the garden only five days ago.

"They'll split up, won't they?" Rachel asked.

Tim shook his head. "I don't think so, I think this is it."

Paul looked at Elinor. "I ought to go back."

"I doubt you'll be able to," Rachel said.

"He might," Tim said. "All the traffic's going to be coming the other way."

"What, refugees?" Rachel sounded alarmed.

"Why not? Civilians under fire, there's always the possibility of panic."

"Well, as long as they don't land on us."

"Not very patriotic," Elinor said.

"I've done my bit."

It was so obvious what Rachel meant that they all looked round for Kenny, but he'd seized the opportunity to take the last two slices of gooseberry tart and was nowhere to be seen.

"I wouldn't have thought there's much point going back

tonight." Tim was looking at Paul. "It'll be over by the time you get there."

It was easy, once the drone of bombers had receded, to accept what he said, settle back and enjoy the last of the sun. The shadows now had swallowed more than half the lawn. A single star clung to the topmost branches of the fir tree, and the sky above the distant hill, where the stricken German plane had gone down, was fading to a pale translucent green.

"This is perfect," Elinor said.

But then, a short time later, a plague of midges descended on bare arms and legs and they were glad to pick up their plates and cups and run for the shelter of the house. Only then, surrounded by the familiar walls and furniture, did the reality of the war reassert itself.

"I wonder if there's any news," Tim said.

They all gathered round the wireless, while Tim fiddled with the knobs, producing a great buzzing and crackling interspersed with short bursts of music. After a while, he gave up and tried to telephone several people in London, but it was impossible to get through. He was starting to look uneasy. "I'll drive up in the morning, see what's going on."

As if that was going to make a difference, they all silently thought. They went through into the drawing room, where they decided the sun had definitely fallen over the yardarm and it was high time they had a drink.

Two glasses of whisky later, Rachel was already slightly slewed. She squinted at Elinor, as if a sea fret had suddenly blown into the drawing room. "You're not really going to drive an ambulance, are you?"

"Ye-es."

"But, Elinor, you can't drive."

"I can, actually."

"She's rather good," Paul said. *Well, decisive, anyway.*

"I simply can't imagine it."

"They wouldn't let her do it if she wasn't competent."

Poor Elinor. When he'd first met her family, Paul had been inclined to think her complaints about them were unjustified, but over the years, he'd seen how consistently her mother and sister undermined her, though he didn't quite know why she was singled out for criticism in this way.

Mrs. Murchison appeared in the doorway. "I'm off now, madam."

"Oh, yes, thank you. Where's Kenny? Is he in bed?"

"I don't know, madam. I thought he was in here with you."

"I expect he's still in the garden. Elinor . . . ?"

"He won't be out there now," Elinor said. "It's dark."

Rachel waved a hand vaguely at the blacked-out window. "He catches moths."

"God, yes, and he uses a lamp." Tim made an unconvincing show of getting out of his armchair. "We'll have the air-raid warden down on us like a ton of bricks."

Rachel said, "Frightful little man, always looking for something he can tell me off about, he just can't wait."

Paul put his glass down. Elinor said, "No, look, you stay here, I'll go."

IT WAS A relief to get out of the house. Rachel had been starting to needle her, as she always did when she'd had a few drinks.

The moonlight and the blacked-out windows behind her made the garden seem a wild, even dangerous, place. She could see the attraction being out here at night would have for a child. At Kenny's age, she and Toby had been great bug hunters: soaking sheets of purple paper in sugar water then arranging them around an oil lamp under the trees. Moths had been Toby's speciality. She remembered herself as a girl in a white dress with moths fluttering all around her, a blizzard of moths, and Toby saying: *"Keep still."* She froze, instantly, and he pointed to a huge dark moth that was clinging to her chest. He bent to look more closely, his pupils in the lamplight tiny pinpricks of black. "Do you know, I think it's a Death's Head." "I don't care what it is, get it off me." Jigging up and down, afraid to touch the moth that clung and clung and rubbed its *things* together. "No, keep still, they're rare." So she kept still, while he came closer and closer until she could feel his breath on her neck, almost as if he were the moth and she the flame . . .

But it wasn't fair. Middle-aged, now, searching through a moonlit garden for a child who wasn't hers, she wanted to protest: he was older than me. Two years older. How could I possibly have known? Decades too late for that. *Forget,* she told herself. Some things can only be forgotten.

"Kenny?"

No reply. She walked round the side of the house to the gate and looked up and down the lane. The moon was bright enough for her to see the black squares of gun emplacements on the river banks. No guns fired tonight, though; no fighter planes in the sky.

Paul came out of the house. "Any luck?"

"No, he might just have gone to bed."

"No, I've checked." He joined her by the gate. "I hope the little bugger hasn't run off. Bet he has."

"No, I don't think—"

"There was too much talk at teatime about the East End being bombed. His mother's there, for God's sake."

Rachel had come to the door. "No sign?"

"No." Elinor was trying not to sound worried.

"He'll have gone to the station," Paul said.

"Well, he'll be out of luck, then." Tim, peering over Rachel's shoulder. "There'll be no trains running tonight."

"Would he have any money?" Elinor asked.

"*Oh, yes*," Rachel said.

Tim explained: "He steals."

"When did we last see him?" Elinor asked.

On the lawn at teatime, that was the general opinion. Nobody could be more precise than that.

"So he's been gone for hours," Paul said.

Elinor chafed her bare arms as if the night had suddenly grown colder. "I think he's still here. He's probably up there now, laughing at us."

"I'll just check the station," Paul said.

"Hang on, I'll come with you."

"No, you stay with Rachel." He lowered his voice. "And for God's sake, try to get her to lay off the booze, she's half-cut already."

"You won't be long?"

"No, you go on in, I'll be all right."

Reluctantly, she let go of his arm and went back into the house.

DRIVING DOWN THE long tunnel of trees with only the thin beams of blackout headlights to guide him, Paul felt a small sense of relief at getting away from the house and the empty bedroom upstairs. To have something concrete to do—find the little bugger and bring him back—helped enormously. He told himself he wasn't seriously worried: a boy that age couldn't have got far. On the other hand, Kenny wasn't most boys.

At the station, Paul parked in a great spray of gravel

and ran on to the platform. Despite Tim's certainty, there might still be some local trains running and if he'd got on one of those he could be anywhere by now. The platform was deserted. Standing on the edge, Paul looked up the line towards London, where an ominous red glow was lighting the underbelly of the clouds. His fear, now—because his fears kept shifting—was that Kenny had come to the station, realized there were no trains, and had simply jumped down on to the track and started walking. That would solve one problem: finding his way. Walk along that line and, yes, you would reach London, in the end. He could be miles away by now. Or—*let's be optimistic*—he might have decided to wait till morning.

Finding the door of the waiting room unlocked, Paul went in and flashed the dim needlepoint of his blackout torch around the walls. Posters advertising day trips to the seaside: children building sandcastles on beaches, buckets, spades, swings, roundabouts: all as innocent and far away as childhood itself. Only one poster, newer than the rest, warned of the dangers of careless talk. No Kenny. It was beginning to look as if he had set off to walk. Paul closed the door and went to the end of the platform. The more he thought about it the more obvious it seemed: Kenny would simply follow the lines.

Paul jumped down on to the track and started to walk, his footsteps loud on the gravel. Moonlight sliding along the rails beside him made him feel as if he were wading through water. He was treading on the heels of his own faint shadow. At the bend in the line, he stopped, the tracks stretching out ahead of him into the far distance. It was pointless to go on, when he didn't even know whether Kenny had chosen this route or not.

He turned and started to go back, but then a movement

in the buddleia bushes by the side of the track caught his eye. There was no wind to account for the movement, but it could be an animal, a fox out hunting, though something in the waiting silence felt human. Quickly, he darted up the bank and dragged out a struggling Kenny, a little, yelping, spitting ball of fury who kicked at his shins and, finally, bit his hand. "Ouch, you little sod."

Kenny went still. "I'm not going back."

"What are you going to do, then? Stay here?"

"Getting the train."

"Not tonight you're not."

"There'll be one in the morning."

"All right, then, but what's the point of staying here tonight? When you could be sleeping in your own bed?" A mulish silence. "Look, why don't we talk about it in the morning? Just let's get you home and—"

The boy wrenched himself free. "*That's* home." He jabbed his finger at the red glare in the sky.

It was Paul's turn to be silenced. At that moment, he knew he had to take Kenny to see his mother. Not necessarily to stay with her, but at least to see her. "She'll be all right, you know."

"No, she won't, she's only got a shelter in the backyard and she won't even go in it."

"Why won't she?"

"She says she can't breathe, she just—" He shook his head, on the verge of tears.

"Tell you what, come back now and—"

"*No.*"

"*Listen.* I'll take you to see her."

"Now?"

"No, in the morning, it's too—"

"She could be dead by then."

Deep breath. "Kenny, you can't go tonight."

Kenny heaved a great sigh of resignation, his shoulders dropped and he started to trudge back towards the station.

Paul relaxed. "There's a good lad."

Then, without warning, Kenny dodged round him and raced away along the track. *Oh for God's sake.* Paul set off after him, lurching from side to side, gritting his teeth against the pain in his knee—running on gravel was almost impossible. *Mad*, he thought. *And dangerous.* Local trains might still be running and like everything else these days they operated with dimmed lights. If there was one on the other side of the bend, it could be on you before you knew it. And Kenny was already well ahead.

"Kenny, all right!"

The boy looked over his shoulder, tripped and fell. But he was up on his feet again in a minute, brushing gravel from his knees, by the time Paul came panting up.

"You stupid little bugger, if a train had come round that bend you wouldn't've stood a chance."

"Thought you said there weren't any."

"*Local* trains."

"Well, why can't I get on one of them, then, and walk the rest of the way?"

"Because it's *miles.*"

He realized Kenny had no idea where he was, or London was, or—supposing he ever got to London—where the docks were . . . Nothing. Not a bloody thing. And yet, if Paul forced him back to the house, he'd just wait for the first opportunity and run away again. He needed to see his mother.

"Look, all right, we'll go tonight, but you've got to go back and tell everybody, do it properly. Right?"

Kenny nodded. "You promise, though?"

"I promise."

"All right."

THEY FOUND THE family still in the drawing room, slumped in armchairs with the dazed, disorientated look of the recently bereaved and the totally pissed.

"I'm taking him home," Paul said.

Elinor looked up. "You mean, to our house?"

"No. Well, yes, that first. Then his."

She shook her head. "You can't do that."

"He wants to go."

"And that's a reason? Paul, it's mad. Oh, all right, if he wants to see his mother, fair enough . . . But surely it can wait till morning?"

Paul felt the boy's eyes on him. "No, it's got to be tonight. I promised."

"Then you shouldn't have done!"

Rachel stood up. "I'll just pack a few things."

Holding on to the backs of chairs, she made it to the door. She was making no effort to postpone their departure, nor even to assert her right to take the decision. The truth was, she was as keen to get rid of Kenny as he was to go. And Tim said nothing. It was all rather disgraceful, but it did at least confirm Paul's view that the boy would be better off with his own family. While Rachel moved around upstairs, Paul and Elinor stood a few feet away from each other, Elinor with her bare arms clasped across her chest, Paul smoking furiously.

"You will ring when you get there?" she asked.

"If I can get through."

A few minutes later, Rachel came down with a small battered suitcase, the same one Kenny had arrived with a year ago, though the clothes inside were all new. She'd given him a few *Boy's Own* annuals and the toy soldiers. Kenny's eyes widened when he opened the paper bag and saw them.

"What do you say?" Elinor asked.

"Thank you."

He was hugging them to his chest as if they might be taken back at any moment.

"Come on, then," Paul said.

Kenny went round the circle, shaking hands. "Thank you for having me."

It was an oddly stilted performance, heartbreaking in a way. It brought tears to Paul's eyes. Perhaps Kenny had, after all, grown fond of this family who'd taken him in so reluctantly?

But he didn't look back or wave as they drove away.

❋ EIGHT

As they were leaving the village, Paul glanced sideways at Kenny. "I'd try to get some sleep if I were you. It's a long way."

But Kenny was wide awake, both hands resting on the seat, surreptitiously stroking the leather. Of course, he wouldn't have been in a car very often, if at all. Even in these circumstances it was a treat to be savored. He leaned against the glass, peering at passing trees and fields. Once or twice, Paul thought he might have nodded off, but no. Kenny's eyes were strained wide with excitement. No hope of sleep there.

He didn't seem to want to talk, which was probably just as well: Paul needed to concentrate on the road. So far, he'd managed to avoid blackout driving altogether. In London, if he had to be out late, he took a taxi or walked. Now, he drove slowly, his headlights casting narrow beams of bluish light in which moths and insects constantly danced. On either side of the lane, hedges and ditches shelved steeply into darkness. He crouched over the wheel, straining his eyes to see into the gloom. So far the blackout had killed more people than the raids; and no wonder: you couldn't see people until you were right on top of them. But the trouble with staring into darkness, if you do it long enough, is that you start seeing things. Like looking into no-man's-land in the last war: in the end, you could imagine anything lurking out there. *Don't look straight at it,* he used to tell sentries, the young, inexperienced ones who were almost too terrified to blink. *You'll see more if you look slightly to one side.* Unfortunately, looking slightly to one side of the road wasn't an option. Though there was this to be said for it: the need to concentrate stopped him thinking about the possible idiocy of what he was doing. *Possible?* Elinor might have asked. And he had to admit it: this did feel like driving into a trap.

He looked at Kenny. *Ha,* eyelids drooping, and about time too. He went on driving as smoothly as he could until, at the next bend, the boy slid sideways and slumped against his arm. Asleep, at last.

CENTRAL LONDON WAS reassuring. The streets, though quiet, seemed almost normal, or what passed for normal these days. The few cars he saw had little, piggy, red eyes; they puttered cautiously along, while taxis careered past, as if they owned the entire city—as indeed they did. Petrol rationed for private cars, buses scarce. This was what you saw everywhere. The change was in the sky: beyond the black ridges of the rooftops, a red, sullen glare was growing and spreading, lit at intervals by the orange flashes of exploding bombs. Searchlights everywhere, but no fighter planes that he could see; and no guns.

He parked the car and persuaded Kenny to get out. At first the boy was groggy with sleep, but Paul knew he'd need to keep an eye on him. Kenny was wound up to such a pitch of excitement he was quite capable of slipping away and trying to reach home tonight. He'd have no trouble finding the docks; all he'd have to do was walk straight towards that red glow. But into what kind of hell?

Paul tried several times to turn the front-door key, but it no longer quite fitted. Perhaps the wood had warped, something like that; you couldn't get a locksmith for love nor money. He sucked the key, pursing his lips against the sourness of the metal, but when he tried again, it turned. A breath of cool, stale air. The house had been empty only a few days and yet already it had started to forget them. Letters and newspapers littered the mat. Stooping, he picked them up and put them, unopened, on the hall table. Kenny stepped over the threshold as cautiously as a cat. Now the drive was behind him, Paul felt suddenly very tired.

Closing the door on the merciless moonlight, he went round the drawing room checking the blackout curtains were in position and switching on the lamps. Then he turned to look at Kenny, who was staring blankly around the strange room. *Now what? What on earth am I supposed to do with him?* The sirens were sounding for the second time that night. They ought, really, to go to one of the public shelters, but he couldn't face going out again and he didn't think Kenny could either.

"We'll sleep in the hall," he said. "We'll be safe enough there." A few weeks ago, when the nuisance raids started, he and Elinor had dragged a double mattress downstairs. They'd lined the walls with other mattresses and cushions from the sofa and he'd made sure all the windows were taped against blast. Of course, none of this would protect them from a direct hit, but then neither would most of the shelters. "Why don't you settle yourself down? I'll see if I can find us something to eat." *And drink.*

In the kitchen, he opened and shut cupboards, found half a loaf of bread (stale, but it would have to do), a couple of wizened apples, a slab of Cheddar just beginning to sweat and a bottle of orange juice. Then he poured himself a large whisky and carried the tray into the hall.

Kenny had tipped the toy soldiers out of the bag and was arranging them on a strip of wooden floor between the mattress and the drawing-room door. He looked up, white-faced, on the verge of tears again but blinking them back hard. "Why can't we go tonight?"

"Because it'll be absolute chaos and we'll only get in the way."

"We could help."

"I don't think so. Anyway, I doubt they'd let us anywhere near." Thumps and bangs in the distance. "Look, I'll take you first thing in the morning, soon as it's light. Sorry, Kenny, best I can do." A nearer thud shook the door. "Come on, have something to eat, it'll make you feel better."

Kenny was tearing off a chunk of bread with his teeth. "We could play."

"Play?"

Kenny nodded towards the soldiers. Well, why not? It would take his mind off it. So they munched apples, cheese and bread, drank whisky and orange juice, moved cohorts of little figures here and there until, eventually, even Paul became absorbed in the game. The background clumps and thuds blended in really rather well. Kenny was the officer, of course. Paul was a not-very-bright NCO. Now and then, an explosion rattled the window frames—and, yes, he was afraid. Nothing like the fear he'd experienced in the trenches; though, in one way, it was worse: he was experiencing this fear in the safety of his own home, and that meant nowhere was safe. More than once, he was tempted to go out and try to see what was happening, but he didn't want to interrupt the game—it was so obviously helping take Kenny's mind off the bombs—and so they played on, metal armies advancing across strips of parquet floor, rather more quickly than they'd done in life; Passchendaele and the Somme played out on the floor of a house in Bloomsbury. "Yes, sir!" Drifting clouds of smoke obscured the salient. "Right you are, sir!" A shell landing in a flooded crater sent sheets of muddy water thirty feet into the air. "Going out to take a look, now, sir!"

Kenny would have to sleep soon, his eyes were rolling back in his head, but my God he fought it. Finished his orange juice, asked for more . . . This time, Paul tipped a little whisky into the glass and, although Kenny wrinkled his nose at the funny taste, he drank it all down and shortly afterwards curled up on the mattress and went to sleep.

Paul began to clear the soldiers away, then stopped, selected two and looked at them, lying side by side on the palm of his hand. Somehow, last time he'd seen them, he hadn't quite realized what it meant. *My God,* he thought. *We've become toys.* He wanted to share the moment, the shock of it, but there was nobody who'd understand.

He slipped the little figures into his pocket, lay down beside Kenny and went to sleep.

In the middle of the night, Kenny woke up and shook Paul's arm. "You hear that?"

Paul struggled to wake up; he must've gone very deep, he could hardly force his eyes open. They lay listening to the thuds until one blast louder than the rest made Kenny cry out. He was too big to ask for reassurance, too young not to need it. Paul touched his arm. "Don't worry, it's all right."

"Is it true, you don't hear the one that hits you?"

"*Yes.*" Said very firmly indeed, though he'd certainly heard the shell that had hit him; he'd heard it shrieking all the way down. Still did.

Kenny was sitting up, wide-eyed, quivering like a whip-pet at the start of a race. "Can we go now?"

"Soon as it's light."

"What time is it?"

"Three thirty. Come on, go back to sleep."

"I can't sleep."

Nor could Paul.

"You know, we mightn't be able to get there. There won't be any buses or taxis. And I'm not driving through that."

"We can walk."

No point arguing. And anyway he didn't know. No more than Kenny could he guess what they would have to face. "Well, I'm going back to sleep," he said. "And if you've got any sense at all you'll do the same."

He turned on his side and lay in darkness, waiting for the change in Kenny's breathing. Only when he was sure Kenny was asleep did he let his own eyes close.

THE ALL CLEAR went at four thirty. Kenny woke instantly, alert and wary, more like an animal than a child. Paul fetched the last of the orange juice for Kenny and two cups of black tea, one for each of them. "Here, drink this. No, I know it doesn't taste very nice but you need something hot."

Paul stepped across the mattress and opened the front door; his eyes, gritty with tiredness, flinched from the sudden light. Yet another monotonously blue sky, but over there above the docks, the red glow lingered, mixed in with plumes of billowing black smoke. Even at this distance he could smell burning.

Kenny joined him on the step. "Look," Paul started to say, wanting to warn him again that it mightn't be possible to get anywhere near his house, but the words dribbled into vacancy before the boy's fixed, hard stare. He was going, no question; no hope of deflecting him either.

"Come on," Paul said. "Let's get your case."

A CABBIE AGREED to take them part of the way. When a warden waved at them to turn back, Paul and Kenny got out and walked for a while before Paul begged a lift in an ambulance from Derek James, one of the drivers Elinor worked with.

Oily black smoke drifted across the wet roads. Many of the warehouses were still on fire, dwarfing the exhausted crews who still, hour after hour, directed white poles of water into the heart of the blaze. Other buildings had been reduced to charred and smoldering ruins in which, at any moment, you felt a fire could break out again. So many streets lay in ruins he couldn't understand how Kenny was finding his way, and yet he rarely hesitated. Bodies lay by the side of the roads, lifeless, sodden heaps of rags. No child should be seeing this, but then, some of the bodies were children.

Once, he tried to persuade Kenny to turn back, but the boy just shook his head. "No, no, it's just along here." He grabbed Paul's sleeve and started dragging him along. He had such a strange, haunted look on his face that Paul was frightened for him, though at least the intensity of his drive to get home seemed to prevent his taking in the horrors on either side. They were walking along the river now, or as close to it as they could get. On the opposite bank, a wall of flame half a mile long leapt into the lowering sky. In midstream, burning barges, loose from their moorings, drifted hither and thither with the shifting of the tide.

Ahead of them a cluster of little terraces, still apparently more or less intact, ran up to the dock gates, like a row of piglets suckling a sow's teats. As they got closer, they saw that most of the houses were badly damaged and a few had collapsed altogether, leaving gaps through which further destruction showed. "Kenny . . ."

"No, it's not far. Just along there."

As they turned into the first street Paul heard Kenny's intake of breath. It seemed, at first sight, as though all the houses had been hit. Kenny began to run, weaving his way around piles of rubble until at last he stopped in front of one of the houses. The windows had been blown in, a mattress hung out of an upstairs room, most of the roof had gone. Paul tried to push the front door open. It was a struggle—the door was jammed shut by debris from a fallen ceiling—but he managed it at last.

Kenny pushed past him and was clambering across the mess of bricks and plaster in the passage.

"Don't," Paul called out. "It's not—"

Safe, he had been going to say, but the word meant nothing here. He followed Kenny into the devastated sitting room, through the almost-untouched kitchen and out into the yard at the back. Fleeting glimpses along the way of where and how Kenny had lived.

"Mam?" Kenny was calling. "Mam?"

A body was lying outside the coalhouse door, a woman's body, facedown, and for a moment Paul thought: *Oh God it's her,* but Kenny paid it no attention. Farther along, by the yard door, a man's head rested on the concrete, severed neatly at the neck, one eye closed. Kenny pushed it to one side with his foot and opened the door into the alley. A big jump down and he was on the cobbles, staring up and down a row of washing lines, from some of which, incredibly, shirts and pillowcases still hung. Dazed-looking people were wandering up and down, lost, waiting for somebody to get hold of them and tell them where to go. A few, braver or harder than the rest, were rescuing their possessions from ruined houses, carrying tables and chairs into the alley and setting them down, with sheets and blankets and pots and pans, small heaps of possessions fiercely guarded. Somebody had stuck a Union Jack on a pile of rubble, but most of these people were too exhausted and shocked for gestures of that kind.

Kenny looked around him. "It's all gone."

Paul opened his mouth, but had no idea what to say. He was about to suggest that Kenny should come back inside the house, when, at the far end of the street, they saw a woman walking towards them with a baby in her arms. Kenny ran towards her shouting, "Mam! Mam!" She stopped, but then came on more quickly. Her clothes were black and torn, her face blackened too. She might even be burnt, Paul thought. At any rate she'd lost her eyebrows. She looked dully at Kenny. "Oh, it's you."

A dark-haired, cadaverous man with yellow skin and deep furrows in his cheeks followed along behind, holding a tiny red-haired girl by the hand. "What you doing here?"

Kenny ignored this and went on tugging at the woman's sleeve, but she shook him off. It's the shock, Paul thought, she'll be all right in a minute, and indeed, a few seconds later, she pressed the boy's head against her side and ran her fingers distractedly through his hair. But then, immediately, she looked accusingly at Paul. "What you brought him back for? I can't have him—you can see for yourself there's nothing left."

"Kenny." Paul put his hand on the boy's shoulder but he squirmed away and burrowed his head deeper into his mother's side. "Your mam's right. I think you'd better come back with me, just till your mam gets a bit more settled."

"I'm not going." He looked up at his mother. "You can't make me go with him, he's been mucking me about."

It took Paul a moment to realize what he meant. "You little toad. You know bloody well that's not true."

"Mam, it is, Mam. He's been putting whisky in me orange juice and all sorts. Ask him. No, go on, ask him. *And* we slept in the same bed last night."

"Kenny? No-o, Kenny, look at me, look me in the eye and say it, go on." When there was no response, Paul looked directly at the mother. "It's not true."

"No, I know, it's all right, he's always making things up." She leaned in closer. With a slight shock he saw the moist, puckered anemone of the baby's mouth tugging at a huge brown nipple. Almost whispering, she said, "The thing is, he doesn't get on with his stepdad." She glanced over her shoulder, then made a sharp, sideways gesture with her free hand: *hopeless.*

The cadaverous man was starting to take an interest in the conversation—perhaps thinking there might be a fiver in it for him, if he played his cards right. And why not? Plenty of girls, and not a few boys, changed hands for a lot less than that. This was not quite the family reunion Paul had been expecting.

"Where are they taking you?" he asked.

"I don't know." She looked helplessly at a small crowd that was gathering a few feet away at the end of the alley.

"School on Agate Street!" somebody shouted.

"Is it far?" Paul called back.

" 'Bout a mile."

A hell of a distance for these shattered people—some injured, some with minor burns, many in pajamas and dressing gowns—to walk. He looked down at their feet. Not all of them had shoes; some limped over the cobbles, blood-shod.

He turned back to Kenny's mother. "Look, I'll help you carry." He was desperate to do something, anything.

"I've got a suitcase packed," she said.

So Paul followed her into the house and dragged it out of its hiding place under the stairs. God knows what she'd got in there. Lifting it almost wrenched his arm out of the socket, but he wasn't going to give in. If they could bear this, so could he.

Air-raid wardens, white-faced with plaster dust, had already started shepherding the crowd along.

So they walked. And what a rabble they were. Red eyes stared out of gray faces; some ranted and raved, others were hysterical or mute with shock. He'd witnessed all these reactions in casualty clearing stations in France and Belgium, only he'd never thought to see them here. *London's burning, London's burning* ... Bloody tune skittered round and round his brain as he lugged and tramped, try as he might he couldn't get rid of it, so he made himself look outwards, to notice and remember.

They walked along rubble-strewn roads, through puddles of water filmed with oil, over fire hoses that lay across the black and glistening pavements as gray and flaccid as drowned worms. On their right, buildings blazed out of control; others, black and skeletal, wavered in the heat. Once, looking ahead, he saw the tarmac come to life and move. He thought it must be a trick of the light then realized it was a colony of rats, thousands of them, fleeing a burning warehouse. Sometimes the ground underfoot was hot and the people whose feet were lacerated or burned cried out as they limped across it. The really terrifying thing, the one he knew he'd never forget, was when the road behind them suddenly ignited in a long, slow, leisurely lick of flame.

The things people carried. An old lady's wrinkled forearms covered in claw marks, beaded with blood. A tabby cat, its pupils wildly dilated, peered out from the neck of her dressing gown. A clock. Photographs—yes, of course you'd try to save those, but a black hand grasping a bunch of plastic lilies of the valley? Or an elephant's tusk in a brown leather sling?

At last they reached the school. After twenty minutes' hanging about, they were guided down into the basement. They found a place by the wall and Paul was finally able to relinquish the suitcase and chafe his hands to get the blood flowing again. "I'll see if I can find out what's going on."

Pushing his way through the crowd, he saw how packed the basement was. The smell of hot human bodies mingled with the fumes from oil lamps snagged in his throat. Wardens were setting up latrine buckets behind a screen of blankets, men one end of the corridor, women the other, though how people were supposed to get to them through the crush . . . He spoke to one of the wardens, who said buses were coming to take everybody away that afternoon. "Where to?" The man didn't know; nobody knew. But it was some consolation to know they weren't going to have to endure these conditions for more than a couple of hours.

When he got back Kenny's mother was sitting on the suitcase feeding the baby, a tiny, wizened little mite with a bright orange face and a shock of straight black hair. Two weeks old, apparently, and he hadn't been due till mid-October. Looking away to give her some privacy, Paul caught the expression on Kenny's face. Love? Yes, that certainly. But also the pain of exclusion. A gap of twelve years or more between him and these children, and that sallow-skinned, silent man was very obviously not his father. Had they sent him to the country for his own safety, or because the family worked better without him there?

All around them people were settling down, arranging bags and coats, staking out small territories, though as more and more people pushed down the stairs these fragile boundaries were being continually breached. "Where are we going?" was the question on everybody's lips. "Where are they taking us?" But there were no answers from the wardens or anyone else, only offers of more tea. Nobody knew. People were guessing Kent, the hop fields, where there was accommodation for migrant workers. "I've had some good holidays there," Kenny's mother said. The thought of the hop fields seemed to cheer her up. She really didn't look at all well.

More and more people crammed themselves into the airless space. Many people had lit cigarettes and a bluish pall of smoke hung on the stagnant air. The wardens shouted at them to put them out, but only a few did. Along with sweat, cigarette smoke, dirty nappies and latrine buckets were all the smells they'd brought with them on their clothes: burnt brick, charred wood, the carrion stench of high explosive. Paul's chest was tightening all the time, but he didn't feel he could just walk away.

He found the chief warden and offered to help with first aid, though with no clean water or bandages there was very little he or anybody else could do. Wardens and voluntary workers were everywhere, trying to help, but the press of bodies defeated them. By now, moving was almost impossible. No Underground train at the height of the rush hour had ever been as packed as this. He could see Kenny and his mother, who now had the grizzling toddler in her arms, at the other end of the main corridor, but there was no hope of reaching them. He pointed to the stairs, mouthing: *Got to go.* Kenny raised his hand to wave good-bye, then turned to his baby sister, who stopped crying and held out her arms.

At first, getting upstairs against the crush of people surging down seemed impossible, but then somebody at the top started organizing those coming down onto the left. Paul and another warden edged up step by step, persuading people to move to one side. At the top of the stairs Paul looked around for somebody in authority. An exhausted little man with a gray, bristly mustache bleated, "What am I supposed to do? They can't stay up here, it's not safe."

When, finally, Paul struggled out of the playground into the street he held on to the railings and watched the stream of the shocked and homeless going through the gates. It wasn't all bad. That basement was deep enough to withstand even a direct hit. But then, just as he was about to leave, he noticed the building was already bomb-damaged. One wall had a crack running from the roof down to the ground. Immediately, he wanted to go back and get them out, but it was impossible and anyway they'd be all right, the buses would be here in another hour, the wardens would get everybody organized and they'd be off to Kent, and safety. And Kenny was back with his mother, where he'd wanted, and needed, to be.

❈ *NINE*

ack at the house he picked his way across the
mattress in the hall, remembering Kenny's out-
rageous accusation: And *we slept in the same bed last night.* It
was difficult not to feel a certain reluctant admiration for the
boy's single-minded and utterly unscrupulous determination
to get what he wanted. *Little toad.*

He ought really now to go straight to his studio and start
work but he was finding it unusually difficult. That walk
with the suitcase had taken a lot out of him. So he went out,
bought milk and bread and made himself a pot of tea and
toast. He was just finishing the last mouthful when he heard
the front door open.

"Elinor?"

It had to be: the only other person who had a key was
the housekeeper, who'd gone to stay with her sister in Dorset
and God alone knew when she'd be back. He went upstairs to
the ground floor and found Elinor in front of the hall mirror,
unpinning her hat. She raised her cheek for him to kiss.

"This is a surprise."

"Yes, Tim gave me a lift; I thought it was too good an
opportunity to miss. And I need some more clothes anyway."

"Oh, you're going back?"

She pulled a face. "Well, I've got to, really. I can't leave Rachel to do it all."

"I thought Gabriella was supposed to be coming?"

"Yes, but she's eight months pregnant. She's not going to be doing a lot of running around. Where's Kenny?"

Paul looked surprised. "With his mother."

"So you took him back?"

"Well, yes, of course. That was the point."

"Are they all right?"

"So-so. The house was bombed, but they're being evacuated this afternoon."

"Was she pleased to see him?"

That was not a comfortable question. It forced him to weigh his impressions. "No, not very. I don't think he gets on with his stepfather and she's got two younger children."

"And she kept them with her?"

"Well, yes, obviously."

"I wonder what Kenny thinks about that."

"He doesn't seem to fit in, but on the other hand, he obviously loves them."

"I don't think you should've taken him back."

"He wanted to go."

"He's a *child.* Anyway, it wasn't your decision."

"No, it was Rachel's. And Tim's. Tim said bugger-all and Rachel couldn't wait to see the back of him."

She turned back to the mirror and started fluffing up her hair where the hat had flattened it.

"You think it was about me, don't you? *My* mother?"

She met his eyes in the glass. "Wasn't it?"

The conversation disturbed Paul. Kenny had wanted more than anything to be back with his mother. Wasn't that justification enough? He remembered the way her soot-blackened arm had come round to press his head into her side. No, absolutely, he didn't regret it. A lot of this uneasiness was no more than the shapeless anxiety that comes from extreme tiredness, and he couldn't afford to give in to it. He was on duty tonight, and the next night. And the next. No, he'd taken the decision, and now he just had to forget about it and move on.

BY THE END of the second night on duty tiredness had become another dimension. He snatched an hour or two of dozing on the bed between coming off duty and walking round to his studio, but during the long, golden, sludgy afternoon he had to force himself to go on painting; it was dangerous even to think about sleep.

On the morning after his third night, he was standing in the kitchen, drinking a cup of hot sweet tea and idly flicking through the newspapers. There was a certain grim fascination in seeing how officialdom packaged the destruction of the night before. He was about to turn a page when a headline about a direct hit on a school in the East End caught his eye. Seventy-three people dead. Well, there must be hundreds of schools in the East End. Under the headline there was a grainy photograph of the ruined building with a heap of rubble breaking through iron railings onto the pavement. *Was* that Agate Street? Well, even if it was, Kenny and his family would have long since moved on.

He opened the door, intending to walk round to his studio as he did every morning. Another fine day, though the smell of burnt brick dust tainted the bright air. Farther along the street, an old man was sweeping up the first of the autumn's fallen leaves, a sight you saw every year around this time, only this September the familiar rustle was sharpened by the scratching of broken glass. If you closed your eyes, it sounded exactly like waves seething between the pebbles of a shingle beach. Only he daren't close his eyes. Even the action of blinking brought with it the strong, dark undertow of sleep.

A crowd had gathered at the entrance to a side street, people who'd spent the night in shelters returning to find access to their homes denied. He looked across the road. From where he stood, the tape cordoning off the street was invisible, so the people seemed to be pressed against a glass wall—like insects splatted across a windscreen. Lured by the attraction of that forbidden space, he crossed the road and stared up the empty street. At first nobody spoke, and then a few whispers began to break the cathedral hush. There was a time bomb in the street. Nobody was allowed to go home and, after the long night in a cramped, foul-smelling shelter, that was hard. Some of the group were in pajamas and dressing gowns; one of the women had thrown a mackintosh over her nightdress. An old lady with her hair in thin, gray plaits was trembling with shock, or perhaps it was just the general frailty of age, and yet she seemed positively cheerful; defiant, even. She touched his sleeve—her hand as skeletal as a dead leaf on a bonfire, but God how she crackled and sparked as the flames licked round her. "That's my house," she said, pointing. "The one with the blue door."

It was odd; when he'd crossed the road to join the little group staring into the sunlit silence of the cordoned-off street, he'd fully intended going to his studio to do a normal day's work, and yet, minutes later, as he turned away, he knew he had to go to Agate Street. At the corner of the road, he turned and looked back. There they still were, haloed in light, as if the air had somehow solidified in front of them. How would you paint them—convey that sense of suspended motion—or of an infinitely slow, noiseless collision—when there was nothing visible to account for it?

He took a taxi as far as he could, then walked. All around were signs of last night's destruction. A burst water main with a group of boys egging each other on to run through it, their shrieks, sharp as seagulls' cries, slicing the crisp air. Farther along, he passed a broken shopwindow with mannequins inside, all prudishly shrouded in brown paper, one leaning out into the street, arm and wrist elegantly posed, smirking at devastation. All the time, now, you noticed these oddities. What survived; what didn't. And that first feeling of indecency at peering into other people's lives—their bedrooms, their bathrooms, their toilets—had already begun to fade.

As he walked, he thought not about Kenny—he still felt there was no real reason for anxiety—but about that cordoned-off street, the way a perfectly ordinary road acquired, merely because access to it had been denied, an air of mystery. He remembered looking through a periscope into no-man's-land: the inhabitation of rats and eels, and of the corpses, submerged in flooded craters, whose slow, invisible decomposition sent strings of bubbles spiraling to the surface. But, no, that wasn't it. It wasn't the obvious horrors that made the hairs on the nape of your neck stand up. It might be a country lane: not bombed, not devastated, pretty, even; but a lane you couldn't walk down, because it was enemy territory. And that lane, merely by being forbidden, acquired depth, mystery and terror. It seemed shocking to him that now there were streets and squares in London that aroused the same prickling of unease. He'd never before felt that he wanted to paint London, or any other built-up area, and yet those roped-off, silent squares and streets had started to haunt him. Perhaps because blacked-out and bombed London felt less and less like a city?

Agate Street wasn't difficult to find. A corkscrew of black smoke twined into the sky above it, almost like a question mark reversed. This was the school in the photograph. Even before he turned the corner, he knew that.

Despite the coil of smoke, the fire service must have declared the building safe, because teams of rescue-squad workers, wearing overalls and tin hats, were clambering over a scree of rubble, slipping and slithering as they tried to get a footing. The school seemed to have imploded; there was a crater at the center where the roof had crashed through onto the floors below. Whoever had been in the basement when the upper floors collapsed was dead now. Nobody could have survived tons of brick landing on them like that.

The scene in front of Paul was oddly static. Heat and dust everywhere, but no sense of urgency. The rescue workers with their covering of white dust might have been carvings on an antique frieze: a funeral procession, though, not a wedding feast. There was no sound. Four ambulances were parked by the side of the road, the drivers leaning against their vehicles, smoking, occasionally wiping sweat from foreheads or lips. They looked as if they'd been there for hours.

Still wearing his warden's coat and tin hat, Paul ducked under the tape and strode confidently towards the ambulances. A tin hat could take you almost anywhere. Close to, it was obvious the drivers had been there all night. Red-eyed, exhausted, stubble sprouting from their chins, lips parched from the long hours of chain-smoking, none of them looking as if they expected to be going anywhere in the next few hours. As he approached, the door of one of the vehicles opened and a figure he recognized jumped down on to the road. Derek James.

"My God," Paul said. "They're keeping you busy."

"Twelve bloody hours I've been stuck here."

"What's happening?"

"You can see what's happening—bugger-all." He fished a packet of Woodbines from his pocket and offered it. "What you doing here anyway?"

"You know that lad I was with when you gave us a lift—Sunday?"

"Yeah?"

"Well, it turned out his house had been bombed and they were sent here." He could tell from James's face that something was wrong. "That was Sunday. They were just waiting for the buses to take them away."

"Bloody long wait."

Paul stared at him.

"They didn't come. Apparently, there was some mix-up over the address, Canning Town, Camden Town, God knows. And then, when they finally did show up, a raid started so they decided to postpone the evacuation. They were still here last night."

"But that's three days."

James shrugged. "Another bloody cock-up. They've had years to get this right. *Years.*"

Paul pictured Kenny and his family at the end of the crowded corridor, how at the last moment the little red-haired girl had turned and held out her arms. "How many?"

"They're saying seventy-three."

Paul twisted sharply to one side. "I was *there*, it was bloody well jam-packed."

James said, slowly: "To begin with you could hear them crying out . . . You know? And every now and then they'd call for silence and everybody stopped and listened, and then the last time . . ." He shook his head. "Mind, we did get two babies out. Tough little buggers, babies."

"Nobody else?"

"Not that I saw."

The rescue squads had started gathering in small groups around their leaders, the men who'd been climbing across the rubble sliding down and walking across to join them.

James nodded. "I think they're calling it."

"What, pulling out?"

"What else can they do? It's going to take weeks to clear that lot. Hundreds of bodies, this heat?"

He was right, of course. Every night these rescue squads were needed to dig out people who could still be saved. How could you possibly justify using them to retrieve dead bodies? No, the only thing to do with this was cement it over. Walk away. Paul patted James's shoulder and walked across to the railings. Now he was closer to the building, he noticed a smell that was not the stench of high explosive. The rescue workers wore masks against the plaster dust, but others, this side of the railings, were pinching their noses and covering their mouths with their hands. No, James was right, that was all you could do, declare it a mass grave. But my God . . . All those people. Kenny, the little girl, the baby. Kenny.

Resting his forehead against the railings, Paul realized he was looking at the small area of playground that was clear of rubble. Somebody, perhaps a teacher but more likely a child, had chalked out squares for a game of hopscotch. He saw, for a moment, with the clarity of hallucination, a stick of yellow chalk gripped in a small, pudgy hand.

Blinking the image away, he looked instead at the wrecked building and above it to the sky, where the corkscrew of black smoke was beginning to change shape. Again, he saw Kenny raise his hand and wave; again the little girl stretched out her arms, while flakes of soot, whirled around on the slight breeze, fell onto his upturned face like snow.

✥ *TEN*

*C*rappit heid. Dear God, fancy being reduced to that after all these years. Fishmonger just now give her a funny look—you'd think it was in his own best interest to be civil, wouldn't you, but oh, no. Just stood there in his straw hat and his white coat, fag end stuck to his bottom lip, bloody great turd of ash ready to drop—*and* he was leaning over the fish. "Cod's head?" he asked. She felt like saying: *You want the business or not?* Didn't, of course, just raked about in her purse for the coppers and handed them across. As she walked away, she felt his gaze stitched to her back, though when she turned round she saw he'd already moved on to the next customer, wasn't watching her at all.

She was sat on a bench in Russell Square on this September afternoon because she didn't know what the fuck else to do. In prison the only fresh air you got was an hour in the exercise yard every day, and even then all you did was trudge round and round, nothing much to look at except the wobbling backside of the woman in front. Still, on the inside, there were people all round you, you could hear them and see them even if you didn't talk to them, and then she come out and there was nobody. Oh, she could've gone back up north, set herself up again in a small way, people's front rooms, that type of thing—she didn't want to go attracting attention to herself. She knew she was going to have to be very, very careful.

So, in the end, she decided she'd make a complete break of it. Plenty of work in London, masses—*and* it was easy reach of the south coast. That's where the real money was, the ports, only she didn't want Gladys and Mrs. Buckle getting their fingers in the pot—bloodsuckers, the pair of 'em—so she told them she was packing it in altogether. "Can't face it without Howard," she'd said.

"What about Albert?" Gladys asked.

"What about him?"

"What's he going to do?"

"Oh, he'll move on." Stubborn silence. "You know as well as I do, Gladys, spirit guides do move on."

Albert hadn't. He was in and out all the time. Mind you, she hadn't dared risk the ports, though it was a big temptation, that lot at the Temple paid her a pittance. Absolute bloody disgrace, the amount they gave her. She filled the house—they didn't. Hence the frigging cod's head.

Which didn't half pong. Probably ponged a bit herself, to be honest, in this heat. God, it was hot. She could feel the sweat soaking through her dress shields, and the Vaseline she rubbed into her thighs to stop them chafing had long since melted into a claggy mess. No fun being fat this weather— and totally unfair, too. The amount she ate she should be thin as a rake, 'stead of which she was piling it on. It upset her, sometimes, the size she was. So to cheer herself up she started singing. "Wider still and wider, shall my bounds be set . . ." She was on stage, now, at the Alhambra, belting it out: "God, who made me mighty, make me mightier yet . . ." Waving her trident at the audience. "God who made me mighty, MAKE ME MIGHTIER YET!"

She looked around—people always seemed to think it a

bit odd when you sang like that—and saw a tall, thin man, with a limp, approaching. Not bad-looking, coat a bit shabby, but his shoes were good and he'd given them a bit of a polish. She noticed the limp, she always picked up on things like that, last war, probably, but it wasn't just the limp making him wobbly on his pins. Bugger was pissed, had to be. She pursed her lips disapprovingly, thinking of the bottle of gin under her kitchen sink. Never touched a drop of it before six o'clock. Eh, dear me, the state people let themselves get into. She hoped he wasn't going to sit near her, but, of course, Sod's law, he did.

He was a funny color, mind. "You all right?"

"Yes, I'm—all right. Went a bit dizzy there for a minute."

"Be the heat."

He agreed that yes, very probably, it would be the heat, then lapsed into silence.

Least he spoke. The way some of them went on down here, you couldn't pass a civil remark without them thinking you were giving them the glad eye or something. Bloody cod's head wasn't half stinking the place out, she only hoped he couldn't smell it, though the way he kept glancing her way she thought he probably could. It reminded her of something, that smell, and she couldn't quite place it—but then suddenly it dawned on her. And all at once she was back in the big classroom at Castle View Board School—skinny little thing with long black hair—nobody would credit it, but she had once been very thin, even a bit *too* thin—looking up at tall, angular Miss Brackenbury, who'd been drafted in to deliver her famous domestic science lecture: "Five Ways to Stuff a Cod's Head for a Penny." Forty little girls sat on stools and listened; forty little girls who knew their place and never seemed to wonder who was eating the cod's body while they were stuffing the head. But she did. She wondered.

And before she knew what she was doing she was on her feet and telling Miss Brackenbury exactly how she could stuff the cod's head—and where.

Six strokes of the cane she got for that. The minute school was out, she ran all the way along the shore to the castle and stood right on the edge of the cliff, clouds whirling around above her head, the sea boiling and churning in the Egyncleugh beneath her feet. One step. *One step.* She knew there'd be another good hiding when she got home. Nothing more certain. Dad believed in supporting the school. "Don't you go telling me you did nowt . . . You must've done summat." And off would come his belt, whipped from round his trousers, fast as a snake.

Eh, dear me. She heaved a sigh and closed her eyes, but then almost immediately opened them again and looked around the square. Amazing how many kids there were. A boy and an older man—dad or granddad—were kicking a ball around the grass. The boy couldn't have been more than twelve or thirteen, still young enough to be evacuated. Another lot, over there, were even younger, charging around having a whale of a time. Nice seeing them.

The lad playing football was a right little ginger nut. Couldn't really tell about the father, he didn't have enough left.

"Nice to see them happy," she said, with a sidelong glance along the bench. When he didn't reply, she thought at first: *Stuck-up git;* but then she looked more closely, and realized he was in a terrible state. She could feel it, she could feel his misery; it was coming off him in waves. And he was looking so intently at the ginger boy and grinding one clenched fist into the palm of his other hand. Didn't even know he was doing it, you could tell. She wondered for a minute if he wasn't one of the peculiar fellas you get hanging round school playgrounds, but she didn't think it was that. There was hunger on his face—or grief, pretty much the same thing, really—but she didn't think it was that sort of hunger.

"Surprising how many bairns there are."

She saw him register the word "bairns" and thought his face softened. He was a northerner.

"Have you seen the posters?"

She shook her head. "No."

"There's one that shows Hitler whispering in a mother's ear: *Bring the children back*."

"A lot have done."

"Yes, I know. But there's nothing for them here, is there? The schools aren't open, it certainly isn't safe."

"No, look at that school. Seventy-three dead."

"And the rest."

She looked a question.

"Four or five hundred. I was there."

"My God, doesn't bear thinking about, does it?"

"No." He was watching the boy again. "It doesn't."

She looked from the boy to the man on the bench and back again. Now what was all that about? "They're right, you know, the mothers—bringing them back. It's bloody bedlam down there, at the minute. You see . . ." She leaned forward, confidentially. "People think it's like they were taught, pearly gates and harps and Saint Peter running round with his little list, but it's not. Charing Cross Station in the rush hour more like, people running round like headless chickens, half of 'em don't even know they've passed. No, I say, stick together and if you've got to die, die together. Believe me, you don't want to let go of a child's hand in that."

He was looking at her rather uneasily. Oh, well. Should've known, should've kept her trap shut, people were frightened, they didn't want to know. And anyway why should she do it for nothing?

Only the expression on his face as he looked at the boy worried her. After that, they sat in silence, but then, a couple of minutes later, she started to hear something, an all too familiar sound: the peevish muttering the dead go in for, whenever they think they're not getting enough attention, which of course is most of the time, poor sods. And then she looked past the man, and there he was. Not very clear, but definitely there.

She had to say something. "Who's the lad?"

"What lad?"

"The one behind you."

He started to turn round, but checked himself. There was no space behind the bench for anybody who took up space.

"There's nobody there," he said.

She went back to watching the children. After a while, she said, "Skinny, white face, freckles, red hair?"

"That's a description of the boy you're looking at." The next words seemed to be dragged out of him. "What does he want?"

She looked, and shrugged. "Gone now."

At that, he seemed to lose patience; stood up, walked a few paces, then stopped. Every bit of color had drained from his face.

"Here, sit down," she said. "You're not well."

She got a hand under his elbow and helped him to sit down, but he was no sooner down than he was up again. "I think I'll be better walking it off."

Couldn't wait to get away, although, to be fair, he did smile and thank her as he left. He stumbled several times before he reached the end of the path—he certainly wasn't walking in a straight line—but he kept on going. At the gate he turned and looked back. "You take care now," she called out, but he was too far away to hear. A second later he disappeared into the press of people rushing past.

She thought: *I'll be seeing you again.*

No reason to suppose so, in this vast, overcrowded city, but she knew absolutely—no question at all—that she'd see him again.

ELEVEN

Neville answered the door half naked and slightly drunk. The former was a surprise.

"Tarrant!" He sounded startled, even a little put out, although it was he who'd suggested the meeting.

"I'm not early, am I?"

"No, sorry. Fell asleep in the bath."

He led the way across the hall, Paul following a trail of wet footprints, averting his gaze from the gyrations of Neville's arse under the damp towel. The hall was lit by a small window, taped against blast, letting in only a dim, stripy light, through which Neville padded like a huge, pink tiger.

Opening a door on the left, he showed Paul into the drawing room, before continuing up the stairs, in search—Paul devoutly hoped—of clothes.

Left alone, Paul looked around the room, his gaze as always drawn first to the paintings. Several good landscapes: the one above the mantelpiece—*Dunstanburgh Castle at Sunset*—was particularly fine. He thought he could identify the exact spot the painter had been standing on. In 1920, a war artist without a war, he'd spent a month in Northumberland scratting and scraping about for inspiration—and not finding it, in Dunstanburgh or anywhere else, not for a long, long time. Meanwhile, Neville, the minute he was released from hospital, left for America in a blaze of publicity. No hesitation, no groping about for inspiration there. Within a couple of years, every boardroom in Chicago and New York seemed to have one or other of Neville's "vibrant," "challenging," "futuristic" cityscapes hanging on the wall. Mind, he hadn't been doing so well recently. Of course, his Great War paintings still hung in galleries alongside Paul's own, but he wasn't getting much critical attention these days. In fact, he was probably better known to the younger generation as a critic than an artist. Paul's reputation as a painter was higher than Neville's now, though they did share a problem: their best work—at least their best-known work—was behind them. It was a strange predicament, to be remembered for what everybody else was trying to forget.

"We should've got ourselves killed," Neville had said, bitterly, more than once. "They'd be all over us then."

On the mantelpiece, there was a framed photograph of a little girl, five or six years old: Neville's daughter, presumably. Anne, was it? No resemblance to Neville, or none that he could see, but then he'd almost forgotten what Neville looked like. *Used* to look like. No photograph of Catherine, and he thought he remembered somebody saying they were separated. Where had he heard that?

Feeling suddenly that he was prying, he turned his back on the fireplace and looked around. A pleasant, slightly old-fashioned room, comfortable chairs and sofas: nothing wrong with any of it. Though he couldn't see much trace of Neville's own taste. The one discordant note was a broken blind, which drooped like a half-shut eyelid, making the room look as if it had suffered a stroke.

Footsteps on the landing. A second later, Neville appeared in the doorway, more or less dressed, though still without a tie and bringing with him a swimming-baths smell of damp skinfolds and wet hair.

"Sorry about that. Just nodded off."

"Bad night?"

"Busy." He went straight to the drinks table. "Whisky?"

Paul nodded. "I've just been admiring your paintings."

"Job lot, I'm afraid. Dad used to collect them."

Job lot? Unless he was very much mistaken the one above the fireplace was a Turner. "I painted Dunstanburgh Castle once."

"Any good?"

"Not really."

"I keep meaning to get rid of them, but nothing goes for anything these days; I'd be giving them away." He handed Paul a glass. "Same with the house, I wouldn't mind selling it, but . . ."

Paul looked at the ceiling. "You must rattle around a bit."

"I do."

"Catherine not coming over?"

"No, she'll stay in America."

"You must miss them."

"I miss Anne."

Ah.

A slightly awkward pause. Then Neville said: "Tell you what I've got that might interest you."

He led the way across the hall into a small study. Above the desk hung a framed pastel portrait of Neville himself, though not Neville as he was now—as he had been when he returned from France in 1917. Striving for some kind of objectivity, Paul looked at the drawing.

An eye like a dying sun sank beneath the rim of a shattered cheekbone, the lips were pulled back to reveal teeth like stumps of dead trees, and right at the center, where the nose should have been, a crater gaped wide. This was less a face than a landscape: a landscape Paul knew very well.

Neville stood, four-square, nursing his glass. "Best thing Tonks ever did, those portraits."

"How did you get it?"

"From Tonks, he gave it to me. I don't think it was his to give, actually; I think it belongs to the War Office. But . . ." He shrugged. "I suppose he just stretched the rules."

"Kind of him."

"Yes, very. Normally all you got was a couple of photographs. Fact, I think I've still got mine somewhere . . ."

The vagueness was a pretense. He went straight to the top-left-hand drawer of the desk, took two photographs out of a brown envelope and handed them across. Paul looked down. One profile, one full face—both utterly shocking. He looked up and found Neville watching him. Keeping his face carefully expressionless, he handed them back. "This was a parting present?"

"Yes, I think they're meant for if you go in a pub and some silly cow chokes on her drink, you know? You're supposed to whip them out of your pocket, point at your face and say: 'You think this is bad, love? Well, just look what they started with.'"

"It *is* remarkable, you know, what they did."

The surgeons, he meant. Was that the right thing to say? Well, if the pursing of Neville's lips was anything to go by—no, it most certainly was not. Paul handed the photographs back. This had been a rather disconcerting episode. It was a relief when Neville led the way back into the drawing room.

"So, what have you been up to?" Neville asked, settling himself into an armchair.

"Oh, you know . . . Working quite hard."

"Painting?"

"Aeroplanes, you know, dogfights, that sort of thing."

"Yes, I believe I've seen some of your recent stuff. Vapor trails?"

Why was it, when Neville said "vapor," Paul heard "vapid"? Because Neville bloody well meant him to, that's why.

A silver clock on the mantelpiece began to chime. Immediately, Neville put his glass down. "Blackout."

He crossed to the windows and began pulling down blinds, each tug of the cords contributing to a premature descent of night until finally only a sliver of sunlight remained. Paul felt a small stab of grief as that, too, was extinguished.

Neville was now merely a moving column of deeper shadow. There was a rasp to his breathing, a side effect of surgery, perhaps; you noticed it more in the dark. He was going from table to table, switching on lamps. As he bent over a side table near Paul's chair every scar and suture line showed. And yet what Paul had just said was true: the surgeons had done a remarkable job.

Only it was not his face, just as this was not his room.

"So . . ." Neville picked up his glass. "Where were we?"

Starting to needle each other, Paul thought. Painting wasn't a safe area. Yes, it was what they had in common, but it was also what divided them. Time for a change of subject. "I had a rather strange experience this afternoon. I think I met the Witch of Endor . . ."

Quickly, he told Neville about his meeting with the fat woman in Russell Square, emphasizing the absurdity of the occasion, recounting it, more or less, as a joke against himself.

Neville was amused, but he was also good at detecting

pain. "Well," he said, when Paul had finished, "she certainly got you rattled."

"No—"

"Oh, come *on*."

"No, really; actually, I felt quite sorry for her."

"I don't see why. I mean, you say yourself she was describing the boy you were looking at. She just picked up on it, that's all. She was obviously having you on."

"But that's just it, you see, I'm not sure she was. Oh, I'm not saying she actually saw anything but . . . Oh, I don't know. She was . . . she was . . . doing *something*—and I'm not quite sure what it was."

"I suppose the real question is, why have you suddenly got interested in boys?"

Paul didn't want to talk about Kenny but he could see an explanation was required, and once he'd started it was surprisingly easy to go on. When, at last, he stopped, Neville said, "There's no doubt he's dead?"

"None at all. Nobody got out."

"Still, you mustn't let that woman get to you."

"I don't think she was trying to, to be fair."

"Oh, of course she was! If you'd gone along with it she'd have been asking for money in no time at all. I can't stand the way these people crawl out of the woodwork whenever there's a war on, battening on people's grief—it's horrible. Do you know, my mother used to hold seances in the last war—in the dining room just along there. And I mean she was a *highly* intelligent woman, very forward-thinking in all kinds of ways, and yet she couldn't seem to see through it. I actually went to one of them—" He shuddered. "Appalling stuff. 'Auntie Maud likes your curtains.' I'm glad I didn't die, it would've been me coming back to say I liked the curtains.

You don't seriously think—?" He threw up his hands in disgust. "It's all *fraud*."

He came over to refill Paul's glass. As he bent down, the lamp threw his shadow across the far wall. Bull neck, massive shoulders, a whiff of the Minotaur's stable. The beast in the brain. But it wasn't just his physical bulk. It was that impression of baffled pain. An animal's pain. That invitation to go and see the Tonks portrait had been decidedly odd. It was almost as if he'd been reaching out, trying to get past the rivalry that had always prevented them from being, in any simple or uncomplicated way, friends.

No sooner had he finished pouring than the siren set up its nightly wail.

"What do you do in a raid?" Neville asked. "You know, if you're not on duty?"

"I walk."

"Not all night?"

"You might be surprised."

"What does Elinor think about that?"

"Well, I don't do it when she's here."

"We haven't seen much of her recently."

"No, she's still in the country, helping her sister sort things out."

The siren had stopped wailing. In its absence the silence of the deserted streets began to ooze through cracks in doors and window frames, a silence so deep the whisper of blood in your ears became more and more difficult to ignore. And then they heard it: that awful, desperate, edge-of-darkness buzzing, the sound a kettle makes when it's about to boil dry.

"Ours," Neville said.

"No, it's not."

And immediately, from Hampstead Heath close by,

came the hysterical yapping of the guns. A thud, followed by another, closer, the end of the next street, perhaps. Above their heads, the chandelier gave out a soft, silvery chime.

Paul said, "You need to get that bloody thing bagged up."

"Spoken like a true air-raid warden." Neville got to his feet. "Well, unless you want to stay inside . . . ?"

"I never want to stay in."

In the hall, there was a brief hiatus as Neville fumbled for his keys. Paul was starting to feel dizzy again. He'd been suffering from episodes of vertigo ever since a particularly nasty bout of flu in January. Inflammation of the labyrinth, the doctor said. Nothing to worry about, he'd said, most people get over it quite quickly; only an unlucky few get stuck. It was beginning to look as if Paul was one of the few. The walls spun round him; Neville's breath grated in his ears. He put a hand out to steady himself. Neville had switched the light out before he opened the door and, for some reason, the dizziness was always worse in the dark.

"Bloody key."

He got the door open at last. They collected hats and gas masks from the hall table and stepped out into the noisy night.

THEY WERE SHOWN to a quiet table in the corner of the restaurant. Menus were produced, a bottle of wine ordered. It was all really rather pleasant, except Paul's appetite seemed to have deserted him. The soup went down easily enough, but he struggled with the game pie, refused a pudding and merely picked at the cheese, content to let Neville do most of the talking. He could be very amusing, when he chose: scurrilous gossip about other painters, bizarre goings-on at the Ministry of Information . . . "Complete loony bin."

"For God's sake, keep your voice down."

Neville looked round the room and shrugged. Nobody was paying them any attention, and actually, to be fair, he'd said virtually nothing about his work—while contriving to imply his contribution to the war effort was second only to Winston Churchill's. But then—he was well into the second bottle by now—he embarked on a great rant about Kenneth Clark and the War Artists Advisory Committee. None of the commissioned artists had any talent whatsoever, *not a glimmer.* Moore, Sutherland, Piper: all rubbish. Clark was the problem, of course—Clark and his coterie of arse-licking toadies.

"He's commissioned one or two women as well," Paul said, hoping to divert the flow of bile.

"Elinor?"

"No, not yet, though—"

"Then she should think herself lucky. It's an insult to be commissioned by that man."

Paul was one of the people "that man" had insulted, but obviously it suited Neville to forget that. "Laura Knight, she's—"

"Poisonous old bat."

Paul gave up. Let him rant, if it made him feel better, but Neville seemed to have finished with Kenneth Clark, for the time being, at least. He glanced at Paul's plate. "You're not eating your cheese."

"No, I've had enough."

Immediately, a predatory fork descended and impaled the Cheddar. Neville munched in silence for a while.

Paul's vertigo was getting worse. Fresh air, that's what he needed, he'd be all right once he was outside, but the bill was a long time coming. When, finally, he staggered out into the street, the buildings started revolving around his head. He'd gone only a few paces when he found himself sitting on the pavement, trying not to be sick.

Neville stood over him. "You can't be drunk."

"Vertigo."

Even the effort of saying the word made it worse. If only things would *keep still*. He fixed his gaze on a crack in the pavement and, for a moment, the spinning did slow down.

"Can you stand?" Neville offered Paul his hand and then, when that didn't work, went behind and levered him to his feet. "Come on, my place. You need to get to bed."

Slowly, with Neville's help, Paul managed to take a few steps. He could walk, though he seemed to have only two paces: so slow he was threatening to sink into the ground, or so fast he was almost running. *"Whoa!"* Neville kept saying, as if to a skittish horse. Now he *was* drunk.

Blotched into a single shadow, they staggered from side to side in the road. Once, the wavering beam of a blackout torch came towards them, nothing of the man behind it visible except the hand holding the torch. An old man's hand, with thick, raised, bluish-gray veins. "Good night!" he said. Seconds later, the murk swallowed him.

Not long after, they arrived back at the house. Neville lowered Paul into an armchair. "Well. That was a surprise."

Unable to speak, Paul gripped the arms of the chair and willed the room to stop spinning. Neville stood looking down at him. "Who was the Witch of Endor anyway?"

"Saul," he tried to say, but it came out as "sore."

Immediately Neville's fingers were round his throat. "Yes, it will be, your glands are up. Is there anything I can get you?"

"No, I'm all right, thanks."

"Has it happened before?"

"Off and on since January. I had the flu and this started

a few days later. But, you know, I've seen a doctor and he says it's nothing to worry about. It's just the room keeps spinning every time I move my head."

"That'd worry me. Wouldn't you be better off in bed?"

During the time he'd been sitting in the chair the spinning had slowed down, though he knew it would start again the moment he moved. It was tempting to stay where he was, even to sleep in the chair, but he knew Neville wouldn't be happy leaving him downstairs on his own. "Yes, probably."

With Neville behind him, pushing him every step of the way, he managed to get upstairs and across the landing into a guest room, where he immediately collapsed onto the bed. Neville's voice came and went, now booming, now barely audible: the effect you can get by pressing your hands rhythmically against your ears. He remembered doing that in the hall at school, a small boy, lost and frightened, dumbfounded by the noise. In, out, loud, soft—and suddenly it was all right, everything was under control.

This wasn't. He just prayed he wasn't going to vomit all over the counterpane. Neville was pulling his shoes off now. *Clunk:* one of them hit the floor. And again: *clunk.* A blurry face bent over him. "You all right?"

This had gone on quite long enough. "Yes, thank you." He enunciated the words with great precision, and immediately, as if in response to his efforts, Neville's face swam into focus, though his voice still boomed and vanished. "I'll be . . . door . . . don't . . . if you . . . thing."

Then he switched off the light, and Paul was left alone.

※ TWELVE

Nightmares crawled across each other like copulating toads. He was walking with Neville along a shingle beach, the rasp and roar of waves loud in his ears, but then he realized it wasn't the waves, it was Neville's breathing. Humped shapes lay at intervals along the shore. He assumed they were seals, and expected them to heave and lollop into the water, but they didn't, and as he got closer he saw they were corpses, some stranded on the shoreline, others drifting to and fro on the tide: all too badly burned to be identified. Then, as he probed them, one stood up and seemed about to speak, its lipless mouth struggling to form words . . .

The dream shifted. He was going through the front door at home, throwing his school satchel down on the floor by the stairs. His hand was on the living-room door, but he hesitated, afraid to go in, afraid of what he would find. She'd be standing by the window and, though he knew she'd heard his footsteps, she wouldn't turn round. She never turned round. Always, he had to touch her, pull her back, *make* her notice him. Then, slowly, she would turn—and turn and turn and turn, day after day. He never knew which face he was going to see: blank with misery, blubbery with tears, contracted into a hard, angry knot. Sometimes she didn't turn at all, merely brushed his hand away as if it were an insect crawling across her skin. At other times, but rarely, she managed a smile: always with that curious string of saliva at the corner of her mouth—it should have been repulsive, but it wasn't, not to him; it was one of the things he loved most about her—and then sometimes she'd say his name, but tentatively, as if she couldn't quite remember who he was.

On the day they came to get her, she was sitting in a chair by the fireplace, and so, for a moment, he thought she must be better. But his father was home from work and he shouldn't be—he was working two till ten—and Gran was in the kitchen, banging pots and pans. "I thought you were going to tea at your Auntie May's?" she said. "Why, what's happening?" "Nothing." He looked at Dad, who just shook his head. It was bad, Paul knew it was. So he went straight to his mother and knelt beside her.

She had tears trickling down her face. Back when things were normal, before the standing-at-the-window began, she used to sing, and so he sang to her now: hymns—she knew hundreds of hymns—music-hall songs—she loved the music hall—and so he sang all her favorites, every single one. He was afraid to stop; he knew if he stopped something bad would happen. He even had a go at the "Hallelujah Chorus." "Jesus Christ!" Gran muttered in the kitchen. At first, it didn't seem as if his mother were listening, but after a while she reached out and squeezed his hand.

A knock on the door. Wiping her hands on her pinny, Gran went to answer it. His father hung back. A horse-drawn wagon had pulled up outside; he caught only one glimpse of it before Dad grabbed him by the shoulders and pushed him into the front room. From the window, he saw them helping her into the wagon. The driver flicked the reins, the wheels started to turn, and, as if realizing what was happening for the first time, she turned to look back.

Meeting him in the street a few weeks later, the vicar said, "Why've you stopped coming to choir practice, Paul?"

Because. Because, because, because, because . . .

He went on seeing her standing by the window. She lingered like an after-image on the retina, except that after-images fade and this never did. There she stood, looking out onto a yard where nothing grew, where there was nothing to see except brick walls imprisoning a patch of sky. Still, even now, he had to touch her, make her acknowledge him: *Mam, Mam.* Still, he never knew which face he'd see. The angry face was the one he dreaded most: the shout, the slap that sent him flying . . . She was angry now and he was frightened, really frightened this time—only, thank God, he heard Dad coming up the passage, the door opened, and there he was—

"*Dad!*"

A cold hand touched his forehead. He opened his eyes and it wasn't Dad, it was a man he'd never seen before, a man whose face, like a reflection in ruffled water, slowly settled and resolved into—

"Neville."

"You were shouting."

"Was I?" He stared round the room. "I'm sorry, I—"

"You were shouting, 'Dad!' "

"Was I?" He struggled to sit up, but the movement set the vertigo off and he was glad to sink back onto the pillows. "Poor old Dad, he was never much use when he was alive. What time is it?"

"Ten to four."

"Oh, I'm sorry. Look, you go back to bed, I'll be all right."

But he couldn't stop looking at the window, afraid of finding her there, or something there.

"I'll get you some water."

Even in the few minutes Neville was gone, Paul must have drifted off to sleep for the next time he woke Neville was at the window pulling up the blinds. Hard, scouring light flooded into the room and, like slugs sprinkled with salt, the nightmares shriveled and died.

"Let's get you into these pajamas, shall we? You'll feel a lot more comfortable."

Before helping him into the jacket, Neville took a flannel soaked in tepid water and gave Paul's arms and chest a quick rub. Paul knew it made sense, his skin was slick with sweat, but he hated it all the same, the enforced intimacy, and withdrew, as far as he could, turning his head to one side, disowning the stinking carcass on the bed. When it was finished, though, he did, admittedly, feel a whole lot better.

Neville threw the towel over his shoulder and picked up the bowl. "I think I should phone Elinor."

"There's no need, she's got enough on."

"I think she should know where you are, at least."

"I'll be home in a couple of hours."

Neville looked doubtful. "Let's see how you get on."

Though the nightmares had gone, their fetid darkness stained the day. Paul kept looking at the window, expecting to see her standing there, or his father coming through the door, shambling and inept. As you get older, you think you're moving further away from your parents, leaving them behind, but it's not like that. There's a trick, a flaw, some kind of hidden circularity in the path, because suddenly, in old age, there they are in front of you again, and getting closer by the day.

This particular day dragged. Neville closed the curtains

because the brightness hurt Paul's eyes. He couldn't read: even the movement of his eyes across the page was enough to bring the dizziness back. He could do nothing, in fact, except lie with his eyes closed or every now and then glance apprehensively at the lighter square of gray that was the window.

Surprisingly often, he found himself thinking about the woman in the square. How she must've noticed him watching the ginger-haired boy kicking the football around. No other explanation of what she'd claimed to see was possible. But the woman herself haunted him. Her singing. "Land of Hope and Glory" of all things, one of the songs he'd sung that day. She'd had remarkable eyes—blue with the merest hint of mauve, the color of harebells—and all the more remarkable for being sunk in wads of fat. And my God she stank.

Yet, somehow, this ludicrous woman had seen him watching the boy and put her finger—possibly a rather mercenary finger—on his grief.

If "grief" was the right word. He'd scarcely known Kenny well enough to grieve for him. No, what he felt was regret; guilt, even. Taking Kenny back to his mother had been the wrong decision, arrived at for the wrong reasons. Elinor was right: he hadn't been thinking about Kenny at all. It had been about *himself* and *his* mother. A kind of proxy reconciliation; a reconciliation that in his own life had never been achieved. So he'd failed in the most basic human task: to shield the present from the deforming weight of the past. And now, lying in a strange bed, in the hot, close darkness of a strange room, his condemnation of himself was absolute.

By midafternoon he was starting to feel hot again. Neville brought him a cup of tea, but he couldn't drink it. *Sleep,* that was the thing—and no more nightmares, please God. Throwing off the covers, he tried to ignore the images that clung to the inside of his skull, thousands of them—black, furry, insistent, clicking . . .

"*Ridiculous.*"

"What's ridiculous?"

"This. Me."

"Blame the Witch of Endor."

"Oh, so you think I'm cursed, do you?"

Neville tapped him on the head. "Go to sleep."

And, abruptly, as if he'd been waiting for that word of command, he fell asleep.

THIRTEEN

The bell's doleful clanging brought Kit to the door. Elinor wasted no time on small talk. "How is he?"

"Asleep."

He turned and led the way upstairs. Paul was lying with his eyes closed, propped up on three pillows. The pajama jacket—Kit's presumably—was open and each breath delineated the structure of ribs and sternum. Sitting on the bed, she clasped his slippery fingers in hers and, after a while, he seemed to feel her presence. His eyes dragged open. "Oh, hello, I didn't expect to see you."

She kissed him. "I'd have come sooner, only I was down at the cottage and nobody told me you'd rung."

"That was Neville, I didn't want to bother you."

Standing just inside the door, Kit stirred. "Elinor, would you like a drink?"

"Tea would be lovely."

He left the room. They were silent for a moment, listening to his footsteps going heavily downstairs. Paul said, "He's been very good."

That sounded like a plea: *Don't be nasty to Kit*. Well, no, of course she wouldn't be. "Thing is, can we get you home?"

"There's only one way to find out."

Pushing the covers back, he swung his legs over the side of the bed—and sat there, motionless, swallowing hard. She reached out to help, but he waved her away. After several attempts to stand up, he admitted defeat and lay back on the pillows. "Dunno what's wrong with me."

"Well, don't force it. Why don't you have a sleep?"

"Because I've been sleeping all day."

"Perhaps that's what you need . . ."

"What I need is to go home."

But his eyelids were already closing, and by the time Kit reappeared with the tea he was asleep. Kit put the tray down, glanced at the bed, and mouthed: "See you downstairs."

Left alone, Elinor poured herself a cup of tea and settled back to drink it. *Damn*, she was thinking. Paul obviously wasn't well enough to be moved, but she couldn't just leave him here—and that meant her spending an evening with Kit. Something she'd so far managed to avoid. Her relationship with Kit, never easy, seemed to become more and more complicated. He'd been serving with Toby in the months leading up to Toby's death, but he'd never written to her about it, and when she wrote to him, he hadn't replied. An omission Paul had described at the time as "unforgivable." Later, he'd told Paul as much as he knew about Toby's death—or as much as he could bring himself to tell—but he'd never directly told *her* anything. She'd found that hard to forgive, and for a long time, even after he married Catherine, her closest friend, she'd seen as little of him as possible. Avoiding him had not been too difficult, since she and Paul spent a lot of time in Spain whereas he and Catherine had lived in Germany for a number of years before finally settling in America. An occasional encounter in London or New York— strained civility—and that was it: friendship over.

Only now Kit was back in London, working as an ambulance driver in the same Tottenham Court Road depot as Elinor. This proximity added a new dimension to what had always been a difficult—well, what could you call it? Association? They were now members of the same team: they'd trained together, grumbled together, drunk endless cups of stewed tea together; and now—almost nightly, when she was in London—faced danger together. All this inevitably produced a sense of comradeship that was both intense and impersonal. But it was the same with all the drivers. It hardly seemed to matter whether you liked the person or not. You just jogged along together, because you had to. This was something altogether new in Elinor's experience, though she supposed the men were familiar with it from the last war. Even so, she'd managed to avoid anything in the way of direct contact with Kit. If they went to the pub, it was always in a group of five or six other people. Sitting around in the depot, waiting for calls, she talked to Violet or Dana. She doubted if she'd exchanged a single personal word with him in the last few months—nor had she wanted to. So she wasn't particularly looking forward to this evening, but it needn't last long; she could always say she was tired and needed an early night.

On her way downstairs, she paused to peer into an aquarium that stood in a recess on the half-landing, but, though well stocked with plants, it seemed to be empty. Kit had come out of a door on the right and was looking up at her.

"I can't see any fish."

"That's because there aren't any." He came upstairs and took the tray from her. "It's all for him." He pointed to a small terrapin lurking at the bottom of the tank.

"Oh, I didn't see him."

"No, well, he's very well disguised, isn't he?" He hesitated. "When I was a child I used to think that was me."

"What, rattling around on your own?"

"Felt like it sometimes." He nodded towards the stairs as if to emphasize the size of the house.

"Must feel a little bit like that now."

"It does, rather. I mean, I suppose I could live at the club, but . . . Oh, I don't know." He led the way into the drawing room. "Would you like a drink?"

She suppressed a smile: he so obviously *needed* her to have a drink. "What are you having?"

"Whisky."

"Go on, I'll join you."

The glass he handed her was rather large. Never mind, she could always take it slowly. He was busy drawing the blinds.

She took a sip of whisky and recoiled from the peaty taste. Kit didn't seem to have heard of water. "Don't you think the blackout's worse in summer? In winter you can kid yourself it feels cosy, but . . ."

"I don't think I ever managed that." He sat down, about as far away as he could get while remaining in the same room. "How did you find him?"

"Not good."

"He had a bad night. *We* had a bad night."

"No, he's not been sleeping well."

"What's wrong?"

"Did he tell you about the dizziness?"

"He didn't have to, he fell over."

"Oh, as bad as that?"

"He said something about flu."

"Yes, that's when it started. Apparently there's nothing much wrong. I mean, we were terrified at first—well, you can imagine—but it's nothing like that. Nothing serious."

"What do you think's causing it?"

"Well, like the doctor said—flu."

"You don't believe that."

She hesitated. "No, I don't, not really. I mean, it's certainly worse if he gets upset about something."

"He was upset last night."

"Was he?"

"Yes, he was hiding it well, but looking back, I think he was in quite a state. He met some sort of weird woman in the square—the one weird sister, I think—and she said she could see a ginger-haired boy standing behind him. But Paul was actually looking at a ginger-haired boy at the time—staring at him, in fact—and she obviously picked up on that."

"Did he tell you about Kenny?"

"He did, yes."

She closed her eyes. "Oh, poor Paul. That's the last thing he needed."

"As I say, he was in quite a state." He raised his empty glass, asking her if she'd like another. When she shook her head, he got up and refilled his own. "Are you back in town now?"

"Yes—though there's an awful lot of sorting out still."

"I was sorry to hear about your mother."

She thanked him, and then the talk turned to other things. Not, as she'd expected, their shared experiences of driving an ambulance. No, by mutual, unspoken consent, they went right back to their student days at the Slade, before the last war, before his silence after Toby's death divided them. Rather to her surprise, Elinor began to enjoy it. All those fancy-dress parties, what was all that about? And they'd put so much effort into it . . .

"Do you remember the last one?" she asked. "We must have been sewing costumes for a week."

"Was that the one where you and Catherine went as Har-lequin?"

She smiled. "Yes, both of us."

"And you wouldn't take your masks off, or say anything, so nobody could tell which was which. And you danced with each other all evening, wouldn't let any of the men break in."

"Funny, Paul remembers that too."

"Elinor, every man who was *there* remembers that."

"Yes, you were all standing round the edge of the dance floor with your tongues hanging out."

"Ah, so you did know? Thought you did."

"Wasn't why we were doing it though . . ."

"No, you never took your eyes off each other—all evening."

Elinor looked down into her glass. "How is she?"

"Pretty good. Well, as far as I know."

"I'm sorry."

"Don't be. I've never regretted the marriage. It gave me Anne."

"How old is she now?"

"Six. She's got two gaps in her front teeth. Just here." He tapped his own teeth. "She's very proud of them; she was one of the last people in her class to get them. I think she thought it was never going to happen."

"It's a nice age," Elinor said, vaguely. She found it hard to imagine Kit as a father.

"Do you know, I was thinking the other evening—well, the middle of the night, really—the last time the three of us were together—I mean, under the same roof—was the start of the last war."

"Yes, we went for a bike ride. To see the Doom."

"And I fell off."

"So you did."

"And asked you to marry me."

An awkward pause. "So you did."

"God, that was so humiliating."

"Oh, don't be silly, Kit, you didn't mean it . . ."

"No, I meant falling off. Poor old Dad, he used to take me round and round the heath, must've run miles. And the minute he let go, off I came. I never did get the hang of it."

"Well, you seem to have got the hang of proposing."

"E-vent-u-al-ly." He moved the lamp a few inches farther away from his face. "Oh, and by the way, I did mean it."

She shook her head.

"I was trying to remember who else was there. Paul, of course, and, er—"

"Toby."

Abruptly, it was between them: Toby's death; Kit's long silence. But then, just as he was about to speak, the siren set up its awful tooth-jarring wail and so she never did find out what he was going to say.

Sitting like this in silence, listening to the sirens, you felt the darkness deepen. Even with every lamp in the room lit, you were aware of it, pushing against the windowpanes, seeping through cracks in doors and walls, dragging the city back into barbarism. London: no longer one of the world's great centers of civilization, but merely a settlement on a river, lit by guttering candles after dark.

"I've just realized something," he said, as the banshee howl wound down into silence. "You're the only person who still calls me 'Kit.' "

"Really?" How impossibly self-centered men were. No, she corrected herself: not "men." *This* man.

"Since my mother died, yes."

"How extraordinary. What does Catherine call you?"

" 'You.' If Anne's there, 'Daddy'—or, if I'm really in the doghouse: 'Your father.' "

Elinor didn't know how to respond to that and was glad when it was time to go through into the dining room to eat. Cold cuts on the sideboard, a surprising amount of meat. Apparently his housekeeper knew somebody. *Oh, yes,* Elinor thought, restored to something of her original dislike: Kit's housekeeper would know somebody. Over the meal, he talked about his time in Germany. Catherine hadn't wanted to leave, though she seemed perfectly happy in America. In fact, she was probably more American than he was. Perhaps that was why the marriage had broken down? Elinor wasn't sure she believed in all this "drifting apart" nonsense. There was always a reason.

Outside the raid went on, various thuds and bumps, none very close. Her glass seemed to be emptying itself rather quickly. The clock ticked towards midnight. She thought it had been an altogether strange evening, full of emotional undercurrents, things said, things left unsaid, she didn't know what to make of it. But at least it ended in laughter. They'd been reminiscing about the dances they used to go to when they were students, when—it was a shock to remember—they'd been, actually for quite a long time, each other's best friend. They'd spent virtually every evening together, in fact: going to exhibitions, theaters, music halls . . . But, above all, dancing.

"Do you remember the turkey trot?" Kit asked. "We used to go in for competitions."

She put her hands over her eyes. "Oh my God, yes. The turkey trot. What were we thinking?"

Kit stood up, spread his legs—more frog than turkey—and hopped a few paces to the left . . . Then, tucking his thumbs into his braces, a few paces to the right. He looked so ridiculous she burst out laughing. He joined in, but then stopped and looked at her.

"Do you think we could still do it?"

"No, of course we couldn't."

"Bet you we could."

He was holding out his hand and, for a second, anything seemed possible—she was on the verge of getting up—but then she smiled and shook her head, and turned away.

❊ FOURTEEN

Paul hated the Underground stations that had been turned into shelters. For a long time, the authorities had resisted using the Underground in this way, but after the destruction of the school in Agate Street, people took things into their own hands: they forced their way in. And so at night the Underground became almost indistinguishable from the underworld, with hundreds of people asleep or inert under their blankets. You had to clamber over them. And always, for Paul, there were memories of other tunnels: humped bodies in half-darkness, sleeping or dead. Increasingly, the two worlds—France, then; London, now—met and merged. It was a relief to escape the fetid darkness of the shelters into the tumult of the upper air.

Darkness was falling, a hot, clammy darkness that made it hard to breathe. He still didn't feel well, though the dizziness had gone; and he was constantly afraid. He quickened his steps. The only solution to fear was other people. A few jokes, a game of cards, and things didn't look quite so bad.

At the corner of Guilford Street, he bumped into Walter Harris, who was just going out on patrol.

"What's happening?"

"Nothing much," Walter said. "Very quiet."

Incendiaries were drifting down like huge yellow peonies. The two of them stood at the center of a web of shadows, reluctant to part. People clung to each other these days, as if the mere fact of being known, recognized, addressed by name could protect you from the random destruction of bombs and blast. But after a few minutes, Walter ground his fag out, said, "So long"—nobody these days risked saying "Good-bye"—and set off in the direction of Russell Square.

As Paul turned the corner, he saw a stick of bombs come tumbling down the beam of a searchlight onto a building fifty yards ahead, an extraordinary sight, like a worm's-eye view of somebody shitting. He was close enough to feel the blast wave suck at his eyeballs, but already he'd started to run, arriving on the scene in a smog of black smoke. Charlie Web was there and Brian Temple and shortly afterwards Nick Hendry came shambling up.

As Paul turned to greet him, there was another explosion farther down the street. The windows behind them shattered and they crouched down, shielding their faces and arms from a shower of broken glass. "Bloody hell," Charlie said. "You all right, lad?" This was directed at Nick, who was looking more dazed than frightened.

Cautiously, Paul straightened up. The road was filling with civilians, swarming out of the burning buildings, many of them barefoot, treading on broken glass, impervious to pain. There must've been a shelter in one of the basements. Sandra Jobling, bent double, was leading a group out, waving at them to come on. *Come on.* There was another shelter not far away in Gray's Inn Road, but it was going to be a terribly long walk for some of those people.

Within half an hour, Sandra was back. "All right, love?" Charlie asked. She nodded, without speaking. It was difficult to tell how she was, or how anybody was. They were all white with plaster dust, their eyelids crusted and inflamed.

Nick was in a bad way. Charlie pointed to the basement of a nearby house. "There's an old man lives down there, I think we ought to check on him."

"No, he's in hospital," Brian Temple said.

"Nope, came out yesterday."

Nobody questioned it: Charlie knew everything and everybody on his patch.

"Won't he have gone to a shelter?" Paul asked.

"Can't walk."

"*Bloody* hell."

They found him in the living room. Plaster had fallen from the ceiling and lay in clumps all over the floor, but the old man didn't seem to be injured. He was sitting on the edge of a sofa bed, stick-thin, rodent-faced, a plastic bag full of urine dangling from his side, but as they helped him to the door he was positively cackling with triumph. Apparently, they'd told him in the hospital he might never walk again. "And look at me now." He paused for breath, hanging on to Charlie's arm. "Shows how much the fuckers know."

"*Oi*, you, language." Charlie jabbed his finger at Sandra. "*Lady.*"

"Sorry, love. Didn't see you."

Sandra smiled. " 'S'all right."

"Thought she was a lad," they heard him say, as Charlie pushed his skinny arse up the stairs. "They all wear trousers these days, you can't tell hes from shes."

They got him into one of the ambulances that had drawn up on the other side of the road and were just turning away when somebody said there was a man trapped on the second floor of a building farther down the street. "Why the fuck wasn't *he* in a shelter?" Brian asked. It didn't matter why; they still had to go in. Inside, there was total devastation, illuminated at intervals by flares that shone through the broken windows. A crater, twenty feet deep, had opened up at the center of the building and they were having to edge around its rim. "Like that school in Agate Street," Brian said. Twenty yards farther on, they heard a slithering thump, exactly like snow falling off a roof in a rapid thaw. They looked at each other, as the seconds ticked past. Charlie had stopped, mid-stride, one hand raised. He seemed to be on the point of turning back, but then he lowered his hand and they started to move forward again.

They found a man on the first-floor landing, his head and shoulders sticking out of the rubble, eyes glazed, that unmistakable look of nobody at home. But was this the man they'd been told about, or was there somebody else? No way of knowing. Charlie decided to press on. Paul swept the torch from side to side, training the light on their feet, as they crept up the stairs, each tread complaining under their combined weight. At any moment, now, you felt the whole bloody staircase was coming down. Paul opened his mouth to say they ought to think about going back, but at that moment Charlie raised his hand again.

A man was lying across the top of the stairs, unconscious, barely breathing, short, middle-aged, with a paunch that strained his shirt buttons, and cheeks like a hamster's full of nuts. Brian blew his whistle, and the sound carried Paul back to the trenches. *Stretcher-bearers!* Trying to fix himself in the present, he swung the torch over gilt picture frames and velvet curtains. "Keep it steady, mate," Charlie said. "Can't see what I'm doing here."

No stretcher-bearers appeared in response to Brian's whistle; nobody had seriously thought they would. "All right then?" Charlie said, and they positioned themselves at the unconscious man's head and feet.

It took them an hour to get him out. Paul helped the

woman ambulance driver lift him onto the top bunk. The bunk below was already occupied, by a terrified man who kept whimpering that he'd broken his arm and it was a disgrace—an absolute bloody disgrace—that he hadn't been taken to the hospital straight away. "There's plenty worse than you," the driver said, in a ferociously clipped accent. "If you don't keep quiet I'll dump you in the road."

"I'd do as I was told if I were you," Paul said. "I think she means it."

The driver slipped off her right gauntlet and held out her hand. Automatically, Paul took it, though it seemed an odd gesture in the circumstances.

"Thank you," she said. "Bit of a dead weight, wasn't he?"

Or just dead. "It's Miss Tempest, isn't it?"

"Oh, Violet, please. I trained with Elinor."

"Yes, I remember."

He was just about to jump down into the road when she took hold of his sleeve. Puzzled, he glanced down and saw the cloth was stiff with blood. "Oh, it's all right," he said. "It's not mine."

She pulled the edges of the tear apart and peered inside. "I think you'll find it is."

Immediately, his arm began to throb, though up to that moment he'd felt no pain. "I'd no idea."

"No, I'm serious now, you go and get that seen to."

He looked at her. A painfully thin, wiry, indestructible woman in late middle age. Far too old to be driving an ambulance, but nobody had the nerve to tell her that. Before the war she'd taught—classics, was it? At Cambridge. Very ivory-tower, the sort of woman whom normally he might not have taken seriously, but in the confusion of the moment any sufficiently firm suggestion acquired the force of a command. He sketched a salute. "Yes, ma'am."

He thought he might as well get the cut seen to, though he didn't think it was anything serious and felt a bit of a fraud, crunching along Gower Street over a river of broken glass. This same route he'd taken every morning as a student at the Slade. Now, shocked people huddled in doorways or wandered around in the middle of the road, purgatorial shadows with their white, dust-covered faces and dark clothes. Some, in pajamas and dressing gowns, limped along on bloodied feet.

Reaching his station at the School of Tropical Medicine, he staggered down into the basement, where he found Nick Hendry being treated for a cut to his forehead. Lucky lad—another inch and it would've been his eye.

When Paul's turn came, he rolled up his shirtsleeve and discovered, as he'd rather expected, that the cut, though still oozing blood, was not deep. "Looks worse than it is," the first-aid worker said. "Go and have a cup of tea."

He retreated to one of the two battered sofas that lined the walls. Nick Hendry was stretched out on the other and was snoring softly, his upper lip vibrating with every breath. Paul tried to read a newspaper, but couldn't concentrate. He forced down a cup of orange tea, and though his stomach rose in revolt, immediately began to feel better.

After a brief respite, he started to feel he was shirking and forced himself to go out on patrol again. One good thing, he hadn't suffered any spells of dizziness all night and that was reassuring because this was his first night back on duty, and he'd been half expecting it to return.

Two hours later, he returned to the station, eyelids gritty with tiredness, yawning and scratching his neck. Nick was still on the sofa, face averted, though Paul could tell from his breathing he wasn't asleep. A few minutes later, Sandra

Jobling came in and took off her helmet, bending forward to run her fingers through her sweaty hair. Her face was still covered in plaster dust, but at some time during the night she must have reapplied her lipstick without the aid of a mirror, because she now had two huge, glossy, smiling red lips, with smears of lipstick all over her cheeks and chin. She waved to Paul, then went straight through to the cloakroom next door.

Charlie Web and Brian Temple came in not long after. Charlie put his mug of tea on the table and pulled up a chair. "Gone quiet."

"Not long now," Paul said.

They waited for the All Clear with hardly less tension than they'd waited for the warning sirens the night before. Charlie jerked his head in Nick's direction. "He's making the most of it." He slurped a mouthful of tea. "What about that old geezer, then, the one with the plastic bag? Bloody thing burst, you know. I was lifting him onto the top bunk and . . . *Pish*. All over me. Could've done with a bloody umbrella."

Nick sat up, ostentatiously rubbing his eyes.

"Hey up," Charlie said. "Sleeping Beauty's back. How are you, mate?"

He carried his mug across to the sofa and sat down. Nick had seemed very jittery all night; Charlie had been virtually carrying him. Their voices sank to a low murmur. Paul was already nodding off to sleep when a hand on his shoulder jerked him awake.

Charlie: "I'm taking Nick round the corner for a pasty. You coming?"

Brian stood up at once, but Paul shook his head. "No thanks, I think I'll be getting off home."

But it was hard to make himself get going. He'd only just levered himself to his feet when Sandra came back into the room, her face pink and shining, forehead plastered with tendrils of wet hair. She came straight over to him. "I don't know. *Men.*"

"What have we done now?"

"How could you let me walk round like that?"

"Like what?"

"Lipstick plastered all over me face."

He smiled. "I thought you looked amazing."

"I looked like a clown."

It seemed the easiest, most natural thing in the world to grab her by the shoulders and kiss her. Only when it was too late, when she'd taken a step back and was gawping at him, did he realize what he'd done. *My God.* He tried to come up with something to say, something that would shrink the kiss, turn it into a friendly, casual, comradely gesture, the sort of thing he might have done to Charlie or Brian, but the words wouldn't come. To his relief, he saw she was looking amused rather than offended. "I'm—"

Sorry, he was going to say, but at that moment a voice at the door said, "Is there any tea left in that pot?"

Walter Harris, gray-faced, ready to drop.

Sandra felt the curve of the pot. "Past its best, I'm afraid. Yeah, no, you can't have that. I'll put the kettle on."

Walter lowered himself into a chair. "Thanks, love."

"Well," Paul said, deliberately including both of them. "I'd better be off. See you tomorrow."

"You not on tonight, then?" Walter said. "Jammy bugger."

Paul waited for Sandra to say something, but she was busy at the sink. "See you?"

She looked over her shoulder. "Yeah, right."

Outside on the pavement, breathing the tainted air, he relived the kiss. Had there been a second's yielding before she pulled away? *Nah, wishful thinking. No fool like an old fool, et-bloody-cetera.* He began to walk home, but slowly, in no hurry to get there, noticing cordoned-off streets, gaps in terraces, some new, some already familiar. Relief at having survived the night fizzed in every vein.

But it was Sandra he thought about, as he walked along. Sandra, with her long, coarse, dark hair, the fringe that was always getting into her eyes, so she had to keep pushing it back. What with that and her short, stocky, little legs, she reminded him of a Shetland pony. Oh, she wasn't pretty, but he thought she had something better than prettiness: it was almost impossible to look at her without smiling. He wanted—oh, very badly, he wanted—to lie naked with her in a bed, to feel her young, strong, firm body under his. And, at first, he thought, sheer exhaustion might make lovemaking difficult, but then, in small touches and movements, the heat between them would grow, until at last sex became not merely possible, but urgent, necessary, unavoidable.

He was close to home now, but walking more slowly all the time, until at last, turning into the square, he was forced to acknowledge the truth: that he didn't want to go home at all.

FIFTEEN

Over the last few weeks, Neville's dislike of the Ministry of Information had become an almost hysterical loathing. He dated the change to one apparently endless afternoon when it first occurred to him that the ministry was alive; that its corridors were the intestines of some flabby, flatulent beast farting memos, reports and minutes that always had to be initialed and passed on, though as far as he could tell no action was ever taken.

Once you started thinking the building might be alive, the evidence for it rapidly accumulated. It was always on the move, always changing shape. Literally, from one Friday afternoon to the following Monday morning, whole corridors would appear or disappear. His own room, which was hardly big enough for one—though he shared it with two other people—had been carved out of another, much larger, room. The half-window let in scarcely any light, and the partition kept out no noise at all. So he was privy to the conversation of half a dozen shorthand typists, listening in—involuntarily, if not reluctantly—as they talked about their boyfriends, nightclubs they were going to, which dresses they were going to wear . . . How far they were going to go. "Who is it tonight?" he heard one girl say. "Somebody nice?" Giggles all round. "Is it somebody you want to die with?"

That shook him. It made him think: *Who would* I *want to die with?* *Nobody;* but even as he said, or rather thought, "nobody," he was back in the dining room with Elinor, holding out his hand, inviting her to dance with him. Totally unexpected, that evening they'd spent together. At first, he'd experienced no more than a slight awkwardness, a few tweaks of nostalgia perhaps, and yet by midnight it had been far more than that. When she smiled and turned away, he was immediately back on a dusty road with his head in her lap, seeing, as she bent over him, how her nipples formed two dark circles against the thin white lawn of her blouse, as unexpected and mysterious as fish rising to break the smooth surface of a lake.

Hilde sat next to him: a sad Austrian woman. He'd have liked to practice his German on her, but, except when discussing the finer points of a translation, she stuck resolutely to English. The only other inhabitant of the room was an old man with the streaming white hair of an Old Testament prophet, Bertram Somebody-or-other, but he appeared less and less frequently. They were supposed to be translating a series of pamphlets collectively entitled *Life Under the Nazis,* but progress was slow, and the material unpromising. Hilde, he suspected, knew far more about life under the Nazis than any of the authors did.

Every morning, as he entered the building, along with hundreds of other identically dressed men carrying identical briefcases, his spirits sank. By midafternoon, he was desperate, his eyes full of grit, his mouth dry, every muscle aching. As the golden light crept across the parquet floor, he daren't think about sleep. To try to keep himself awake, he went along the corridor to the Gents, where he splashed his face with cold water. There was a mirror behind the washbasin, but he avoided looking at his reflection. He'd long ago mastered the art of washing, combing his hair and even shaving by touch alone. Each basin had a cheap plastic nailbrush chained to the wall behind the taps, for all the world as if they were priceless medieval Bibles. The irritation this caused him was out of all proportion; he wanted to wrench the bloody things off the wall, but of course he didn't. Though as he walked back to the stuffy little room, he was nursing fantasies of escape. After all, he wasn't obliged to stay here. He could leave—leave London, for that matter—go somewhere else, anywhere else, and paint. Accident had made him a journalist and a critic—and a good one, too—but it was not who he was.

Hilde hardly looked up when he came back into the room. She wore her hair pinned up in a rather untidy bun; as he squeezed past he looked down at the nape of her neck and wondered why it should be that exhaustion increased the desire to fuck. Logically, it should have had the opposite effect, but it never did, not with him anyway. In fact, a lot of his time in this room was spent weaving fantasies about Hilde or the typists next door or . . . Well, anybody really. There was nothing to take his mind off it. When talking to Tarrant he'd emphasized the importance of his work, but really anybody with fluent German could have done it. Yes, he dealt with classified information, but only because all information here was classified. The lowest classification was "Secret" and that was applied to the requisitioning of toilet rolls. Sighing, he sat down, pulled a stack of files towards him and began to sort through it.

The clock ticked towards six. The Indian-summer afternoon was slipping away and that mattered so much these days, when people lay in the parks and squares basking in the sun like lizards, or stood in doorways and windows, raising their eyes to the light, storing it up against the blackout.

Nobody dared think about the coming winter, when days would be shorter and air raids longer. As he crouched over the files, he could hear Hilde's stocking-clad legs—where did she get them?—whispering to each other as she walked across to the filing cabinet. She bent to pull out the lower drawer and he gazed hungrily at her backside. A minute later, she found the file she was looking for and straightened up. As she turned, their eyes met and he saw her flinch as she registered the full force of his melancholy lust. Quickly, not looking at him, she returned to her desk.

Ah, well. She wasn't even noticeably attractive, though to him at the moment almost all women were attractive, at least to some degree. On his last free night, he'd gone out walking. It was one of the paradoxes of his present exhausted state that on the nights when he wasn't on duty, he sometimes found it difficult to sleep. After tossing and turning for an hour, he thought: *To hell with it,* and went out. Though he was London born and bred, he found the blacked-out streets not only startling, but confusing. More than once he got lost. Piccadilly, after dark, felt particularly strange, because in peacetime it had always been so brightly lit. He stopped to light a cigarette and heard the tapping of a prostitute's heels on the pavement. High heels, on these lightless nights, always sounded erotic, but a prostitute's especially so because they hammered tacks into the heels and toes, to make them stand out. And stand out they certainly did, beating an urgent, unmistakable tattoo. This wasn't the only way prostitutes defeated the blackout. Another was to lurk in shop doorways and, whenever a man approached, shine their blackout torches on exposed breasts or the triangle of darkness at the apex of their thighs. He found these spotlit body parts disturbing: they reminded him of an incident he'd attended near King's Cross where a railway arch, being used as an unofficial shelter, had suffered a direct hit. When the ambulances got there, heavy rescue squads were pulling arms, legs, heads, hands, feet from the rubble, lining them up on the pavement. Somebody had flashed a torch along the line and it was exactly like this. Revulsion and a kind of excitement. The girl whose *tap-tapping* footsteps he'd heard—he could see her now, walking towards him, or at least he could see the shape of her, which was all he needed or wanted to see. As he came closer, she shone her torch down onto her slim legs—the ankles almost feverishly thin. They found each other in a shop doorway. He pushed up her skirt, his fingers snagging on her stocking tops, slipping across her bare thighs into the warm, moist darkness between, moaning now, gasping for breath, over in seconds, laughing shakily as he withdrew. From beginning to end, he hadn't seen her face.

Promptly at six, Neville closed the file he was working on and reached for his hat. Hilde was already putting on her jacket. They walked to the lift together, or if not together then at least not ostentatiously apart, but then she met one of the secretaries from the room next door and stopped to chat so he waved and went on alone.

The lift took ages to arrive; it always did at this time of day. He killed time by looking at the paintings on the wall, which were quite possibly, for all he knew, selected by Kenneth Clark himself. His office was farther down the corridor. One, in particular, Neville objected to: a landscape, a beauty spot somewhere in the Lake District, precisely the sort of painting that had no reason to exist. A bit like some of Tarrant's early stuff. Oh my God, it might even be a Tarrant. He peered at the signature, but it was illegible, and then stood back, determined to give the painting a fair chance. *No*, nothing there at all, just a picture-postcard view of a lake. Couldn't even tell which one. Ullswater? *Wet*, anyway.

The sight of that scrawled, illegible signature—*was* that a "T"?—reminded him he was having supper with the Tarrants that night. Probably not a good idea. The continued silence from Kenneth Clark had begun to prey on his mind. Of course it shouldn't matter that he—Neville—was being continually passed over. Every night when on duty he saw lives ended prematurely, people injured, mutilated, in terrible pain. What possible importance could personal ambition have in such a context? Oh, but it did, it *did*. It hurt that Tarrant's reputation had overtaken his. And yet somehow the friendship survived, though it was an odd relationship. Sometimes it hardly seemed like friendship at all.

Whatever it was, he was in for a whole evening of it. The original invitation—when they finally managed to hit on a date when nobody was on duty—had been for dinner at their house, but then Elinor had telephoned to say the house had been damaged by blast—kitchen window blown in, something like that—so now they were going to a restaurant in Dean Street instead.

Elinor was already at the bar when he arrived. She raised her cheek for him to kiss and then they settled down to wait for Tarrant, who'd been unavoidably delayed. No sirens yet.

"So you've been bombed?" he asked.

"Just blast. Kitchen window came in, I've been running round all day trying to find a glazier . . ."

"Still, you've got it boarded up all right?"

"Oh, yes, no problems there, it's secure."

"Well, that's the main thing."

"The clocks have stopped. And the electric went off for a time but it's back on now."

She was looking tired, he thought. Understandably. "Shall we have a drink while we wait?"

"Oh, yes, please."

While the barman poured, she sat clasping and unclasping her hands. "You know, I was expecting Paul to be upset. About the clocks, I mean. He's very fond of them, he's always polishing them and winding them up, and he wasn't at all. In fact, he was rather excited. 'We're outside time,' he said."

"Is that why he's late?"

"No, he'll be painting."

"How has he been?"

"Not too bad, he's not falling over or anything, but he does seem very unsettled. You know that woman he met—?"

"The Witch of Endor, yes."

"He keeps talking about her."

"I'm surprised he doesn't see through it."

"It's Kenny; he blames himself. I don't know what to say anymore, he's got me at my wits' end."

Tarrant arrived a few minutes later, wearing an opennecked blue shirt and a shabby, expensive jacket. "Sorry." He settled into the chair beside Elinor. "I lost track of time."

Oh dear me. The artist at work.

"You still have an outside studio?"

"God, yes, I couldn't work at home, never could."

"I've got a room in the attic," Elinor said.

Neville raised his hand to summon the waiter. "What'll you drink, Tarrant?"

"I think I'll stick to wine."

"Well, make the most of it. I drink whisky all the time now. No chance of that running out. Unless he invades Scotland first."

"Oh, don't talk about invasion," Elinor said. "Do you know Violet's got a cyanide capsule? She has, she showed me."

Bloody hell. It had come to something when middleaged, dried-up old spinsters took to carrying cyanide capsules. What did she think was going to happen to her, for Christ's sake?

"She's a Communist. Was, anyway."

"*Violet?*"

Elinor bristled. "Why not?"

"You never really know people, do you?"

The waiter brought them a menu, which showed a surprising range of choice. "They're good here," Tarrant said.

Elinor began reminiscing about food in Spain. "It's so easy, you know, you go to the market every day, everything's so fresh."

"It's becoming a bit of a legend, our time out there," Tarrant said.

"Yes," Elinor said. "It is a bit; it's our Land of Lost Content. Well, mine, anyway."

"When did you come back?"

"We gave the place up in '36," Tarrant said. "A man we knew very well—he used to keep an eye on the house when we were in England—was shot in the marketplace and nobody was charged though everybody knew who'd done it—so we thought: Right, that's it, time to go."

"I still think about sitting out on the terrace in the early morning, having coffee; the sun used to catch the top of the church and everywhere else was still dark." She seemed to be on the verge of tears.

Tarrant said, quite sharply, "I think we can be just as happy here." No response. "Elinor's inherited her mother's cottage and it's . . . Well, it's really rather nice."

"Roses round the door."

Tarrant put his glass down. "I think you'd like it if you'd only give it a chance."

Elinor seemed to become aware that Neville was being

virtually excluded from the conversation—excluded, but also used as an audience. She said lightly, or with an attempt at lightness, "Paul wants to pack me off to the country, away from all the nasty bombs."

"Yes. I do—and I'm not ashamed of it either." He looked directly at Neville. "I'd just find everything so much easier if I knew she was safe."

"She? I am still here, you know."

Tarrant was looking increasingly exasperated. "People didn't take their wives into the trenches with them."

"No, but the trenches didn't run through the family living room."

"And now they do?"

"Paul, the kitchen window was blown in last night! Anyway, I'm not going and that's that."

A tense silence.

"You'd be missed," Neville said. Not perhaps the most tactful thing he could have said, but true all the same.

She looked at him and smiled, and immediately he was back in the country lane, seeing her nipples, hearing a loud *plop* as a frog, affronted by the invasion of his territory, leapt to safety in a ditch . . . And for all the hope *he* had of kissing the princess, he might as well have been the fucking frog. All the same, this marriage was in trouble. Oh, they'd both deny it, but all the same it was. He knew the signs.

Fortunately, at that moment, the waiter arrived to tell them their table was ready, and over the meal the talk took a less abrasive turn.

GOING HOME in the taxi, Elinor said, "I wish you hadn't mentioned the cottage."

"Why?"

"Because I don't want him telling the other drivers and them thinking I'm suddenly going to not show up or something."

"I don't think he'll do that."

"He's a gossip."

"No, he's not. He's not interested enough in other people to be a gossip." He gave her a sidelong glance. "Tell you one thing, though, he's a bit in love with you."

A yelp of disbelief. When she saw he was serious, she said: "Actually, I used to think he was a bit in love with you."

"What, Neville? No, he's not like that."

She shrugged and stared out of the window, though there was little to be seen except a circle of blue warning lights around a crater in the road.

While Paul paid the driver, Elinor opened the front door and went through into the drawing room, where she was immediately confronted by the carriage clock on the mantelpiece, its hands stopped at twenty past three. Oddly enough, the grandfather clock on the upstairs landing disagreed, putting the time of the explosion at twenty-five to four.

She remembered how strange Paul had been, how almost . . . elated. She'd watched him bending over the clock, shaking it gently to see if it would start, getting out the key, trying to wind it up. She'd been so sure he'd be upset, even perhaps disproportionately upset, but when he turned to face her his eyes were shining. *We're outside time,* he'd said.

She heard the taxi pull away and a moment later Paul came into the room. "Do you fancy another drink or . . . ?"

"No, I think I'll go up now."

Undressed, stretched about between the sheets, she waited for him to join her, worrying about the broken window and where, in this city of broken glass, she was going to find a glazier willing to take on a small domestic job. Paul got undressed quickly, and as soon as he got into bed turned on his side away from her. Cautiously, not sure if she'd be welcome or not, she rested her cheek between his shoulder blades, feeling a raised mole pressing into her skin. She could have drawn, from memory, the position of every mole on his back. She rested her hand on his hip, then let it slide across his stomach until she was gently cupping his balls. His breath quickened, but he didn't turn to face her, or, in any other way, respond, and after a while she took her hand away.

✻ *SIXTEEN*

Elinor came off duty, her hair gray with dust and her trousers sticking uncomfortably to the backs of her thighs. She'd tried shampooing her hair in the showers, but it didn't work. If you weren't careful you risked turning the plaster dust into a paste. People were aged by it, the dust in their hair, that and the rings of exhaustion under their eyes. Women who, before the war, had worn no makeup plastered themselves with it now. Even Violet had been seen dabbing girlishly pink lipstick on her mouth. Dana, like Elinor, went the whole hog: vanishing cream, powder, rouge, eye shadow, the lot.

Elinor walked quickly. She wanted to get home, make tea, have a bath, fall into bed and snatch a couple of hours' sleep before starting on the shopping and cooking and the hundred and one other things that had to be fitted in as if everything were normal. Painting? Ah, well. Somehow, in these changed circumstances, Paul went on painting. She didn't.

The sun was only just rising over the rooftops of the still-intact buildings, casting a cruel light on ruins that had already become familiar, no longer novelties to be gawped at. There was a gap on the corner, and it was an effort to remember which shop used to be there, though it couldn't be more than a week since that bomb fell. Everywhere, there was the crunch of glass under tramping feet as people came up out of the shelters, blinked, took deep breaths, tried to decide between heading home or going straight to work. The streets glittered, hurting her eyes.

Farther along, she stopped, then almost ran the rest of the way, because now she could see yellow tape stretched across the entrance to the square. Somebody's house must've been hit, and though really it was no more than a nameless, mouth-parching fear, the conviction grew on her that this time her luck had run out, this time it was her house that had gone.

A group of people, among them many of her neighbors, was standing at the tape. An old man with white hair tried to duck under it, but a warden yelled at him to get back. There was a time bomb at the center of the square, under the grass, and another in the middle of the road. She could see a sort of boil under the tarmac. Until those bombs were dealt with, nobody was going home.

From this angle, she couldn't quite see her house, though she could see that a house three doors farther up had been virtually demolished—that must be where the bomb had fallen. So her house—hers and Paul's—had to be badly damaged. It couldn't not be.

Everybody stood looking into the familiar square, which seemed as strange now as the cratered surface of the moon. People whispered. Why? There was no reason for it, and yet not one person spoke at a normal pitch. A deadly silence emanated from the broken houses, the piles of rubble, that menacing blister in the surface of the road. Men clambered across the ruins like black beetles. A woman lit a cigarette and a warden shouted at her to put it out. Gas mains had burst, did she want the whole bloody street to go up? The woman blushed, pinched the cigarette between thumb and forefinger and replaced the tab end in the packet.

Elinor looked round for Paul and saw him approaching, with that distinctive loping stride of his. He hadn't seen her yet, hadn't seen the yellow tape. When he did, he stamped out his cigarette and broke into a run. They met and embraced and she started crying, which surprised her because she hadn't known till then how close she was to tears.

Paul pulled on her elbow, indicating they should walk round to the back of the square: they might be able to see their house more clearly from there. She followed him, stumbling over bricks, hardly able to keep up with him: he was striding ahead as if his life depended on it. Now she could get a closer look at the house that had received the direct hit. It had been sliced in half with almost surgical precision. On the first floor, a green brocade armchair cocked one elegant cabriole leg over the abyss. There was a bathroom with a washbasin and toilet, looking somehow vulnerable, touching even, like a fleeting, accidental glimpse of somebody's backside. You wanted to cover it up, restore its dignity, but there was no way of doing that.

She knew the three girls who lived in the basement flat—they didn't go to any of the public shelters. They were all young nurses working at University College Hospital. She remembered their laughter on summer evenings, the parties that used to go on half the night, how irritated she'd been. Now she felt her additional years, the years they wouldn't have, as a sagging of the skin, a weight pulling her down, and she was ashamed.

"Can you see what's happened?" she asked.

"No, but I'm going to find out."

Of course, Paul knew all the local wardens. He simply put his tin hat on and ducked under the tape. She watched him stride across to the man who seemed to be in charge, heard a mutter of conversation, then saw Paul walk on a few steps and peer up the street. He stood staring for a minute, then turned and came back to her.

"There's no hope of getting back in tonight. We're going to have to find somewhere to sleep."

"Could you see the house?"

He pulled a face. "Not good. The roof's caved in. I don't think they're going to let us live there, even after they've dealt with the bombs."

"But it's still standing?"

"Well, just about. Basically, it's collapsed in a V shape." His hands were making the shape as he spoke. "We might be able to get something out, depends how stable it is. But it's not looking good."

Instantly, Elinor felt smaller, less competent, as dependent on Paul as a small child might have been. "Where shall we go?"

"Oh, there's plenty of B&Bs around. Look, why don't I put you in a café while I go and book us in somewhere? At least then we'll know where we're going to be. *Or . . .*" He turned to face her. "I could take you to the station and you could stay with Rachel, just for a few nights, then you can move into the cottage. Have your own place."

"What about you?"

"I'm all right, I can sleep in the studio."

"But I don't want to leave you."

"Well, yes, all right. First thing is, to find a room. And there's clothes . . . You know, you've still got a few things at Rachel's . . ."

"No, absolutely not."

"All right."

He sighed, the slump of his shoulders telling her she'd become a problem, something he had to worry about, a distraction from other, arguably more important, matters. That sigh weakened her, undermined her, as almost nothing else could have done.

"Come on," she said. "We'll find somewhere together."

THE ROOM THEY FOUND, in one of the side roads off Oxford Street, was small with yellowish-brown paper on the walls. The one window looked out into a basement yard so at all times of the day they were in semidarkness. Their faces loomed pale in the brown-spotted mirror, like fish in a badly maintained tank.

By day, Elinor had nowhere to go—it was almost impossible to stay in the room—so she spent a lot of time just wandering around, always drawn back to the square where she'd spent so many years of her life. It was still cordoned off; she stood, with other lost souls, looking across the tape at the bulge in the road, and the wrecked houses. Apparently quite a few of them would have to be demolished, including, Paul seemed to think, their own.

She couldn't face going on duty from the B&B or leaving it to go to one of the public shelters. So when Paul was on duty, she simply lay on the bed and waited for him to return. But then, on the fourth night, she gave herself a good talking-to and reported to the ambulance depot, as usual. Dana and Violet welcomed her with open arms, and other people too—people who in normal circumstances she would probably never have met—went out of their way to be kind. They seemed to care about her—as she did about them.

Next morning, exhausted, but determined to spend the

day looking for more permanent accommodation, she went back to Oxford Street and found the B&B had been bombed. So there they were, for the second time in a week, homeless.

Or rather, she was. Paul could always move into his studio, which—as he never tired of pointing out—wasn't big enough for two.

They stood in a doorway on Oxford Street surrounded by yet another group of shocked, disorientated people. The newly risen sun glinted on the silver barrage balloons and silhouetted the broken outline of bombed and partially demolished buildings. The usual smell of charred timber and burning bricks. On the other side of the tape was sunlit emptiness. A man, standing halfway up the road, shimmered in the heat from a still-smoldering building. He seemed almost to be walking on water. The woman standing next to Elinor had long, Rapunzel-like hair, loosely plaited, reaching to her waist, though it was iron-gray. Elinor noticed these things, but blankly, unable to attach any meaning to what she saw.

Paul stood beside Elinor, his elbow lightly touching hers. She realized, without the need for speech, that this second bomb had settled the argument. She would go to Rachel's and then to the cottage, not because she thought it was the right thing to do, but because her tired mind couldn't come up with an alternative. In front of them, closer to the tape, a young girl was brushing her long black hair, trying to get rid of the dust, but soothing herself too, perhaps. As she bent and swayed, her whole body followed the movement of her arm. How slender and supple her waist was. Elinor was aware of Paul following the girl's every movement, and she'd never felt more distant from him than she did at that moment.

"I want to go back to the house."

"Is that a good idea?"

"I'll go to the cottage, but I want to see the house first."

"All right, I'll see if I can find a taxi."

EVEN IN A few days, her memory of the square had started to fade. She struggled now to remember what number 35 had looked like, what color its front door had been. Next year she supposed buddleia and rosebay willow herb would throng the empty spaces where people had once lived. She closed her eyes. Everywhere—every step she took, every step anybody took—was the crunch of broken glass.

The time bombs' detonation had inflicted further damage on their house, but at least they were allowed access to the square. They could see at first hand the extent of the damage by climbing cautiously over the outer fringes of the rubble. She could even see into her kitchen. The dresser had somehow become jammed at an angle to the wall. She caught a glint of knives and forks, the blue-and-white fragments of a serving dish. They would be able to get a few things out, but it wasn't pots and pans she wanted, it was the paintings from her attic studio, the portraits of her father and Toby. All gone. And, with them, so much of her past.

She and Paul picked their way around the ruin separately. At one point, she saw him straighten up and look around, and the expression on his face was, unmistakably, one of relief.

She slid down the last slope of rubble and waited for him in the road.

"Well," he said, coming across to join her. "Worse than you thought?"

She couldn't look at him. "I don't think I can face another B&B. I think I'd be better off in the country."

A hint of satisfaction. "I'm sure that's right."

Straggling apart, they walked away from their house, past the crater where two nights ago one of the time bombs had exploded. Trudging along with her eyes on the road, Elinor was startled by an unexpected flash of light, and looked up to see sunshine streaming through a gap in the terrace. The light gilded the tops of trees and bushes that only a week ago had been struggling to survive in deep shade. Oh, yes, all kinds of opportunities for new growth. Only not for her.

She stopped and looked around her, wanting to remember the moment. Then, needing reassurance, she glanced at Paul, but against that dazzling shaft of light he'd become merely a silhouette, featureless.

It might have been anybody standing there.

❄ *SEVENTEEN*

Left alone in London, Paul felt increasingly rest-
less. Partly this was because of his constant
involuntary searching for Kenny. He scanned the faces of
children he passed in the streets, and somehow, despite the
raids, London seemed to be full of children. He watched
them during the day, playing in the parks—the schools were
still closed—or queuing outside the Underground stations.
Children were often sent on ahead to claim the family's
favorite spot; you would see them, laden with sleeping bags
and blankets, sometimes laughing and messing about, but
waiting for hours.

Paul's studio was only ten minutes' walk from his station,
so on the nights when he was on duty he went straight to the
School of Tropical Medicine basement after finishing work,
and played cards or darts till the sirens went and it was time
to go out on patrol.

The evenings when he was not on duty were more of a
problem, because he found it quite impossible to stay indoors
during a raid. He could remember feeling exactly like this
during the last war. Very often at night he'd shunned the
comparative safety of the dugout for walks between sentry
posts. Anything was better than the dank, grave-smelling
murk of life underground, where a single candle, guttering in

the blast from an exploding shell, would send panic-stricken shadows fleeing across the walls. The dugout was safer, yes, but it never *felt* safe. Now, he felt the same way about the public shelters. On the nights when he wasn't on duty, he walked miles through the blacked-out city, sometimes not getting home till two or even three in the morning, by which time he was too exhausted not to sleep.

The darkness turned London into a palimpsest. That knot of boisterous young men by the crush barriers, they were probably soldiers home from Dunkirk, or just possibly stragglers from Boudicca's army. After all, from the perspective of the poor bloody infantry, one cock-up's pretty much like another. You had a sense on these nights of long-buried bones working their way to the surface: London's dead gurgling up through the drains. Perhaps in these thronging shadows the living and the dead met in fleeting, unconscious encounters. Why not? *How would you know?*

On one of these walks, he found himself in a side street near Coram's Fields. On the corner there was a pawnshop, its three brass balls suspended over the pavement, a symbol so evocative of his youth he had to cross the road for a closer look. In the window, as he'd expected, were rows and rows of little white cards offering rings—most poignantly, wedding rings—for sale. Probably they'd been pawned over and over again until some worsening of an already desperate situation meant they couldn't be redeemed. Ah, *redeemed*. The religious language of pawnbroking had always fascinated him.

When he was a boy, his grandmother had owned a pawnshop, conducting business with her usual rapacity. Many of her clients were pawning goods in order to pay the rent on the ramshackle properties she owned. Yet Gran hadn't been the bloated capitalist of socialist theory, but a half-literate working-class woman who'd got many a black eye from her handsome, philandering husband until she stopped loving him and learned to hit back—or rather, since she was a tiny, birdlike woman, to wait till he was too pissed to know what he was drinking and then jollop him till his arse bled.

Paul's first job had been behind the counter of her shop: he'd done his homework in between customers. When he leaned forward, he could see his reflection in wood that had been polished to a hard conker-shine by the weight of human misery that passed over it. But it was a job, a proper job, and he had been proud of it.

God, how it all came flooding back. He was about to move on when he saw a notice in the bottom-right-hand corner of the window. Bertha Mason, materialization medium, would be giving a seance at eight o'clock this evening. The accompanying photograph was creased and grainy—obviously cut from a newspaper—but there could be no mistaking the woman. It was the Witch of Endor, no less. He bent down to make sure, but, yes, it had to be. There couldn't be two women in London who looked like that. Eight o'clock—just time for a pint of beer and a sandwich. He thought he might as well give it a go, as much from nostalgia as anything else, though he was curious about the woman who had made a disagreeable but powerful impression on him. He wasn't finding her easy to forget.

RETURNING AN HOUR later, he stepped into a shop whose smells stripped away the intervening years till he was fourteen years old again. A single bulb cast a pallid light over the detritus of hopeless lives: musty-smelling clothes hung from racks, some, with pink tickets, waiting to be redeemed; others, with blue tickets, up for sale. Racks of shoes pressed out of shape by other people's bunions, dresses with other people's sweat stains under the arms, a hatstand from which hung a solitary bowler hat, shiny with age. Despite the downtrodden, shabby air of it all, he kept experiencing exquisitely painful tweaks of nostalgia. Not for when he was a child serving in the shop for the first time—no; for a year or so later, when he was a pimply adolescent with hairs on the palms of his hands. The hairs hadn't been real hairs, of course—they were what you were threatened with if you didn't stop doing *it*—and try as he might he never could stop. There were some mornings when he could virtually have combed those hairs.

There'd been a girl called Gemma Martin who'd come in every Monday morning on her way to work to pawn her father's Sunday suit. Long blond hair, the greenish color of unripe wheat, and slightly prominent blue eyes. Gran didn't like the Martins. "I knew her mam when her knickers were that raggy she was ashamed to hang them on the line. And as for her nan—she used to sew bacon fat in her vest and bloomers every December, didn't take them off till March. I've seen dogs follow her down the street." The Martins, he gathered, gave themselves airs: a worse crime than murder in Gran's book.

What with Gran's beady eyes and vitriolic tongue, it had taken him nearly six months to summon up the courage to ask Gemma out. Oh, but it was worth it. And the reason he found all these smells erotic was that one evening, hours after the shop had closed, he'd managed to persuade Gemma to go nearly all the way, on a pile of unredeemed coats.

It was five to eight; he ought to be taking his seat. A thin man with round spectacles appeared and guided him past the racks of clothes and up a rickety staircase. At the top was a small landing packed with people waiting to buy tickets. More people were coming up the stairs behind him. Since that basement in Agate Street he'd hated overcrowded spaces and might have left, only at that moment the couple in front moved on, and he was level with the table. A woman with mournful brown eyes was taking the money, attempting to look deeply spiritual while counting notes with the help of spit on a well-practiced thumb. He handed over a ten-shilling note, was given a ticket and asked to surrender his blackout torch.

"Why?"

She looked at him. "When the medium's in a trance, her eyes are very sensitive to light."

"But there's hardly any light." Blackout torches were notoriously dim.

Rolling the notes into a wad, she snapped an elastic band tight around them. "*Very* sensitive." He gave her the torch.

The seance room was cramped and stuffy, lit only by three small, red-shaded lamps set at intervals along the far wall. An usher guided him to a seat near the back, though he noticed there was a whole row of vacant seats at the front. It was so dark he could hardly see to get to his seat and had to apologize constantly for trampling on people's toes. When, finally, he was settled, he took a deep breath and looked around. Eight rows of chairs faced a stage on which stood some kind of cabinet, not unlike a nightwatchman's box. Black curtains had been pulled back to reveal a wooden chair with arms. He noticed another chair near the front of the stage, which seemed to have black clothes draped over the back. The room was about two thirds full, and it was well past eight o'clock, but for a long time nothing happened, except whispers and coughing and more muttered apologies as late arrivals tripped over people's feet. He could see slightly better now. In the third row, he noticed a middle-aged shelter warden, Angela Langdale, very jolly-hockey-sticks, but rather nice, with a lot of mousey-fair down on her upper lip and a genius for organization. When he was on patrol, he often called in at her shelter for a cup of tea and a cigarette. Next to her was Sandra Jobling. Now that was a surprise. He didn't think of Sandra as the sort of person who went to seances, but then he didn't think of himself as that sort of person either.

The thought of a cigarette, once planted, quickly blossomed into a craving, though when he looked around he saw that nobody else was smoking. Perhaps the organizers were so wedded to darkness that even the striking of a match seemed threatening? He tried to ignore the craving, but it wouldn't go away, so he repeated the stumbling and apologizing, receiving in return some decidedly disgruntled looks.

Downstairs, he found the front door locked, but there'd be a back entrance and almost certainly a yard. He pushed between the racks of clothes, releasing a smell of mothballs which made him want to sneeze, and found himself in another much smaller room, hardly more than a passage really, with three doors opening off. The first door led into a broom cupboard containing an ironing board, a bucket and a mop. The next door opened onto a room where at last, *at last*, there was enough light to see by, though what he saw defied belief. He stood, rooted to the ground, jaw unhinged, gawping like an idiot.

Bertha Mason sat, naked, on a table, facing him, surrounded by three middle-aged women, all dressed in black, but he had eyes for nobody but her. The sheer size of her: chins, neck, breasts, belly—all pendulous—the sagging, wrinkled abdomen hanging so low it almost hid the fuzz of black hair beneath. Like a huge, white, half-melted candle she sat, eyes glazed, a fag end glued to her bottom lip. She made no move to cover herself, just sat there, breathing noisily through her open mouth. He stared, he couldn't stop himself, until one of the women darted forward and slammed the door in his face.

Dazed, he opened the third door and blundered out into a small yard where he lit a cigarette, dragging smoke into his lungs like oxygen. What he felt was neither pity nor revulsion, but something altogether more complex. An image was taking shape in his mind: the Willendorf Venus. That featureless face beneath elaborately styled hair, vestigial arms, roll upon roll of fat, each roll resting on the one below, vestigial legs, no feet. But it's not negative: she has no eyes because she contains the world; she has no feet because everything comes to her. It's an image of power.

At least Bertha Mason had a face, though it had been completely blank. Was she in a trance? Had to be, something like that. He crushed the remains of the cigarette beneath his foot, taking his time, grinding it away to nothing, then went back upstairs to the crowded room, where a buzz of expectation was running along the rows.

His seat had been taken. The back rows were full so he crept down the aisle and took a seat on the end of the front row. Nobody challenged him, though he saw that all these seats were marked "Reserved." Evidently only known supporters were allowed as close to the platform as this.

The lady of the ten-shilling notes mounted the stairs and announced in a markedly nasal voice that she would now invite a member of the audience—"chosen at random"—to step up and examine the medium's clothes. The randomly chosen one, who'd been sitting in one of the reserved seats on the front row, shook the clothes, turned them inside out, ran her fingers ostentatiously along every seam, and then, with a brisk nod, handed them back. The garments were ceremoniously carried out and returned, shortly afterwards, with Mrs. Mason inside them, wheezing from the climb upstairs.

Her breathing was so bad Paul was inclined to shout: *Oh for God's sake, stop messing about, call a doctor!* She had to be helped onto the platform. Once there, she took a moment to get her breath, then entered the cabinet, where she lowered herself into the chair and let her head fall back, shortly afterwards emitting a succession of grunts and snorts as the curtains, with a great rattling of brass rings, were pulled across. Raggedly at first, then with more conviction, the audience began to sing "Abide with Me."

Paul didn't know what to expect. Fraud, yes, of course: only he'd thought it would be subtle. Skilled. What followed was fraud, all right, but blatant, crude, embarrassingly unconvincing fraud. He didn't understand how anybody could possibly be taken in by it, but people were. One woman looked positively radiant as she recognized the face of her dead son, though, to Paul, the returning spirit was very obviously a papier-mâché head stuck on the end of a broomstick and draped in cheesecloth; cheesecloth which smelled strongly of fish.

Mrs. Mason had two spirit guides. The one who appeared most frequently, who acted as a kind of impresario, was Albert, who'd apparently seen service on the Western Front, and had passed over, as he put it, on the first day of the Somme. Albert's voice was convincingly masculine; his public-school accent much less so. This was no more than a music-hall imitation of a toff and even that was starting to slip a bit. The other guide, who popped up from time to time, was a little girl of truly awful sweetness who would keep bursting into song: Shirley Temple, but without the talent. Paul was sickened by it. No, quite literally: he felt sick. Probably he should have walked out, but the memory of that naked figure, the wheeze of her labored breathing, held him back. Instead he closed his eyes, determined to detach himself from the proceedings.

But then the curtains were drawn back. Mrs. Mason, looking decidedly the worse for wear, announced she would give a few individual messages. The audience leaned forward: this was the moment they'd been waiting for. Their turn.

It was the usual trite, banal rubbish. At one point she looked directly at Paul, and he tensed, afraid she was going to give him one of her messages, afraid, irrationally afraid, of what the message might be. At that moment he realized this visit of his was not curiosity about Mrs. Mason, or a trip down memory lane, but something more driven, less rational: part of the endless, exhausting search for Kenny, which still went on even though he knew there was no hope of finding him. He wasn't detached from this: he was just like all the other people here.

He was afraid of her. It was a relief when she turned her attention to the back row, to yet another middle-aged woman with a missing son. A voice began to speak, every bit as convincing as Albert, but offering no banal message of comfort: no reassuring platitudes. The beach at Dunkirk, dunes being sprayed with bullets, sand kicked up into the air, cracked lips, no water, his friend dead in the sand beside him—not a British plane in sight. Where were they? Where were the British planes? The words dwindled to an angry mutter before finally winding down into silence. Seconds later, along came Shirley Temple and "The Good Ship Lollipop."

But now, suddenly, a commotion broke out near the back of the room. People started turning round, trying to peer into the darkness, one or two of them even stood on their chairs. A tall woman, wearing mannish tweeds, strode down the aisle, shining a forbidden torch on the stage—and not a blackout torch either: a proper prewar flashlight. Mrs. Mason ran back into the cabinet and, with a rattle of brass rings, pulled the curtains across. No sooner had she disappeared than the tall woman leapt onto the platform, pulled the curtains apart and revealed an empty chair. Mrs. Mason was on her knees, waving a doll with some kind of vest or camisole attached, and still prattling away in that awful cutesy-pie voice as if unable to grasp what was happening.

The tall woman grabbed the doll, Mrs. Mason refused to let go, and an ugly tug of war ensued in which the doll's head came off. Everybody was on their feet now, riveted by the squalid battle. At last, Mrs. Mason managed to wrench herself free and again ran back into the cabinet, where she could be seen trying to stuff the doll's head up her skirt. At that moment the overhead lights came on, dazzling everybody. Transfixed by the sudden glare, Mrs. Mason was still for a moment, then leapt out of the cabinet, roaring with anger.

The tall woman took a step back, but persisted. "Come on, give it to me, I know you've got it. Come on, I want to see what you've got up there."

"What, and show everybody me knickers? I will *not*. There's men in here, case you haven't noticed."

The tall woman had been joined on the platform by three men, who crowded round Mrs. Mason, demanding to see the doll. Turning swiftly, she picked up the chair and began wielding it as a battering ram. "I'll brain the whole bloody lot of you, bloody buggering bastards!" And then she simply yelled, a great battle cry that seemed to require neither words nor intake of breath.

Paul was pushing his way up the steps onto the platform. Perhaps he should have been pleased to see such cynical fraud exposed, but three men jostling one woman was altogether too much like bullying for his taste. Surprising himself, he fought his way to her side. "Mrs. Mason." Her eyes stared at him without recognition. So she had been in a trance—there was no other way she could have forgotten that encounter downstairs. "Calm down, now. Deep breaths." He turned. "And you lot, back off. Can't you see the state she's in?"

After a while, she seemed to grow calmer. She would get undressed, she said, but only if the men left the room.

The three men who'd been crowding her looked at each other, but made no move. A few others, Paul included, retreated a few paces, though nobody moved very far. Mrs. Mason squatted down and pulled her dress and petticoat over her head. Tangled up in the folds was the doll's head, which fell and rolled across the floor, its china-blue eyes startling in the bristling light. Mrs. Mason tried to kick it behind the cabinet, but was too slow. The tall woman pounced, scooped up the doll's head and held it up for all to see. *"There."*

The sight seemed to enrage Mrs. Mason, who began tearing at her clothes. One enormous breast, the size of a savoy cabbage, escaped her camisole and, despite swearing no man on earth should ever see her knickers, she was now whirling them about above her head, looking, Paul thought, like a corpulent version of Liberty leading the people.

"I'm keeping this." The tall woman waved the doll's head at her. "It's evidence."

"You give that here, it's mine." And, seizing the chair again, Mrs. Mason launched another attack.

Paul tried to restrain her, but she was so beside herself he was beginning to think the whole farcical episode might end in murder.

A short, stocky man with a military mustache said: "Why doesn't somebody ring the police?"

"No," Mrs. Mason said. "There's no need for that."

Slowly, she put down the chair and, after a minute or so, began to get dressed. Her lips were blue. Then, just as everybody started to relax, she charged again, seized the doll's head and ran out of the room.

Paul followed her and found her in the downstairs room, with a group of supporters gathered round her, like drones round a termite queen. One woman pressed a cup of tea into her hands; another fanned her with a copy of *Spiritualist News*, while the randomly chosen one held out a dress for her to put on.

There was a stir in the shop. The forces of law and order had arrived in the form of one bewildered police constable with a fresh, young, freckly face. There wasn't a great deal he could do. Nobody wanted to press charges, though the one man she'd caught a glancing blow with the chair was still bleeding. The tall woman introduced herself as Miss Pole, which amused Paul, though no one else seemed to think it was funny. Fraud was mentioned. Mrs. Mason turned her eyes to the ceiling. "As God is my witness, I know nothing about it."

"What do you mean, you know nothing about it?" Miss Pole demanded. "You had a doll's head in your knickers."

Wisely, Mrs. Mason burst into tears. One of the attendant women touched Paul's arm. "Eh, dear God, that poor woman, she's a martyr, she is. She's been to prison, you know."

Paul could quite believe it.

People were starting to leave. Nobody asked for their money back, perhaps feeling that one way or another they'd had a good show. The policeman left. Somehow, in all the turmoil, the doll's head had vanished, no doubt safely ensconced in somebody else's knickers. And not only the doll; cheesecloth, broomsticks, papier-mâché heads: all spirited away.

Miss Pole glared at Mrs. Mason; Mrs. Mason smirked. She'd got away with it, not for the first time, nor probably the last.

Paul looked around for Angela and Sandra, but they'd gone, so he set off to walk alone. A raid had started, so there was no question of going back to the studio just yet. He was alternately amused and nauseated by the events of the evening, or so at first he told himself, but then as he walked, he realized he was once more separating himself from the experience, which at times he'd found deeply disturbing. Albert's voice, the young man dying on the beach at Dunkirk, stood out from what would otherwise have been blatant fraud, and nothing else but fraud. Papier-mâché heads on broomsticks, fishy cheesecloth—fishy in every sense of the word—but was that the whole truth? He didn't think so. He thought she'd been doing something else, though he didn't believe the something else had much to do with contacting the dead.

He'd been afraid she'd tell him about Kenny, describe his last moments in the basement of the school. How could he be so frightened of something he didn't believe was possible? How could that woman, who was in so many ways pathetic—and also, it had to be said, repulsive—have such power? He remembered seeing her in the downstairs room, naked, eyes glazed, fag end stuck to her bottom lip, an image by turns embarrassing, pitiable and nightmarish. He tried to erase it from his mind, but it drew strength from darkness. As he walked from street to street, he found it easy to believe they were leading him to a secret chamber, right at the heart of the blacked-out city, where a white, bloated figure sat enthroned, a grotesque Persephone, claiming to speak for millions of the mouthless dead.

❋ *EIGHTEEN*

Y ou weren't supposed to talk to the patients. The one time they'd caught her at it, Sister Matthews had come down on her like a ton of bricks. "*You* are a *ward maid.*" Lips pursed like a cat's arse. "The patients are nothing to do with you."

Aye, right. But when there'd been a rush on, after Dunkirk, she'd done all sorts, changed beds, emptied bedpans, pushed trolleys full of filthy sheets down to the laundry in the basement—and none of that was her job. Oh, and in between times, yes, she'd talked to the lads, and nobody pulled her up over it. Poor sods, they'd nowt to do all day except watch shadows moving on the walls, check the time to see how long it still was till visiting, strain to hear familiar footsteps coming up the ward.

Once things had settled down a bit, they played cards, talking through lips that hardly moved about stuff that had happened, some of the things they'd seen. Guardsmen forced to shave in seawater before they'd been allowed to get on a boat. "Only in England," one lad said. And then on the train coming back how people had thrown cigarettes in at the windows, treated them like conquering heroes, but they weren't heroes, not in their own estimation. Bloody cock-up—that was the general verdict. She'd never seen so many men so angry.

This poor lad here. Babbling away, but not making a lot of sense, poor soul. God knows what was going on in his head— and his breathing. And she thought hers was bad. First time she clapped eyes on him, she thought: *You're not long for this world, son.* But he had, he'd hung on. And he'd talked, my God he had, how they'd lain in the open under the hot sun, no water, not a British plane in sight. Chap next to him showed him a silk scarf he'd bought for his fancy bit—"bought, my eye, bloody nicked it"—and then he'd died, lying there in the sand. "And I took the scarf. Wasn't stealing, was it?" " 'Course it wasn't, love. It was no good to him."

And that's when Sister Matthews had pounced. Things were back to normal now, apparently. She was just the maid.

So now, though he went on babbling, she turned her back on him, kept herself busy polishing the taps, only then he said the one word that would have made any woman turn round. "Mam."

He was staring round him, wild-eyed, not a clue where he was, poor lad. "Mam?"

She put her hand over his. "It's all right, son. You go off to sleep, now, it's all right."

He closed his eyes. A few minutes later the fluttering behind his lids stopped, and his mouth fell slightly open. Had he gone? Still touching his hand, she watched his chest, saw the almost-imperceptible rise. No, not yet, but it wouldn't be long.

Mam. She knew it was stupid, but the word kept catching in her throat. He could be, she told herself—well, just about. Her son had been born bang in the middle of the last war, so that would make him, what—twenty-four, twenty-five? About right. Of course, it wasn't him, she knew that, but . . . Well, no, actually, come to think of it, you couldn't *know*, could you? Not for certain, you couldn't. She needed to go back and see him again, look for resemblances, but she couldn't. There was another ward to clean, and another. Far too many. Seemed to think you could work bloody miracles.

So she trudged from bed to bed, basin to basin, ward to ward. All the time, floating in front of her eyes, was the memory of the purple, howling dwarf they'd torn out of her all them years ago. She'd never seen a newborn baby before. Little babies, yes, a few days old, but not newborn. And my God it come as a shock, she'd no idea they looked like that.

She'd gone into the home the minute she started showing. For a long time you could cover it up with cardigans and jumpers, but not forever—and you weren't allowed to work in the munitions factory if you were pregnant, something to do with the chemicals, so she more or less had to go in the home. Where was she going to find another job with a belly on her like that? No, it was the home, or starve.

They put her to work in the laundry—laughable, really—lifting buckets, twelve-hour shifts, wonder they didn't all lose their babies—and probably better if they had. But at least the work tired you out. She was asleep the minute her head touched the pillow. And what a lumpy pillow it was. The pillowcase was always spotless—matron saw to that—but the pillow smelled of other people's hair, all the girls who'd slept on it before her. But there it was, lumps or not, she'd drop off to sleep like falling over a cliff, only she didn't stay asleep, not properly asleep. She was aware all the time of the ward: the iron bedsteads, humped bodies under pale green coverlets, gray light seeping through threadbare curtains—and then it all faded, and she was somewhere else.

A place she seemed to know. For some reason, in her dreams—well, she supposed she was dreaming, she didn't know what else to call it—it was always winter. Men huddled under waterproof capes, sheltering from the sleety rain that fell ceaselessly from the evil, yellow sky. On cold nights their eyebrows were rimed with frost. After a while, she found she could hear them speak, taste the chlorine in their tea, feel the heat of the fire—even tell from the sound a shell made as it was coming over how close it was going to land. They weren't aware of her, these men. Stared straight through her. *She* was the ghost.

And then, one night, it all changed. She was with them, watching them, as usual, but now a dark man with heavy eyelids was looking back at her. Watching her. She was so used to being the watcher, it came as quite a shock. At first she didn't believe it, but then, when deliberately she moved a few yards to the right, he turned his head to follow her. She was so new to this, so ignorant, it took her a long time to cotton on that he'd passed.

Next morning, she washed her face as usual, brushed her hair, clumped across the yard to the laundry, where the steamy heat made her nose run. Exactly the same as every other morning, except this time she didn't go alone.

She didn't know Howard then, otherwise she might have sorted it out a bit sooner. Though Howard got things wrong too. He always said Albert was an officer, that he'd been killed on the first day of the Somme. But it was always winter when she saw him, and he wasn't an officer: he crawled out of a funk hole in the side of the trench every morning along with all the other men. Anyway, whoever he was, whenever he died, from that night on he was part of her. Not that he was there all the time, she could go days without a squeak out of him, but he generally took over when things were bad. Gave her a bit of a break—and my God she needed it, because the last few weeks in the home things were very bad.

Mind you, bugger didn't show up when she was in labor. He kept well out of the way then.

Lifting buckets of water all day long, her back ached that much she didn't even realize she'd started till her waters broke. The supervisor told her to walk—*walk?* Was she joking?—across the yard to the infirmary, where she got undressed and hauled herself onto the bed. Sister Mortimer stood at the end, watching her. "Not as much fun getting it out as it was putting it in, is it?" *Wasn't that much bloody fun putting it in,* she wanted to say. Didn't, of course. Oh, and you didn't dare groan. "Shut that noise up. You'll be worse before you're better." Not a shred of sympathy, not a grain. Oh, she could've told them a thing or two, might've done, only another pain was building, and she needed every bit of breath . . . And then, amazingly, all in a great rush, there he was.

Purple. Was he supposed to be that color? Oh, but what a pair of lungs, couldn't be that much wrong with him. She wanted to hold him, but they wouldn't let her. She watched as he was wrapped, expertly, in a white cotton blanket and taken away. She caught one more glimpse of him, just the top of his head, as Sister Mortimer turned to push the door open with her hip, and she whispered, but only to herself: *Good luck, son.*

Back on the streets, with leaking breasts and a craving for sweetness no amount of cake could satisfy, she palled up with a lass called Millie and they went to Glasgow together. Back in munitions, earning good money, she thought Albert might disappear, just fade away, but he didn't. If she got upset—oh, and she did, she couldn't stop thinking about the baby—Albert was there. Some days he was in and out that often she lost track of things. There were holes in her memory, so many holes it was like lace, or a cabbage leaf when the caterpillars have been at it.

But then she met Howard. The best thing that ever happened to her. And the worst. In the twinkling of an eye—Howard's eye, needless to say—she was pregnant, only this time she knew what to do. Howard was more or less disabled—*gas*, he said, though forty fags a day didn't help much, either the budget or his lungs—so she had to work. So there she was, walking round the back streets looking for an address. Mucky old woman come to the door, you could've planted a row of tatties in her neck—now there was a warning—but really there was no choice. Up on the bed, spread your legs. Sometimes, looking back on her life, she thought she'd never done anything else. Well, yes, she had—she'd opened her mouth and let the dead speak through her.

Five days after, she collapsed in the street. Temperature sky-high. "You silly, silly, *silly* girl," the ward sister said. Bit more sympathetic than most.

No more babies after that. Not that Howard minded—he was a baby himself.

Last bed now, last basin. She was free to go, get her hat and coat from the cupboard. Nice hat, she was very fond of it, it always made her feel good—and it hadn't cost a lot, she'd picked it up for a penny in a jumble sale. Still, with a bit of green ribbon and some artificial roses it didn't look too bad. Cheered her up, anyway—she could see the roses bobbing as she walked. She was passing the door of *his* ward now. Perhaps she better leave it? Just walk past? But no, she couldn't do that.

The bed was empty, stripped, the screens folded and pushed back against the wall. Of course, she'd known he was going—but still, it was a shock. For a minute, she just stood and stared, then rested one hand lightly on the mattress. *Mam.* Probably the last thing he'd ever said. Ah, well. Never any hope, not with a head wound like that, the only mystery was why he'd lasted as long as he had. She patted the bed and turned away.

She was just leaving the ward when Sister Wilkinson caught up with her. "Would you mind taking this down to the laundry?"

"This" was a trolley loaded with soiled sheets. *His* sheets, probably. She could've said: *'Course I bloody well mind, I'm off duty.* Still, it paid to stay on the right side of the sisters—and Wilkie was nicer than most.

So she took the trolley and began trundling it along the main corridor. Like a lot of the trolleys, it had a mind of its own and would keep veering to the left. Like a bloody wrestling match, sometimes. So she lurched and swayed along, the roses in her hat bobbing, thinking how nice it would be to put her feet up when she got home, have half an hour on the bed . . . At least, though, she could take the lift—you were allowed to, if you had a trolley.

She hated the basement: so dark, gloomy and deserted, though not, of course, the laundry: that was the same hellhole of hissing steam and clanking buckets she remembered from the home. As she pushed the swing doors open and pulled the trolley through, she was breathing in smells of soap and disinfectant, her eyes were watering—horrible stuff, that disinfectant—and she was remembering the girl whose waters had broken all over the damp floor. *And* they'd made her mop it up. Had they? Now she come to think of it, she wasn't sure. She didn't always remember things right, on account of Albert.

"Can I help you?"

The supervisor, drying her red, wet hands on a towel.

Friendly words, but not a friendly tone, no, not at all. Bertha pushed the trolley in her direction and turned, wordlessly, away. Outside, in the corridor, she stopped to consider. No conveniently empty trolley to take back to the ward, so she was going to have to face the stairs. And she was feeling a bit peculiar, the way she sometimes did when Albert was on his way. Perhaps she could chance the lift? No, better not. She started to walk the length of the corridor towards the stair-case at the far end. No windows, no natural light, the strip light overhead kept flickering, keeping time with the pulsing in her head. She had a headache starting—always one-sided, her headaches. The throbbing turned to muttering, low, at first, but getting louder. She must be passing the morgue. Normally, she'd have said: *Sorry, love, not working.* But not today. After a second's hesitation, standing outside the door, she pushed it open and walked in.

A barred window set high in the opposite wall let in a grudging light, but enough to see three figures, draped in white sheets, and lying stretched out on slabs like huge dead fish. A fan churned up the heavy, lifeless air. The muttering had stopped, probably because he'd heard the door open, but then it started again. It was coming from the nearest slab.

As she walked towards him, she saw the sheet wasn't quite long enough to cover him. He'd grown tall, her boy. Reaching out, she touched the thick yellow soles of his feet. Her fingertips, rasping over hard skin, found no lingering warmth, but farther up, in the folds of his groin, he was warm still. At last, standing by his head, but with no recol-lection of getting there, she pulled back the sheet and looked into his face. Smiling a little, she waited for his eyes to open, for the moment when he'd know her again, and say it, say that word: *Mam.*

"And what the hell do you think you're doing?"

A man in a white coat, Adam's apple jerking in his throat. Dumbly, she stared, then forced herself to say something, anything. *Laundry,* she managed to get out at last. She'd been sent to fetch clean laundry.

"Well, you won't find any in here. The laundry's back there."

She could tell he didn't believe her. Dropping the sheet, she said, "I thought he moved."

"Moved? Good God, woman, are you mad?" Then, when she didn't answer: "Where do you work?"

"I'm a ward maid."

Shouldn't've said that. Now he'd report her to matron and she'd get the sack. There'd been several complaints about her work, already—she was on borrowed time here. She started to edge past him, hardly breathing till she reached the door. He didn't try to follow her or ask any more questions, just stood and watched her go. As the door closed behind her, she looked back, seeing his accusing face narrow to a crack and finally disappear.

She stood for a minute, gasping for breath. The lift? No, she'd be seen, she was in enough trouble already. Instead, she walked in the other direction, turned right along a side corridor and out through the double doors at the end. There was a ramp leading up to a yard in which the mortuary vans turned, but it was a steep climb. She had to keep stopping to get her breath.

"You all right, love?" one of the drivers asked.

She nodded and, not wanting to attract any more attention, took shelter behind a parked van. Well, that's me job down the drain, she thought. But perhaps not; he hadn't asked for her name. Nah, but they'd know who she was. She wasn't exactly easy to miss. What the hell was she supposed to do now? If she lost the job, she'd be depending on the seances, and it wasn't enough. Would've been if she got her fair share of the house, but she didn't. Blood-sucking bastards. No, the only way she was going to make money was to go back to the ports, and give them what they wanted: spirits they could see and touch. More cheesecloth up her fanny. Whatever they'd done to her insides that time, it had left a bloody big hole. Which was . . . convenient. She mightn't have been much use giving birth to the living, but my God she was a dab hand giving birth to the dead.

All this time, while she was worrying about money and paying the rent, she'd been feeling the soles of his feet, how hard and cold they were, and, at the same time, seeing that purple, howling, convulsed dwarf, whose long, delicate fingers had clawed the air. That's it. When you come right down to it, what else matters? *Oh, my boy. My poor, poor boy.*

NINETEEN

The raids came thick and fast, all night, every night. Paul had more or less made up his mind he was going to die and this acceptance freed him from fear and moral scruple. Nothing quite like the proximity of death to make you feel entitled to grab anything that's going. What he wanted, though, was not easily got. He didn't want casual sex, still less commercial sex; he wanted precisely what he couldn't have. The girls he'd kissed and fumbled when he was a boy, the excitement of those first encounters, back home, before he left for London.

Gemma, especially—he thought a lot about her. Buying fish and chips from Sweaty Betty's, newspaper dark with grease and vinegar, kissing her good night on her doorstep, tasting salt on her lips, pushing her not-entirely-reluctant fingers down onto his groin, then her dad throwing open the bedroom window and demanding to know what sort of time they thought this was. Slinking away, after a final, clumsy kiss, exhilarated, sticky and ashamed.

Living, as he now did, in one room with a gas ring and a bathroom down the stairs, it was easy to feel like a student again. Everything: his clothes, his towels, even, for all he knew, his hair and skin smelled of oil paint and turps. Every morning, when he came off duty, he made himself a cup of tea and went to look out of the window at the sunlit street. The houses had a dazed look, as if buildings, no less than people, could marvel at another day of life. But then—unless he was so tired he really had to sleep—he started work, and he worked most of the day. Sleep was for later, for the afternoon, when the light was changing.

On one particularly fine morning, he opened the window and leaned out into the street. No bombs had fallen here last night, so no clouds of billowing black smoke marred the flawless beauty of this day. And there, in one of the houses opposite, was a girl. She was looking out into the street, exactly as he was doing, chafing her bare arms against the morning chill. As she leaned farther out, he realized she was almost naked, no more than a skimpy camisole half covering her breasts. He felt a delight in looking at her that was both sensual and innocent, and then she turned in his direction and he saw that it was Sandra Jobling. At the same moment, she recognized him. He expected her to withdraw in confusion, but instead, to his amazement, she leaned even farther out, raised her arm and waved.

He remembered kissing her, though now it seemed like an episode in a dream. They'd been going off duty, the All Clear had only just sounded, and he'd been light-headed with exhaustion and relief. Kissing her then had seemed the most natural thing in the world. He remembered the dryness of her lips, the mingled smell of smoke and soap on damp skin. That was only eight or nine days ago, though it seemed much longer. With the destruction of his house, a door had clanged shut, cutting him off from his previous life. From his adult life—curiously, his youth seemed to become more and more vivid every day.

With a final wave, Sandra withdrew into the darkness of her room. From then on, it was a matter of waiting to go on duty. But he worked as usual until the light changed, then snatched an hour or so of sleep, before setting off to walk the short distance to Russell Square. He often spent the last hours before going on duty lying on the grass, watching the sun dip below the trees.

Despite the continuing hot weather, there were signs of autumn everywhere. Rows of abandoned deck chairs lined the grassy open spaces, some of them nursing lapfuls of dead leaves. Ignoring them, he lay on the ground, wanting to smell cut grass and crumbly soil, slept for another twenty minutes or so, then, dry-mouthed and sun-sozzled, set off in search of a drink.

The streets were emptying fast, the day's spaciousness narrowing to a single crack of light. Soon would come black-out and the wail of sirens, and people were hurrying home to face another night. He was about to turn into the Russell Hotel when a voice hailed him from the other side of the road. Sandra. Oh my God. For a moment he saw her objectively: a stocky, fearless young woman, bright, amused eyes peering through an overgrown fringe. Not pretty, oh no, God, not pretty. What did he care? She was amazing.

She ran across the road, arriving in front of him, breathless. "Fancy a drink?"

There wasn't an ounce of flirtatiousness about her, but then they were colleagues, co-workers, comrades. Asking a colleague to go for a drink means precisely nothing. He was going to have to play this very carefully.

He nodded towards the hotel. "I was just going in there."

"Bit posh, isn't it?"

"No, it's all right."

"I think I'd rather sit out."

They found a pub that had put benches on the pavement. She asked for a Guinness, though normally she drank bitter:

in fact, she could sink a pint of beer as fast as any man on the team. The area round the bar was packed with business-men, snatching one last drink before returning to wives and children in the safety of the country. He carried the drinks outside and sat opposite her. They didn't speak much at first, just sat in the sunshine, looking around them with the smug-ness of stayers-on. It had become a big part of your identity, whether you spent your nights in London or merely came in during the day to work. More important now than sex or class: whether you got on that evening train. Or not.

"Didn't I see you at the seance?" he asked, feeling the silence had gone on long enough.

"Yes, Angela wanted to go."

"Funny, I hadn't got her down as a—"

"As a what?"

Superstitious, neurotic loony. "I just didn't know she was interested."

"Just curious, I think. I was surprised to see you there."

"I met her, in this square, actually, a couple of weeks ago. I was curious. What about you?"

"She used to come to the Spiritualist Church near us, before the war. Me mam goes now and then. It's not a big thing with her. You know, if she gets a message from me nanna she's pleased, but she doesn't make a lot of it. More of a night out, really. She always says if it wasn't for the spuggies, she wouldn't get out."

How easy it was to settle back. "What about you?"

"What about me?"

"Well, do you think there's anything in it?"

"Not really, though there are one or two things you can't quite explain. I mean, for example, me mam and Auntie Ethel went to a seance—Mrs. Mason—and me Auntie Ethel really doesn't believe in it—I think she's quite frightened of it, though—anyway, me nanna came through loud and clear. "I'm surprised," she said, "to see you sat there, our Ethel, being as how you took the ring off my finger as I lay in the coffin." Well, Auntie Ethel nearly passed out. And as they were going home she says to me mam, 'You told her that. There's no way she could've known. You told her, didn't you?' And me mam just went very quiet. And then she says, 'How could I have told her? You were alone in the room.' So that was a dead give-away. And you've got to admit, it is odd, isn't it? I mean, how could Mrs. Mason have known?"

Well. If Auntie Ethel was flashing the ring round every pub in Middlesbrough and some friend of the dead woman happened to recognize it . . . He nodded. "It is odd."

"It was the finish of me mam and Auntie Ethel, they've not spoken since."

Good old Mrs. Mason, spreading havoc . . . "Can I get you another drink?"

"Aye, go on."

When he sat down again, she said, "I hear you've been bombed."

"Yes, a week ago."

"Bad?"

"Pretty bad. Not liveable in."

"So where's your wife?"

"In the country. We did go to a B&B, but . . ." He shrugged. "We got bombed out of that too. That's twice in one week."

"Will she stay there, do you think?"

"Oh, I think so. The second bomb was a shock."

Sandra's tongue came out and deftly removed a mustache of foam from her upper lip. *"Good."*

He was left wondering what, exactly, she meant. "You know, the funny thing is, I worked really hard for that house.

And do you know, when I looked at it, the only thing I felt was relief? It was like this huge weight..." He flexed his shoulders. "I still feel it. I mean, to be honest, I wish it had been completely flattened because then I wouldn't have to keep going back."

"What does your wife think?"

"Oh, she's devastated." A pause. "I'm not saying I'm proud of it."

"You can't help the way you feel."

"I know one thing, I'm not going to go and live in a bloody cottage in the country."

"No, of course not." She batted away a wasp that was hovering over her glass. "You say you keep going back?"

"Yes, you know, rescuing a few things."

"So it is stable?"

"Not really."

He'd spent hours clambering through the ruins, picking up anything he could find, mainly things belonging to Elinor. He had no great desire to rescue his own possessions. At the weekend, he'd piled it all into the boot of the car and driven down to the cottage to lay what he'd managed to salvage at Elinor's feet. Expiating a guilt he had no reason to feel. *Yet.*

He caught Sandra looking at him, puzzled by his sudden abstraction. "Anyway, that's enough about me. How've you been?"

"Oh, you know." She gave a little laugh. "Busy. Tired."

She wasn't at ease talking about herself. He could see her making an effort to go on, to reciprocate.

"You missed a few duties."

"Yes, I went back home for a bit."

"Nice to have a break..."

She seemed to come to a decision. "Actually, I didn't really enjoy it all that much, but I just thought I ought to go. Me mam's not been very good, worried sick about me brother."

"Where is he? Do you know?"

"Not a clue. He's in the Marines . . ."

"Has he just joined up?"

"Oh, no, before the war. He couldn't get work and when he went down the Labour Exchange they told him he wasn't entitled to anything because his mother and his sister were working. 'Is that right?' he says. And off he goes and joins the Marines. Just like that. And me mam will listen to Lord Haw-Haw. I've told her not to, I'm tired of telling her. 'Where is His Majesty's ship *Repulse*? His Majesty's ship *Repulse* is at the bottom of the sea.' Oh God, that *voice*—it's like scraping your fingernails down a blackboard. Do you listen?"

"No."

"Somebody should shoot the bugger. Oh, and the other thing was . . ." She hesitated. "I had a boyfriend, we weren't engaged or anything, and he was posted missing at Dunkirk. Of course his mam's convinced he's still alive—though I can't help thinking the Red Cross would've found him by now—and of course I have to go and see her, I can't not, and to be honest . . . Well, you know. I don't think we'd ever have got married, but there it is, in her mind we were going to get married, and we still are. I feel such a hypocrite."

"Well, you've no reason to."

"No, I know. Anyway, I just thought I can't go on like this, so what did I do?" She raised her glass. "Took a leaf out of me brother's book."

"And joined the Marines?"

She laughed. "Nah. Joined the Wrens." She drained her glass. "I joined up."

"Good God. I think you deserve another drink." He

picked up the glasses and stood looking down at her. "Something stronger?"

"I'll have a port and lemon."

In the last twenty minutes the crowd round the bar had thinned considerably, so he wouldn't have long to wait. He could see her through the open door. She was tracing a pattern in a puddle of spilled beer, the sunshine finding auburn glints in her brown hair. So she was leaving, then, probably in a couple of weeks. Right from the start the affair, if there was going to be an affair, would be limited; in time and in commitment. Well. He picked up the glasses. That was the one thing necessary to make her utterly irresistible.

He put their drinks down on the table, sat on the bench beside her, closer than before. "Well, there is this: you'll be a helluva lot safer in the Wrens than you are here."

She smiled and they clinked glasses.

"By the way, have you told anybody yet?" He meant other members of the team.

"I told bloody Nick. Do you know what he said?"

"Let me guess. 'Up with the lark, to bed with a Wren.' "

Nick was a strange lad. At times he seemed almost simpleminded, but he could spell any word backwards, and tell you in a second how many letters there were. He never looked you in the eye, so it was difficult to know whether you were making contact or not. And he was especially awkward around young women. He'd sidle up to them, make remarks he clearly intended to be flirtatious, but which many of the girls found offensive, even, some of the younger girls particularly, intimidating. No doubt about it, Nick was a problem.

"I hate all that," Sandra was saying. "You know, the ATS being 'officers' groundsheets'—and the WAAF 'pilots' cockpits.' It's just not true. I know a lot of girls who've joined up and none of them are like that."

"No, I'm sure they're not." He hoped Nick's stupid innuendo wasn't going to produce a backlash of propriety in Sandra. If it did, he'd personally strangle the little sod. "I think a girl who wants to join up should be entitled to respect, same way as a man."

She smiled at him. "I suppose you were in the last war?"

"Ye-es." He wasn't altogether happy to see the conversation turning to his age. "Long time ago."

Twenty minutes till blackout. A noisy group at the bar were bidding each other good night, setting off to the station, to wives and children and safety. Paul slid his hand along the bench towards her and let it lie there, palm upwards. Silence. He felt a pressure in his throat, he couldn't breathe. After a while she glanced sideways, smiled again and covered his hand with her own.

TWENTY

Bloody desperate, this. Picking up her bag, Bertha braced herself to face the stairs. Never liked coming home. Every morning, she plunged onto the streets craving light and space. Every afternoon, she crept back, cowed by the vast expanse of sky. Mind, she wasn't as bad as she used to be. When she first come out, she used to hide in shop doorways, because the bustle was more than she could stand. You didn't get much bustle in prison, only the one hour a day in the exercise yard, trudging round and round in a bloody circle. You weren't supposed to talk to the other women, not that she'd have lowered herself, the riff-raff you got in there.

Needed to do something, cheer herself up. Sing. "Oh Danny boy, the pipes, the pipes are calling . . ." Singing always cheered you up. "But when ye come back, and all the flowers are dying, if I am dead, as dead I well may be . . ." Well, not always. What lifted her spirits was the spirits she had in her bag, but it was a bit early to be starting on that. Gin and cod's head—dear God, what a combination. Hated bloody cod's head, but it was cheap, and if it was a choice between food and gin—and these days it quite often was—gin every time. She was turning into a right old gin-lizzie—her mam would've been horrified. Though, truth be told, she'd liked a tipple herself. She'd been thinking a lot about her mam recently. Well, childhood, really. School. Didn't do to think too much about that. Or anything else back then, really. Only she loved her mam.

Landing. Pause for breath—up we go again. Bloody stairs—they'd be the death of her. Still, the seances were picking up, partly because she was pushing the limits. All the time now. But forty people, ten bob a ticket, not bad, not that she'd see anything like her fair share of it. Howard would have told them. To be fair, whatever his faults, he was the one pushing her along. He'd seen the opportunities—she hadn't. And the first few seances, my God . . . Every bloody spirit who showed up—*manifested*, Howard said—he was always correcting her—was fighting mad. *Furious.* "No use blaming the spirits, love," Howard said. "It's you, you're attracting it." "Oh, so it's my fault, is it?" "Well, it's not exactly your fault, but you're going to have to calm it down a bit, love. Nobody's going to pay good money to get whacked over the head with a chair."

Last lap now. She was looking down at her feet—plod, plod, plod—so she didn't see him at first. But she heard breathing, so she stopped and peered into the darkness. Couldn't see a bloody thing, somebody had nicked the lightbulbs on the stairs, but then a long shadow peeled itself off the wall.

"Oh," she said. "You."

"Now, now, no need to be like that."

He was smiling, big yellow teeth bared in a grin. She wanted to tell him to bugger off, but she didn't dare. Feet squarely planted, he stood waiting for her to unlock the door. Bloody key wouldn't work, her hands were shaking, and all the time he stood there, watching. Weasel-faced little shit.

Said his name was Payne. Didn't believe it. Said he was a policeman—didn't believe that either. She could smell police a mile off, but—and this was the alarming bit—if he wasn't police, what was he?

As soon as she got the door open, he followed her into the room, took his hat off, looked all round, taking his time, finally pulled out a chair and sat down.

"Make yourself at home, why don't you?"

"Well, Mrs. Mason. What a pleasure to see you again."

She wasn't going to dignify that with a reply, so she went over to the window and pulled the blackout curtain across. Attic windows were always fiddly, but at least it give her a minute to think. She switched on the light, checked to see the chamber pot was well tucked under the bed, and turned to face him. "What do you want?"

"You did a seance last night."

"*Gave.*"

"What?"

"You don't *do* seances, you *give* them."

"Bit rich, isn't it, seeing you charge the poor buggers ten bob?"

"Oh, you were there, were you?"

"No, heard about it, though."

"Oh, from Miss Pole, I suppose? I noticed she was there again."

"Nothing to do with me. I believe she calls herself a 'psychic investigator.'"

"She can call herself whatever the hell she likes, she's still a twat."

"Ah, Mrs. Mason, I *have* missed you."

He was leaning forward, elbows on his knees, twirling his hat, a battered trilby, round and round in nicotine-stained fingers. She could see dark stains on the sweatband. His trousers, stretched tight across his bony knees, were shiny, almost threadbare. He had such a seedy, lonely, hangdog look about him—put you in mind of rooms in lodging houses with cracked washbasins and fanny hairs on the bottom sheet. And yet he was a clever man—perhaps "clever" wasn't the right word—*fly,* that was it. It occurred to her, suddenly, that he might be the Devil. In a long and varied career she'd met quite a lot of people who'd seen the Devil and what always impressed her about them was that they described him in exactly the same way—not so much the Prince of Darkness, more a commercial traveler down on his luck. She was reminded of the men you used to see after the last war, selling silk stockings door to door, twitching that much they could hardly count out the change.

She sat down on the bed, folded her arms across her breasts. "It's not against the law."

"Taking money under false pretenses is. And you're not seriously claiming you talk to the dead, are you?"

She sat, mute.

"Pull the other one, it's got bells on. No, Mrs. Mason, what you do is fraud. *Fraud.*"

That word, it put her right back in the dock with that wretched little creep of a man telling everybody they'd got a doctor to examine her. "Every orifice," he'd said. "Every orifice. *And* the rolls of fat on her belly." He'd looked across at the jury and smirked. "You could hide a rat in there."

She looked at Payne, who was also smirking. "I need the money."

"You've got a job. Oh, no, sorry, you haven't, have you? You got the sack. Well, get another one then."

"Where? There aren't any."

"There's always cleaning."

"Too many houses boarded up, and besides it pays peanuts. Nobody could live on that."

"Not with the gin and fags *you* get through."

Bastard knew everything. "What am I supposed to have done this time?"

"Well, it's more of an accumulation, really, isn't it? The boy sailor from the *Royal Oak*? And then there was that soldier on the beach at Dunkirk. No air cover. Remember that. And then last night the boy from the school."

"What about him?"

"You said there were seven hundred dead."

"*He* said, and he didn't say seven hundred, he just said 'hundreds.'"

"The official figure's seventy-three."

"And do you know anybody who believes it? I don't."

"Look, it's one thing to say it in private, it's quite another to say it in public."

"I don't control what gets said."

"'Course you bloody do!" He was leaning towards her again. "Look, Mrs. Mason, I'm going to say something that might surprise you—I don't give a bugger where it comes from, you could be getting it all from the Devil for all I care, the point is: *You can't say it.*"

She caught a flicker in his eye. "This frightens you, doesn't it?"

"*You* frighten me. I think you're a very stupid and *very* dangerous woman. And no, I don't think you talk to the dead. I think you keep your ear to the ground, you ferret around for gossip and speculation and rumor and . . . *Muck.* And you spout it out without stopping to think about security or other people's feelings or public morale or . . . or anything. Except money."

"I tell the truth."

"You wouldn't know the truth if it bit you on the arse. Do you know, I'd have more respect for you if you stood on a street corner and peddled your fanny."

She was up on her feet now. "I think you've stayed quite long enough."

"Think about it."

"What, peddling me fanny?"

"No, keeping the other hole shut."

She couldn't look at him. At the door he paused and looked back. "Because if you don't, it mightn't be fraud next time. It might be witchcraft."

"What you gunna do, burn me?"

"No, I'm serious. You think about it now."

After he'd left, she waited a few minutes then went out onto the landing to check he'd really gone, and wasn't still there, in the darkness, hiding. She was trembling all over—back in the dock, back in prison. They could do it. But not witchcraft—that didn't make any sense. And it was all true, what she'd told him. She didn't control what was said. Once Albert took over, the most she ever heard was a kind of echo.

She switched the light off, pulled the blackout curtains back and lay on the bed. Awkward shape, that window. They'd had one just like it in Newcastle. The night the bailiffs come and took every last stick of furniture, she'd lain on the floor, on a borrowed mattress—Howard snoring beside her—and seen a hand pressed hard against the glass. Her mam's hand. She recognized it straight away from the scars on the palm, scars she'd got in the herring-gutting sheds in Seahouses. And she'd known straight away her mam had passed.

And she'd known something else too: that the dead came to her, sought her out, and there wasn't a bloody thing she could do about it.

She needed to think, but when she closed her eyes and

tried to concentrate, she was back in the dock. *Every* orifice, he'd said, smirking. "*And* the rolls of fat on her belly. You could hide a rat in there." The faces in the courtroom had become a pink blur, she was back on the couch with her legs in stirrups, eyes shut, praying for Albert to come, but Albert didn't come though she called and called for him. And when they let her sit up—take a breather, they said—she pushed them away and ran down into the street. Clinging to the railings, shouting and crying with the pins coming out of her hair and a woman in a fur coat come across to her and said, "What's the matter, love? Are you all right?"

Of course, she had to go back in. Howard said it would look bad if she didn't. So on it went: stomach, throat, nose, ears, fanny, arsehole, and yes, the rolls of fat on her belly. The least of her problems, that day . . . Howard sat outside in the waiting room. She went quiet towards the end, refusing to see the doctor's face, the glint of glasses on his nose, refusing to feel the leather couch that made her back and thighs sweat, refusing to hear the chink of instruments in the bowl . . . And still Albert didn't come.

But he was coming now. The room grew dim as she sank further and further into the hole that was opening up at the center of her being. At first she went slowly, but then faster and faster, swirling round, no longer able to see the window or feel the bed, down down down until at last the darkness covered her.

BERTHA CAME TO herself an hour later, with no sense of time having passed, though the square of sky in the window had faded from blue to white.

She was lying on the bed, though it seemed to have moved several feet across the floor. When she raised her head, she saw a chair lying on its side, plates and cups broken and a gray, sticky mess where the cod's head had been stamped into the rug. Oh God. She didn't blame Albert, not entirely, but didn't he have a shred of common sense? Where was she going to find the money to buy new plates? And that rug was going to have to be thrown out. Of course he hated cod's head, but so did she. Only, when Albert hated something, he went berserk. Always had done, probably always would. And of course, as per bloody usual, he left her to clear up the mess.

Tell you what, she wouldn't be going to the shelter tonight, not with all this lot to clear up—no, not if it pissed bombs.

TWENTY-ONE

After the first few hours you lost track of time. He thought it was about three in the morning, but he couldn't see his watch. In the doorway of a building opposite, a group of people, bombed out of a church basement, was waiting to be found space in other shelters. The usual purgatorial shadows. One of them, a woman, detached herself from the rest and gestured to him to come closer. He crunched towards her over broken glass. She pointed to a house farther down the street, the house she lived in—what was left of it. Her mouth was so caked with dust she had to moisten her lips several times before she could make herself understood. "There's somebody still on the top floor."

Brian Temple joined him and peered up at the house. "Well, whoever it is they're a goner." He was pointing to the side of the roof that had caved in. "If there *is* anybody."

"She seems pretty definite."

Charlie nodded. "Don't see how we can ignore it."

"I bloody do," Brian said. "I'm sick to death of wild goose chases."

"We'll just have a look, right?"

They fetched a stretcher from the back of an ambulance and pushed the front door open. "Rescue-squad job, this," Brian said. Charlie ignored him. He began creeping up the unlit stairs, testing every tread to make sure it would bear his weight. Brian was probably right, but then every available rescue squad had been called to Malet Street, where a bomb had fallen on a hostel. And the building seemed stable enough, nowhere near as bad as the houses on either side. At intervals, Charlie held up his hand and they stopped to listen. Creaks, an occasional louder crack, the grumbling of an injured building.

"I don't think there's anybody here," Charlie said.

But then, on the third landing, they heard a groan and realized it was coming from a room above the attic stairs. These were narrow, room for only one person, and so steep it would be more like climbing a ladder. Charlie gestured to the others to stay back. Halfway up, there was a bend, and there he had to stop: a beam had fallen across the staircase, leaving only the narrowest of apertures. He shone his torch down onto their faces. "So who's the thinnest?" This was a joke. He was grinning at Paul.

Right. Paul took off his coat and helmet, lay down, poked his head under the beam and started pushing with his heels, wriggling into the airless tunnel, inch by painful inch—a bit like being born but in reverse. Once, he got stuck and called back, "This isn't going to work," but then Charlie gave his backside a tremendous shove, his left shoulder broke through and he found extra space. Burrowing into the dusty darkness, mouth and nostrils choked with dust, eyes smarting, he wasn't sure how much longer he could go on, but then, unexpectedly, he felt cool air on his face and neck and guessed the room beyond was open to the sky.

At least, now, he could see, and what he saw, when he finally managed to crawl into the room, was a woman with her nightdress rucked up to her thighs, lying across a mound of rubble. One leg was dark, covered in dried blood, the other fish-white. He couldn't see her face or upper body, but the size of the thighs alone told him she was heavy, quite possibly a dead weight. She wasn't moving. He tried not to hope she was dead. Dead, she could wait till morning. Alive, she was a nightmare.

As he'd thought, the roof was open to the sky. Search-lights probing banks of cloud cast a shifting light across the debris. Table, more or less intact—she must have been sheltering under that when the ceiling came in—bed broken, chair smashed, sink smashed, chamber pot mysteriously intact—and feathers everywhere. A blizzard of feathers. Bright orange flashes—three as he watched—lit up the room, each accompanied by the thud of high explosive. The walls shook. A saucepan skittered across the floor and came to rest by the sink.

Still not knowing if she was alive or conscious, he started saying the usual comforting words. "Don't worry, love, we'll soon have you out." Reaching her ankle, he thought he detected warmth. Not much, but then for God knows how long she'd been lying in a room open to the sky. He crawled along her side till he was level with her shoulders and felt for a pulse in her neck. Irregular, but no mistaking it—she was alive. He tried to assess how badly injured she was, calling out to Charlie on the stairs that he thought she might have broken her leg. He didn't like the angle of that knee.

Her eyes flickered open. "Hello, love," he said. "Well, this is a right pickle, isn't it?" A moan from the white-crusted lips. "Do you think you can stand?"

Before she could answer, a lump of plaster fell from the ceiling, narrowly missing his head. "*Fucking* hell."

Charlie from the stairs: "You all right?"

"Never better."

"We're going to have to dig you out."

They'd never get her down the stairs, not without moving that beam. Lying flat on his back, he stared through the hole in the roof. Flares blossomed and faded, each casting a trembling light across the floor. He listened to the sounds of scuffling and scraping on the stairs, then, propping himself up on his elbow, found himself gazing straight into her eyes. Christ, she was sweating, a slippery, cold sheen bringing with it the stench of fear and pain. "Not long now, love. They've just gone to get the shovels, they'll have us out in no time." No response. "I'm Paul. What's your name?"

"Bertha."

Was it her? My God, it was. He remembered her labored breathing as she climbed onto the platform, and thought: *She's not going to last.*

A few minutes later came a renewed scrabbling on the stairs and Charlie's hand appeared, waving a bottle of water. Paul crawled across to get it, and trickled some into her open mouth until she choked and turned her head away. Then he moistened his own lips. He'd have liked to take a good swig but he didn't know how long he'd have to make the bottle last. He could hear shovels now, digging into the rubble. By rights, they should have left the building and waited for a rescue squad, but he knew they wouldn't do that. They wouldn't rest till they got her out.

Bertha lay motionless, her eyes closed, breathing through her open mouth. He'd wriggled into the narrow space between her and the wall and now lay pressed against her vast bulk. The film of sweat between his body and hers was acutely unpleasant. In the circumstances they were in, that shouldn't have mattered, but it did. He tried to ease himself away from her, but there was no room, and whenever he moved she groaned.

"Yeah, I know," a man's voice said. "She turns my stomach too—all that *lard*."

Paul froze, then made himself turn towards the voice. She looked different. Where before, there'd been only double chins and flabby cheeks, there was now the suggestion of a jaw. How could anybody change physically, like that?

"So, you know, go easy on her." The voice was beginning to slur into silence. "She's a poor beggar."

Charlie's voice from the stairs. "Paul, that you?"

So he'd heard it too. "Yes, don't worry, it's all right."

Paul struggled to sit up, to free himself from the slime of sweat. Looking down at the fat, pallid face, he was inclined to doubt the evidence of his ears. His eyes. She seemed to be unconscious. He pushed up one eyelid, even shone the torch into her eyes, but there was no response.

"Paul, you still in there?" Brian this time.

"No, I've died and gone to heaven."

"Don't worry, mate. Soon have you out."

It was what they said over and over again to people who were injured or trapped, only now they were saying it to him. He'd become a victim, no longer one of the team.

"You OK? Only we thought—"

"Fine!" he shouted back. Easier to say that than try to explain what he didn't understand anyway. More questions; ignoring them, he turned back to her. Her lips moved, but the voice was, once again, not hers. Even in this hot, stuffy darkness, he was drenched in a cold sweat, his own this time. It was a relief when she fell silent.

It took nearly an hour of heaving and shoveling to clear the stairs. They were almost through when a rescue squad arrived and tried to take over. A row broke out as to why the wardens were in the building at all. Paul heard a squeaky, querulous voice laying down the law, or trying to, then Charlie: "You can go fuck yourself, mate, we're not budging."

All this time, Paul had been listening to a constant trickle of plaster dust, the minute creaks and rustles and sudden heart-stopping lurches as the stricken building shifted its center of gravity. Another bottle of water was passed through. He gave some to her, relieved when she seemed to be swallowing, before taking several huge swigs himself. Grit everywhere: between his teeth, in his nostrils, in his eyes. He seemed to be breathing dust. A voice from the past: a doctor he'd consulted a few years ago in Harley Street, after one particularly bad winter. "You have to take better care of your chest. Have you thought of spending the winter abroad?" He was laughing, still laughing when Charlie's head appeared, level with the floor. "Glad you think it's funny, mate."

Paul could cheerfully have kissed him. Charlie inched forward, pressing down hard with his hands before trusting his weight to another foot of sagging floor. When, finally, he reached Paul, he clapped him on the shoulder, then looked down incredulously at the prone woman. "By heck, the size of her." He was whispering, but the sound registered on her face.

"Do you think we can get her down?" Paul asked.

"Bloody got to, mate. Can't leave her here."

"Get some of the others?"

Charlie shook his head. "Floor won't take it." He crawled round to Bertha's other side and wiggled his hands underneath her till his fingers were clasping Paul's in a desperate, painful grip. "Right. Count of three."

As soon as they tried to move her, she started to moan but also, embarrassingly, to apologize. "I'm sorry, I'm sorry," she kept saying. "I'm sorry."

"Not your fault, love," Charlie said. "Blame Hitler."

Finally, they managed to drag her farther away from the wall. Paul got behind her, put his hands under her armpits and heaved her into a semi-upright position, aware, but in a totally detached way, that at one point they formed a perfect, if grotesque, pietà. Then they half dragged, half carried her across the floor, and lowered her through what remained of the doorway into Brian's waiting arms. Still, in between screams and moans, she kept apologizing for her weight. "I'm sorry, I'm so heavy," she said. "I can't help it, I hardly eat a thing." "Sure you don't, love," Brian said. He'd make a joke of it later, but he was tender with her now.

At last, the top of her head disappeared into the darkness and they were able to stand up. Charlie indicated to Paul that he should go down the stairs first.

"No, you go."

Left alone, he took a last look round the room at the detritus of poverty and squalor that had once been a home, then turned and followed Charlie down the stairs.

Then things began to move quickly. Bertha was heaved onto a stretcher and carried downstairs, not easily—it took four men, and even then they grunted and strained. Mercifully, she'd stopped apologizing and lay with her eyes closed, unconscious or dead. Behind them, Charlie was still arguing with the man with the squeaky voice. In the end he simply turned his back and walked away. "Bloody little Hitler."

Outside, fire hoses snaked across the street and pools of black water reflected the sullen, red glare in the sky. Paul followed the stretcher across to the ambulance. He recognized Neville's bull-necked shape as he jumped down from the cab and came round to open the door. They exchanged a few words; terse, impersonal. At the last moment, Paul turned back. "Where you taking her?"

"Guy's."

Paul raised a hand in acknowledgment, splashing through a puddle of stinking water on his way to rejoin the team.

THE ALL CLEAR went just after five o'clock. Back at the depot, they stared into thick white cups of dark orange tea and found little to say. Paul tried to look back over the events of the night, but everything before Bertha and after Bertha was a blur. Of course everything would be carefully timed and tabulated in the incident log, but it certainly wasn't tabulated in his brain.

After a few minutes, Charlie stirred and stretched his legs. "You know what the Chinese say, don't you?"

"No," Paul said, obligingly. "What do the Chinese say?"

"If you save somebody's life it belongs to you. I mean, like you become responsible for that person. Mind, I think it might just be if you stop them killing themselves, I'm not sure. But it's not a very nice thought, is it, when you think of some of the people we've saved? I mean, that poor old bugger pissing in a bag, imagine having him around for the rest of your life."

"He was all right," Brian said. "Happy as Larry. No, the one that'd worry me is that woman tonight. God, the size of her. *And* she'd pissed herself."

"I've met her before," Paul said. "She's a medium."

"Is she?" Charlie said. "Me mam was a great one for the spuggies. Couldn't see anything in it meself." He looked up. "Ah, here they are. We thought you'd got lost."

Walter came towards them, rubbing his hands, his cheeks purplish with cold. "By heck, it's nippy out there."

Paul finished his tea. He didn't fancy going round to

the van for pasties with the others. The ambulance drivers went to the same van and he didn't much fancy bumping into Elinor's friends. Outside, he stood on the pavement taking in deep gulps of air. Alive. It wasn't so much a thought as a pulse that throbbed in every vein in his body. His heart was beating so hard he could see the quiver in his fingertips. A voice hailed him: Sandra. Had she been waiting for him? The thought that perhaps she had, produced more throbbing, but farther down.

"Bad night?" she asked.

"So-so. How about you?"

She shrugged. "All right."

People were watching them. He saw Charlie and Brian exchange a sly grin, then look away, but he didn't care. His previous—very minor—infidelities had been conducted with iron discretion, but not this one. Part of the feeling of being outside time was that nothing seemed to matter very much. Nothing he said or did now would have consequences. If he'd stopped to think about it, even for a second, he'd have known at once it wasn't true, but he *felt* it to be true.

So they linked arms and walked the few hundred yards to his studio. Neither of them said very much. He was amazed by the new day, intensely aware of all those for whom it had never dawned: the dead, lined up on mortuary slabs or lying, still unrecovered, under mountains of rubble. He felt their bewilderment, the pain of truncated lives. So what right did he have to despise Mrs. Mason, her ignorance, her superstition, when in his own experience he knew how porous was the membrane that divides the living from the dead?

Leading the way up to his studio, he remembered the stairs to Bertha Mason's room, the moment when he'd realized he couldn't move, that in all probability he was going to die there, without dignity, without purpose, like a fox in a stopped earth, and the minute he unlocked the door he turned and caught Sandra in his arms, his mouth groping for hers. They fell onto the rumpled divan and there the long night ended, in kisses and cries and, finally, at last, at long last, sleep.

✾ TWENTY-TWO

He couldn't get her out of his head.

Not Sandra; he'd loved every minute of their time together, but after she'd put on her clothes and gone home, he scarcely thought of her. No, it was Bertha Mason he couldn't forget. Bertha, on the table, blank-eyed, fag end stuck to her bottom lip; Bertha, on the platform, whirling black silk bloomers around above her head; Bertha, in his arms, piss dripping down her legs and forming a puddle on the floor. And that voice: the voice in the darkness that couldn't have been hers, and couldn't not have been hers. There she was: old, fat, mad, quite possibly dying—utterly repulsive—and he couldn't forget her.

You know what the Chinese say, don't you?

Perhaps Charlie's remark about becoming responsible for the life you save was preying on his mind. Whatever the reason, he knew he had to see her again. She might, of course, be dead by now, or she could have been discharged from hospital, sent to some hostel for people made homeless by the bombing, but on the whole he didn't think so. She'd been in too bad a state for that. No, with any luck she'd still be in Guy's. If she was alive.

Arriving at the hospital in the late afternoon, he was directed to the third floor. Grim corridors, no natural light, though great efforts were being made to cheer things up: there was even a vase of flowers on a table at the center of the ward. A nurse pointed to a screened-off bed at the far end. Pushing the screen slightly to one side, he saw Bertha sitting up in bed with her head bandaged, looking like a huge, abandoned baby.

"Hello, Mrs. Mason. How are you?"

He'd brought some flowers from the garden of his ruined home: bronze and yellow chrysanthemums, past their best. He couldn't see a vase to put them in, so simply laid them at the foot of her bed, where their graveyard smell quickly spread and filled the small space inside the screens.

At first glance, he thought she looked better than he'd expected: she'd lost that lard-white color; but when he looked more closely, he realized the redness of her cheeks and chin was anything but healthy. He touched her hand—shaking it seemed too formal—and found her flesh hot and clammy. He said, "I don't know if you remember me, I was one of the—"

"Yes, hello."

He could tell she wasn't sure. "I was in the room with you the other night. After the bomb."

Her eyes widened. "So you were. You asked me what I was frightened of."

He couldn't remember asking her that. In fact, he was sure he hadn't. It wasn't the kind of thing you said to injured people in an air raid.

"People think, oh, she knows a lot about the afterlife, she believes in it, so what's she got to be frightened of? If they knew what it's like down there at the moment they'd be bloody frightened. Bedlam, bloody bedlam. People running round in circles, half of 'em don't even know they've passed."

She'd said that the first time he'd met her, only now it made more of an impression. She must've received a Christian education—of some kind—and yet she'd ended up with a view of the afterlife hardly distinguishable from Homer's. Shades, shadows; people who'd rather have life on any terms than endure the insubstantial misery of the underworld.

"They haven't been," she said.

"Who haven't?"

"Mr. and Mrs. Lowe. You know, from the Temple?"

The Temple, he supposed, must be the pawnbroker's. "They probably don't know where you are."

"They didn't come to see me when I was in the nick either, they knew where I was then." She was making curious mumbling motions with her lips: chewing a vile and bitter cud. "Howard didn't come either, said he was ill, I knew he wasn't, he was with his fancy woman."

"Howard's your husband?"

"I wasn't supposed to know about her, but I did, of course, there's always some kind person'll tell you." She looked at him, and her eyes were suddenly sharp. "Won't be long before somebody tells your wife about you."

"Is there anything I can get you?"

"No, I've got everything I want, thank you. Peace and quiet, that's all any of us really want, isn't it?"

Paul stood up at once.

"No, not you. *Him.*"

He glanced round. "Who?"

She was looking at the chair on the other side of the bed, although her eyes seemed to be focused not on the chair itself but on its occupant. Only there was nobody there.

"Is it Howard?"

" 'Course it bloody isn't. Bugger never bloody come when he was alive, he's not gunna show up now, is he? No, it's that fella, he keeps coming round, Payne, whatever he calls himself. Telling me what I should and shouldn't say—only it's

not me saying it—it's Albert—and I just can't get him to *see*."
She was staring at the chair, pleading, justifying herself.

"Why don't you get Albert to talk to him? Well, he'd
understand then, wouldn't he?" She didn't seem to have
heard. "Is he here now? Albert?"

"God only knows, he's a law unto himself. I'm fed up
with it." She lay back against the pillows and closed her eyes.

Paul glanced round again, thinking: *I should go,* but
somehow he couldn't just walk out and leave her here like
this. He looked again and saw her face was changing: the
jaw becoming firmer, the brow ridges more prominent. *How
could she do that?* She couldn't, of course. Nobody could. But
then how did she change the way he saw her?

Albert's voice: "I'm here all the time, it just doesn't register; to be honest, not a lot does register, these days. You should
see the amount of gin she gets through."

"She's not well, is she?" Paul wondered if he was doing
the right thing, going along with the pretense—if pretense
it was. But he didn't know what else to do. "She's not a good
color."

"She's a goner, if you ask me."

"Is she really that bad?"

"You've only got to look at her."

Paul nodded towards the empty chair. "Does he really
exist?"

"Oh God yes, he's the one got her put inside—and he's
been nosing around again. Told her she could be tried as
a witch, scared the shit out of her. She couldn't face prison
again, nearly killed her last time."

In the seance a great deal had been made of Albert's long
service on the Western Front, his officer status, but this was
a music-hall version of an upper-class accent, and even that

was slipping fast. "You know, I met her in Russell Square once."

"I remember. We're not all sozzled on gin."

"She told me there was a boy standing behind me."

"Well, there is, isn't there?" Albert sounded bored. "I mean, it's not as if you don't know he's there."

His voice had begun to slur, vowel sounds elongating until the words became incomprehensible. Paul watched Bertha's face become puddingy again, a doughy, undifferentiated mass in which once-pretty features were submerged in fat. It had never struck him before, but now he thought that in her youth she must have been beautiful. Was she asleep? She was breathing noisily through her open mouth, her eyes half closed, the whites unnervingly visible.

He could do nothing for her, neither save her life nor wrest her back to sanity. Indeed, the longer he stayed with her the more his own grip on reality would slacken. Reaching an abrupt decision, he stood up and retrieved his hat from the foot of her bed. Yet, even now, he lingered. Suddenly he became aware that in the last few minutes he'd unconsciously changed the rhythm of his breathing until it exactly matched hers.

Quickly then, he turned on his heel and walked out.

BERTHA LISTENED TO the footsteps dying away into the darkness. Somebody had been there, just now—they'd brought flowers—but she couldn't remember who. Be glad to get out of this place. Talk about haunted, she'd never in her life experienced such a cluster of unquiet spirits. Now that was a point. Why did they cluster? Something to do with the place, the actual building? Had to be—unless, of course, they recognized a sensitive and were crowding round *her*. But no, that couldn't be true, the night sister said they'd been here years.

Bertha had been surprised when she was on the toilet wrestling with constipation. The door was thrown open without so much as a by-your-leave and a woman came in wearing the dated uniform of a nursing sister in the last war. "Hurry up, now," she'd said. "We haven't got all day." She'd been talking to somebody at the sink, totally oblivious to her, Bertha, sat there, needing a bit of privacy.

There was a child as well, a boy who came in and out of a wall where a door had once been. You could see the outline of the door under the paint. She felt sorry for him, he looked so lost, as did the young man in Victorian dress who sat with his back to the wall in the main corridor, sobbing his heart out, poor soul. She'd have helped them if she could, but they just stared through her. The spirits who came to her in seances—*manifested*—bloody Howard—wanted to make contact. These ones didn't even know she was there.

The trouble was, *she* saw them all the time, whereas other people just caught glimpses now and then—the majority, not even that. Though she had once seen a doctor step aside to avoid the small boy as he came through the wall, and she'd thought: *You don't even know you did that.* But he had, he'd stepped aside.

Payne was back. She thought it might actually *be* Payne this time, though she hadn't heard him come in. On the other hand, she had been dozing, on and off, all day—she could easily have missed him. He was—well, not exactly talking, but words formed in her mind. On and on he bloody went. The school: how did she know how many people had died? Every bugger knows, she said. Just 'cos *you* say something's secret doesn't mean it is. And the boy-sailors on the *Royal*

Oak, how did she know they were dead, when nobody had said the ship had been attacked? And the young men on the beaches of Dunkirk; the men she'd seen crawl out of funk holes in the trenches . . . "Oh, piss off and leave me alone." She didn't know whether she meant the spirits or him.

Somewhere in the lower regions Albert stirred. She was half inclined to let him come to the surface, give Payne a right good bollocking, bloody little pipsqueak. God, just look at him, objectionable little man. "Seedy"—that was the word. *Seedy*. She honestly did believe he could be the Devil, because he wasn't fixed. Whenever you looked at him, he seemed to be a different shape and size. She felt herself start to sink, a sure sign Albert was on his way. She didn't really know where she went when Albert was here, except sometimes it looked a bit like her bedroom at home. At night, when she was huddled up in the narrow bed, with the sheets over her head, she'd hear footsteps on the stairs and see the knob begin to turn, and then, as he came in, a tall, thin shadow would climb the wall behind the bed, and she'd hear a voice whispering: *It's all right, don't cry.* He loved her. He always said he did.

But tonight, letting herself sink didn't seem to work. The thing in the chair, whoever he was—*what*ever—wouldn't let go. She forced herself to go on looking at him. Neat mustache, reddish-brown with a few white hairs, nicotine-stained fingertips twirling his trilby, round and round, round and round, stains on the sweatband, shiny patches on his knees where the cloth had worn thin—oh, yes, he was down on his luck, this one, in spite of his airs and graces.

I see through you, she thought. And immediately, as in a dream, found she could do exactly that. He was still there, very much there, but reduced to an outline, like a child's drawing. Where the solid mass of his face and body had been there was now only a string of rising bubbles, like you get in a pond when something's rotting underneath. She couldn't put her finger on the change, because she could still see him, only now there was a sense that his apparent solidity was a delusion, and the reality was this constant flux. And he was getting smaller; his feet no longer quite reached the floor. He was child-sized now, and still shrinking fast, but somehow this didn't reduce the force of his presence. If anything it increased it. The more he shrank, the more he was reduced to his essence, the more powerful he became.

She wanted to cry out, call for help, but there was no help, not against this, because he was liquid. He could change shape endlessly, fit himself into anything, flow through every crack in every barrier. And flow he does, drenching her in slime.

Look away. She looks instead at her left arm, which is lying on top of the coverlet, but it doesn't seem to belong to her anymore. She focuses on her hand, tries to wiggle the fingers, but they won't move. It's too heavy, too stiff, she can't do anything with it. She feels a spurt of hostility towards it. Is it even hers? It doesn't feel like hers. Is it his hand? Her whole body feels cold along that side and so heavy, so leaden, the bed must surely soon start to tilt. She won't look at the chair. Her right eye can't see anything anyway, but she closes the one eye that still obeys her. Spit drools from the corner of her mouth, she can't wipe it away; she tries to wipe it away with her other hand. The sheets are briefly warm, then cold, oh God she's wet the bed again, she won't half get wrong for that. But she keeps her eye closed, she won't look at the chair. She won't look at the chair.

Voices now, in the ward behind the screens, feet come flapping; a light shines in her eye. *Stroke,* she hears, *stroke,* but makes no sense of it. Nobody's stroked her, not for a long, long time. Oh, six strokes of the cane, yes, she remembers that, remembers running out of school the second the bell rang, along the beach and up the hill to the castle, its towers black against the sky as the sun sinks down behind it. Running across the courtyard, now, stones hard under her feet, flecks of foam drifting like blossom across the grass, her head, her ears, even the marrow in her bones filled with the roaring of the sea. Queen Margaret's tower behind her, she stands on the edge of the cliff. Close, so close she's blinded by the spray and the sea boiling and churning in the Egyncleugh beneath her feet. Oh, and it's nothing now to step forward, to take another step, and then another, to walk on air, and see, in the last moment before the water closes over her head, high above her on the cliff, Dunstanburgh's broken crown.

TWENTY-THREE

ELINOR'S DIARY

14 October 1940

I think. The trouble with my life at the moment is that every day's the same so I end up losing track and forgetting what day it is.

I haven't kept a diary for years and I'm in two minds about it now. I suppose, because I associate it with adolescence, all that endless self-absorption which I'm vain enough to think I've grown out of, though I've no doubt there'd be plenty of people to disagree with me. My entire family, for a start.

So why now? Because I'm lonely. No Paul. No Rachel either—the farmhouse is empty. Rachel's gone to stay with Gabriella, who's had her baby now—a little girl—and Tim's staying at his club, an easy walking distance from the War Office. Rachel's given me a key and told me to take anything I need from the kitchen garden—after all, as she says, it'll only go to waste—she's even told me to raid her wardrobe, though since she's expanded over the years and I've contracted, I can't think that's going to be much use. Still, I'll give it a go. One thing about all that sewing I used to do, I'm quite good at altering clothes.

I found this notebook—completely blank—sitting in the bottom-right-hand drawer of Mother's desk, and I find myself wondering why she bought it, what she intended it for, because it's not at all the kind of thing she'd buy. There are scrapbooks in the kitchen with recipes cut out of magazines and pasted in. They're thick, those books, and they smell of paste, and her thumb- and fingerprints are all over them. Looking through them, I can spot her favorite recipes because those pages are more daubed and crusted than the rest. I can remember the tastes too. Oh, and the ingredients... They're like little messages from another world. But this notebook? No, I've no idea what it was for—and evidently she didn't know either, since it was never used. Another mystery, and not one I'm likely to solve now.

I keep tripping over her presence. Everything here is hers, hers, not mine. The dressing table in the back bedroom... She used to look into that mirror every evening when she was getting ready for dinner. When I was a child, I used to sit on her bed in our old house and watch, though I knew my presence irritated her. Lots of hair-brushing, dabs of scent, the merest dusting of face powder—it was all a great mystery to me, what grown-up ladies did, and I felt I could never be part of it. (Oh, and how right I was!)

The sofa. I sit here in the evenings staring at the fire (lit for company, not warmth—it's still very mild) and if I close my eyes I can actually feel my legs, skinny, little-girl legs, sticking straight out over the edge. It's like one of those trick photographs where a child appears giant-sized because the proportions of the room are abnormal—or rather the reverse, since here I feel dwarfed by giant furniture, though really it's the same size it always was. Only I don't belong with it anymore.

I wonder what Paul's doing. Whether he's on duty. I wonder who he's with. I wonder if Rachel has these thoughts about

Tim—well, yes, of course she does, though in her case I'm pretty sure she's right to be suspicious. I wonder if she minds.

Every time Paul visits, he brings me something, something he's retrieved from the house. He says the house is stable, that there's no risk, though I'm not sure I believe him. If it was stable we'd be allowed back in. I wish these little parcels didn't feel so much like peace offerings. Last Friday, he brought two big portfolios of drawings, which had somehow survived, wedged in between the kitchen dresser and the wall, though I haven't had the heart to look at them yet. Can't open the portfolios. Can't paint. Can't do anything.

I'm a pinprick, a speck, a bee floating and drowning on a pool of black water, surrounded by ever-expanding, concentric rings of silence. I rub my wings together, or do whatever it is bees do that makes a noise, but there's no buzzing. And no echo either, no sound comes back.

15 October 1940

Today I walked as far as the river. It came on to rain, a sudden downpour. I stood and watched raindrops pocking the surface, rings, bubbles, little spurts of water leaping up. And I thought of Paul's mother putting bricks in her pockets and wading in and tried to imagine her last moments, bubbles of water escaping from slackened lips, hair swaying to and fro in the currents, like weeds. And an iron band around the chest, the involuntary struggle for breath—and then, nothing. We have to hope: nothing.

Back at the cottage, I took my wet slacks off in front of the fire and my skin was all gray and purple, goosepimply, and I thought why wouldn't he prefer firm, young flesh? Isn't that what all men prefer, when you get right down to it?

I miss my house. It's like grief for a person—an actual physical craving—and yes, I know it's only bricks and mortar and it shouldn't matter when every day—or rather every night—so many more important things are being lost. Lives, for God's sake. And yet I can't talk myself out of it. There's a particular place—was a particular place—at the bottom of the basement stairs. You turn left and there's a small window looking out onto the back garden and it has a cupboard underneath. I used to keep a jug of flowers there. We bought the jug in Deià, very cheap, but beautiful, and the flowers came from the garden in summer; in winter it was twigs and leaves, hemlock, I used to get it from the riverbank here, catkins...Nothing cost more than a few pennies, but in that particular place, at particular times of day—late afternoon when the sun struck the window at a slight angle and shone through the leaves, delineating every vein on every leaf, it was perfection.

One of the things you notice about getting older is that every loss picks the scab off previous losses. The house is gone, so I miss Toby more. Mad, but true. I feel him all the time now—and I hope that doesn't mean I'm about to join him, because I'm not ready to die just yet.

I think about Violet and her cyanide capsule. She actually offered to get me one, but I said no. I don't want to go to bed at noon.

16 October 1940

Yesterday I got into such a state of gloom and despondency that in the end I just ran out of patience with myself. So I made myself sit down and open the two portfolios Paul brought back last week.

A lot of drawings from last year and the year before, look-

ing rather dated I thought, but then nothing's quite so dated as the recent past. A few shelter drawings, one or two of them quite promising—I might work on those, I suppose. There's one of children queuing outside Warren Street tube station that I rather like, though one of the boys at the front looks exactly like Kenny. I didn't mean it to, but there he is—the resemblance is unmistakable.

I want to go back to London. I don't know what stops me, except I feel I need to get Paul's agreement—consult him at least. I even went up into the loft this morning and got a suitcase down. It'd take me literally minutes to pack. These days I'm like a snail: I carry my house on my back. And though most of the time I feel dreadful, just now and then I get a glimpse of something else, a frisson of something . . . Lightness. Freedom, I suppose.

But I haven't put anything into the suitcase yet, and I don't know what's holding me back. Partly it's fear: going back into that nightly horror, but that's an impersonal fear, shared by everybody. No, I think what I'm really afraid of is being alone, just me, no longer half of a couple. A cold draft blowing down my side where Paul used to be. I don't feel it so much here, because I'm surrounded by all these relics of my childhood, the before-Paul time. But I know in London I'd feel it badly.

Almost enough to keep me here, but I think not quite.

17 October 1940

Another bright, sunny, gritty day, no wind. Water on the marshes steel blue, reflecting light back at the sky, the reeds a vicious yellow-green, the sort of color you feel can't possibly occur in nature, but there it is, you're looking at it.

I came back home to a rare event—a letter, readdressed from the house, of course—just before we left we added our new, separate, addresses to the noticeboard at the end of the street. People don't write to each other much these days, we've all shrunk into our little colonies, the people we see every day, but this was an official letter. And as soon as I saw the Ministry of Information stamp I guessed who it was from. One quick scan of the page, there was his signature: Kenneth Clark, chairman of the War Artists Advisory Committee. Would I...? Could I...? With a view to discussing, etc.... Oh, I would, I could. I will, I can. Though I'm going to have to be quick about it, because the interview's tomorrow morning, the letter having been delayed by the change of address.

If I get a commission—actually, I don't think there's much "if" about it, but let's be cautious—if I get a commission, it'll be on a painting-by-painting basis. Men—Paul, for example— are salaried; women aren't. And I've got a pretty good idea of what he'll want me to do—rosy-cheeked children, safely evacuated from the bombed cities, merrily playing on ye olde village greene. There's a big drive on to get children back into the country, an awful lot of them have gone home. Though we didn't know it at the time, Kenny was one of thousands. Oh, and land-girls, that'll be the other thing. Come to think of it, probably mainly land-girls—something about girls' bums in breeches appeals to the male visual imagination as almost nothing else can—as long as the girl's young and pretty and the bum not so gigantic it fills the whole canvas.

Still, I don't mind, as long as I can do the things I really want to do as well. It'll give me access to materials, and that's no small thing, these days, because they're getting awfully expensive, and scarce. And of course I've lost a lot of mine. Then there's the license—I'll be able to go (almost) anywhere and draw (almost) anything. Status, recognition...I'd love to be able to say they don't matter, but they do. Hear Kit Neville on the subject!

The interview's at ten, so by half past I ought to know one way or the other.

Then what? Go to see Paul, I suppose. It'll feel odd seeing him again in London. I can't tell him I'm coming—there's no telephone in the studio—I'll just have to hope I catch him in.

TWENTY-FOUR

Two or three days later (I could probably work out the date if I really tried but I've been awake all night and I can't bloody well be bothered)

I caught him all right.

But I'm not going to plunge straight into that, because there's Kenneth Clark and the War Artists Advisory Committee and, arguably, that's now more important than Paul.

I know Clark vaguely, as I suppose everybody on the art scene does. He came to the door of his office to greet me, looking taller and broader-shouldered than he actually is—it's amazing what a first-rate tailor can achieve—and shook hands with me very warmly, I think without seeing me at all. Women of my age are invisible to Clark, but, given his tastes, I've probably been invisible for the last twenty-five years at least—so there's no point getting upset about it now!

He started by saying the War Artists Advisory Committee was determined to recruit the largest, most varied, most representative array of talent possible, and as part of this endeavor they were commissioning some of the most distinguished women artists. It was, he said, particularly important that the visual record of the war should include work that conveys the uniquely feminine vision that only women artists can supply.

Etc. I've no idea if he really thinks there's a "uniquely feminine vision," or whether he just thought that would go down well. Rather to my surprise, I found myself arguing against the idea. I said I didn't believe women were necessarily more compassionate than men ... He just sat there looking cool and amused, and when I'd finished pointed out that my best-known paintings are, nevertheless, of women and children. True, of course. Of the three paintings I've got in the Tate, one's a mother feeding her baby on the night-ferry crossing to Belgium, another's of convent schoolgirls in a park, and the other's one of a series of winter landscapes I painted after Toby's death. (Not the best one either!) And then he started explaining that women were paid on a commission-by-commission basis, unlike men, who get a salary. (Part of the "uniquely feminine vision" perhaps: we don't need to be paid.)

And then we moved on to suitable subjects. Children, but only in safe areas well away from the raids; land-girls, bums not specified; women in the forces, though obviously not in any aggressive capacity, definitely no guns; factories, etc.

All very much as I expected, and of course I said yes. So—looking forward to a long and productive relationship, etc.—we shook hands again and off I went. I felt an enormous sense of relief getting out of that building; I can quite see why Kit hates it.

Though I must say, standing there on the pavement, I felt better than I've felt since the house was destroyed. Solider. That awful snail-without-a-shell feeling had gone. I was moving back to London, I was absolutely determined on that, but I also felt I owed it to Paul—and myself—to have one last go at persuading him to rent somewhere big enough for both of us. Not a house, necessarily. A flat would do.

So I set off to walk to his studio. And this is the difficult bit. I'd only just turned the corner when I saw him on the pave-

ment in a dressing gown, accompanied by a girl, a stocky, little figure with long dark hair and short legs. She was standing on tiptoe, reaching up to kiss him. She was so short it was almost like a child reaching up to kiss her father, but there was nothing fatherly about the kiss. His arms were round her, he was laughing, pretending to ward her off, she was tugging at his sleeve, trying to persuade him to go back into the house. He kept shaking his head, pretending to be reluctant, but then, with a shrug of mock defeat, he let himself be led back inside—and the door closed behind them.

I walked a little farther along the road, and then I just stood and stared at the door. My brain was whirring away, trying to come up with an innocent explanation. I just wanted it to go away. Only of course there was no explanation except the obvious, and I couldn't bear to think about that, so in the end I didn't think at all, just tottered off, feeling ancient, frail, as if my bones had turned to glass.

Now I wonder why I didn't bang on the door, force my way up the stairs. But it never occurred to me to do that.

Instead, I went to the house, which was probably the worst thing I could've done. All the outer walls are intact, but the roof's in a bad way, ceilings collapsed on the floors below. And open to the weather because of the roof, so it's bound to deteriorate quite rapidly. I cried. But also I was following Paul and the girl upstairs, into the studio, onto the bed. We made love on that bed once. I wonder if he remembers that when he's rolling round on it with her?

I felt naked, shivering in the sunlight, everything stripped away, not just the house, Paul as well—all gone. And if you take away all the relationships, the possessions, the achievements of somebody's adult life, what they're left with—what I'm left with—isn't youth. I noticed I was walking differently—more slowly, a bit hunched over. I had to force myself to straighten up.

It was a mistake to go to the house—or perhaps not— perhaps I needed that final brutality to be able to stop feeling. Because I did stop. I went to a Lyons Corner House and sat over a pot of tea and gradually the numbness spread. I remembered the first weeks after Toby died, how unfeeling I was, how ruth- lessly efficient. I don't think I've ever been as efficient as that in my entire life. Well—until now.

I drank the tea, paid the bill, checked to see how much money I had in my purse and set off. Two hours later, I'd found a flat on the top floor of a house in Gower Street, two doors down from where I used to live as a student. Huge rooms; one of them, at the back, has wonderful light. I can imagine myself paint- ing in there. Then there's a living room, a bedroom, a kitchen, a bathroom, all good-sized—and it's unbelievably cheap. Of course it's cheap because it's lethal, right at the top of the house, in an area that's seen a lot of bombing, but I don't care about that.

I'm quite clear. This is about survival now. This has the power to destroy me and I'm not going to let it.

But I keep replaying that scene. Paul and the girl kiss- ing, the pretended tug of war, his mock surrender, them going back into the house together. Oh, and then I follow them up the stairs ... It's like a film I'm being forced to watch, but there's no emotion. I seem to have run out of that.

It's a strange feeling. Rather like the cordoned-off roads and squares where a time bomb's fallen. You look across the tape at sunlit emptiness, but you're not allowed in. And you know there are other quiet, roped-off places, all over London, but you also know the life of London goes on, the people, the traffic, all that roar and bustle forcing itself down side streets and alleys, finding new channels, new ways through. And I think my life's going to be like that. I'm not going to be roped off.

It would have been so easy after seeing Paul and that girl to creep back to the cottage, try to pretend it hadn't happened, convert my mother's bedroom into a studio and paint there. Happy children removed to safety, playing on the village green. Do what Paul wants. Do what Clark wants. Hide. And I think: No. This is my place, my city, and I'm not going to let anybody force me out of it.

TWENTY-FIVE

He thought perhaps it was the third incident of the night, but could never afterwards be sure. A pub had been hit—he remembered that. They'd got it roped off and were waiting for a heavy rescue squad to arrive. Three houses adjoining the pub had collapsed and there was minor damage to several others farther up the road. The people who lived in these houses were safe in shelters, presumably; though in for quite a nasty shock when they came out.

Then somebody called from across the street to say there was an old couple living in one of the damaged houses. They turned to see a stout, middle-aged woman with her hair in neat rows of curlers, the metal glinting in the light of flares, as aggressive as shark's teeth.

"She's got arthritis, walks with a stick."

Charlie said: "We'd better just have a look." She was so obviously the sort of woman who knows everybody's business they couldn't afford to ignore it.

Stopping outside the house, Charlie bent and shouted through the letter box. No answer.

"They'll be in there." The woman had followed them and was still watching from the other side of the road.

"You get yourself under cover, Missis!" Charlie shouted back. He turned to Paul. "What do you think?"

Paul shrugged. "She'll know."

Charlie nodded, blew out his lips hard, then wrapped his hand in his coat and smashed the window. He reached through and fiddled with the catch. Often they were jammed under layers of paint, but this one opened. They climbed in, and found themselves in a neat front room. A vase of red plastic roses stood on a sideboard between photographs of children, a boy and a girl, in school uniform. Flashing his torch, Charlie led the way into the passage and opened the door into the back room.

Charlie went in, Paul followed. And there they were, lying side by side on a bed, the counterpane pulled up to their chins; not curled up, as people normally are when they sleep, nor lying chest to back, spoon-fashion, as so many married couples do. No, they lay on their backs, stretched out, an oddly formal position. Stiff. They might have been lying in a double grave. As indeed they were. They'd have woken by now, if this was sleep.

Paul and Charlie looked at each other, Charlie still breathless after scrabbling through the window. Brian followed them in, grumbling as always, though the words died on his lips as he sensed the intensity of their silence. The three of them moved closer to the bed. The old couple lay there, so married, so ordinary—the woman's stick had been hooked over the bedpost so she could reach it easily during the night—and yet infinitely remote, like a medieval knight and lady on a tomb, their blank eyes staring at the vaulted ceiling, unmoving, unchanging, as the slow, murderous centuries pass. Paul felt something like reverence and he thought the others did too. Even Charlie was silenced, and nothing ever stopped Charlie cracking jokes.

Automatically, Paul touched their necks, felt for a pulse, shook his head. What had killed them? There were no obvious wounds. Gently, feeling he was invading their privacy, he pulled the bedclothes back and saw, with a stab of pity, that they were holding hands.

"Shock?" Charlie said. He had to clear his throat to produce the word.

Paul shrugged. "Suppose so."

He'd seen people die of shock before: healthy young men lying at the bottom of a trench with not a mark on them anywhere. Charlie, who he knew had served in France, must have seen it too. Had the old couple heard the bomb come shrieking down? Had he reached out and held her hand to comfort her in the last seconds before it fell? So peaceful, they were. So quiet. Their silence was a force spreading out around them, trivializing the yapping of the guns and the thud of exploding bombs.

Nick had come in through the window and was pushing to the front, eager to see.

"I'd stay back if I were you," Paul said.

He was tense, expecting Nick to say something utterly crass, but instead he stooped, picked up a cardigan that had slipped onto the floor and, for some reason, draped it carefully over the back of a chair. The others, turning their heads to witness this strange ritual, caught themselves reflected in a mirror, and stood like that, motionless, as if the stillness of the couple on the bed had reached and enfolded everybody in the room.

How long they might have stayed like that Paul never knew. The silence was broken by a whimper that seemed, for one horrific moment, to be coming from the couple on the bed. They looked at each other. The sound did seem to be coming from the bed. Paul shuffled along the wall and felt along the floor. Almost immediately his exploring fingers encountered something disgustingly warm and moist, and he snatched his hand back. Nick, meanwhile, was on his knees peering under the bed. "Come on, boy. Come on." He slapped his thighs, and a small, white-and-brown Jack Russell terrier, ears flattened against its head, crept towards him on its belly. It must have been there all the time, hiding between the bed and the wall, reaching up to lick a still-warm hand.

"Oh, you've got a friend there all right," Charlie said, as the dog leapt up and tried to lick Nick's mouth.

"Gerroff." Nick shoved the dog inside his coat and looked at Charlie, obviously expecting disagreement. "Well, we can't leave it here."

The dog peered out, its sharp face and bright, amber eyes glinting in the light from Charlie's torch.

"All right, but it's your responsibility, mind." He turned to Paul and Brian. "Come on, there's nothing we can do here."

As they closed the door behind them, Nick pointed a stern finger at the dog. "Piss on me, you little fucker, and you're dead."

THE ALL CLEAR sounded early that night; the raid had not been a particularly bad one. And yet, meeting at the wardens' station at the end of the shift, everybody seemed subdued. Nick was slumped in an armchair, staring into space. Charlie came up carrying two steaming mugs of tea and put one on the table in front of him. "What about that dog, then?" He nudged Nick's arm, trying to rouse him, but Nick turned on him a totally blank stare. "What dog?"

Charlie and Paul exchanged glances. Somebody shouted across to Paul: did he want a cup of tea? But he shook his head. More than on most mornings, he was glad to get away.

At the top of the steps, he paused for a moment, wondering what he should do. No Sandra now. She'd left two days ago, to his mingled sadness and relief. He knew he wouldn't be able to sleep. He'd seen so many more horrific things than that old couple, but he knew they were going to haunt him, possibly for quite a long time. Do something—that was the thing. Keep busy. Perhaps he might have a walk round to the house, see what else he could find in the rubble. He was driving down to the cottage at the weekend and it was always nice to have something to give to Elinor.

Scrambling around among the broken bricks and charred timbers, he unearthed some knives and forks—apostle teaspoons, she was quite fond of those—but the real treasures were the paintings—and quite a few of them had survived. No time for that today though. Something was niggling at the back of his mind and he couldn't think what it was. He thought about the old couple—but no, it wasn't that. It was something more recent, something he'd noticed. He straightened up and looked down the street. An elderly man in an antiquated tweed overcoat had stopped in front of the noticeboard and was jotting down one of the addresses. That was it, something on the noticeboard. He threw down the brick he was holding and went to see.

And there it was. Elinor's handwriting. An address in Gower Street. At first, he couldn't take it in. He knew perfectly well she wanted to return to London—they'd argued about it only last weekend—but it had never occurred to him that she might move without consulting him. Or even telling him. It was—well, impossible. Unless . . .

There's always some kind person'll tell you. Won't be long before somebody tells your wife about you.

Who could've told her? Well, almost anybody—he hadn't been particularly discreet. Anybody, really, who was sufficiently malicious, or perhaps just incensed on her behalf. Neville knew. No, he wouldn't.

It didn't matter who. He had to think straight; he had to get this right. He didn't know for a fact that Elinor was aware of his affair with Sandra, or that moving back to London was an expression of her anger. There were all kinds of reasons why she might have decided to return. His affair with Sandra had receded so rapidly into the past he felt it was hardly worth bothering about. The two days since their last meeting might have been years for all he cared. It was easy to think that, because it was over and had meant so little, it couldn't have any impact on his life—or Elinor's. No, it was equally likely she'd just grown tired of the constant arguments and had decided to present him with a fait accompli. *That* was entirely possible.

His first impulse was to rush round to Gower Street and ask her, but if she knew about the affair this would inevitably lead to a confrontation, and he didn't feel ready to face that. No, perhaps he should wait, get rested—that was the most important thing—and then, this evening, he'd come back here and find something—ideally, not knives and forks—a painting or a drawing—and lay it at her feet. That would be the best, the wisest, thing to do.

TWENTY-SIX

21 October 1940

I'd forgotten what living in furnished rooms feels like—the smell of other people's lives: transient lives, passing through. The way the silver plating's always worn off the forks, the cracks in the bone handles on the knives. Oh, I can't put my finger on it exactly, except here I'm a student again. Single. Oh, yes, single.

I've put my address on the board by the house. If Paul's still trying to retrieve stuff he's almost bound to see it and then he'll realize I haven't told him about the move. He'll know I've found out about her.

I lived two doors down from here when I was a student at the Slade. Sometimes when I'm walking down the street I fancy I see her coming towards me, that girl. The girl who lived for days on end on packets of penny soup, made her own clothes, walked everywhere. She doesn't seem so far away now. In fact, I walk through her ghost every time I cross the floor.

And this wallpaper. She'd have had that off the wall in no time. She'd have hated it, the dreary, dingy Victorian fussiness of it, the horrible yellow pattern—paisley, I suppose, a sort of cross between a flower and a praying mantis. No, she'd have been sloshing wallpaper stripper all over that, scraping away at it till her hands ached. How much energy I must have spent

over the years, battling with Victorian wallpaper. Well, not anymore. Let it stay. You see wallpaper like this all over London
where the sides have been ripped off houses. The Luftwaffe's
doing a much better demolition job than I ever could.

And I'd like to talk to Paul about it but, of course, there is
no Paul.

I had to go to the shelter last night. While the house was
still standing, I could use the hall, convince myself it was safe.
Not here: it's a death trap, so off to the shelter I must go.

The usual crowd, mainly women. There's an old couple
who play chess. Rather sweet, really. Oh, and there's the major,
a military gentleman with peppery blue eyes. No nonsense, no
emotion, none of that. Only he has this absolutely marvelous
mustache—a beautiful red-gold color. Titian. He takes tremendous care of it, not in public, of course, but you can imagine him,
in private, combing and trimming it. In some strange way—in
defiance of biology—all the major's feminine qualities, his vul-
nerability, his gentleness, are distilled into that mustache. The
rest of him is very properly hard, masculine, decisive. And of
course he thinks he's boss. Angela, the shelter warden, man-
ages him very well. She always consults him, very deferen-
tially, before going on to do exactly what she was planning to
do anyway.

Angela's tremendous. I wouldn't like her job. The facili-
ties are totally inadequate. We're still using latrine buckets
behind blanket screens—why didn't they realize? Paul says
they thought the raids would be quite short, though very
destructive—thousands dead. Instead of which we have long
raids—thousands homeless.

But it really is high time I stop referring to Paul as the
great authority.

On the rare occasions when I've been here before—generally
because Paul bullied me into it—there was an immensely

fat woman with very beautiful blue eyes—harebell blue. You don't see that very often. But she wasn't there last night. She used to tell fortunes on top of a suitcase, ordinary cards, not tarot. Always good news: unexpected letters, legacies, tall, dark, handsome strangers.

I used to feel sorry for her, especially in the heat. It can't be much fun. And the latrine bucket was harder for her than for most. Her knees wouldn't take the weight, she had a terrible time of it. I don't think I've ever seen anybody quite as fat. I think you can always tell if somebody's always been fat. And she hadn't. There was a thin girl in there. I thought, when she looks in a mirror she doesn't see herself. A bit like Kit, in a way.

Anyway, she wasn't there last night—Bertha, that's her name—and apparently she hasn't been for quite a while. I asked Angela if she knew what had happened to her. She looked round and lowered her voice. "She got bombed, they took her to hospital, but she died a few days later. Poor woman, she was in no state to stand up to anything." I think of her lying upstairs in a pokey little room somewhere, frightened but too tired or too breathless to get to the shelter. Or too embarrassed. I hope she didn't die because she couldn't use the bucket, but it's only too probable. If I'd known where she was I'd've gone to see her.

Our other notable personality is Dorothea Stanhope, who's using the shelter at the moment because she's having the cellar plastered, and a new floor laid. It's going to be wonderful when it's finished, only she can't get the workmen so it's taking longer than she thought. There she sits, with her jewelry case clasped in skeletal hands, diamonds worth an absolute fortune dangling from long, leathery earlobes. She has two daughters. Actually, I think it's an unmarried daughter and a daughter-in-law. The daughter, fresh-faced but no longer young—what can one say? A complete doormat—having failed in what, I suspect, for Dorothea, is the sole business of a girl's life: getting a rich husband. "Gel," as Dorothea says. I don't know if she says "Injun" because I've never managed to bring the conversation round to the Wild West, but I'd bet quite a bit of money she does.

Dorothea's favorite is her granddaughter. Six years old, and very good, she's no bother, a lot less trouble than some of the adults. There was one particularly bad raid when she screamed—but then the rest of us nearly screamed too. The door was shaking with every blast; we thought it was coming in. Dorothea remained totally calm. There's a whiff of the Raj about Dorothea; she's very grand, but also a couple of decades out of date. Anyway, the cellar's finally finished, according to Angela, so we won't be seeing her again.

I slept in this morning, tried to work but couldn't seem to get started, and then the afternoon was so warm I just couldn't bear to stay indoors. So I went and sat in the garden of my old house on a kitchen chair I pulled out of the rubble, no doubt looking very eccentric and rather pathetic but I don't care.

I love my garden. I'm no use at gardening, unlike Mother—or Rachel, for that matter—but some things seem to grow in spite of me. I have Michaelmas daisies and sunflowers peering over the fence into the next garden, almost as if nothing had happened, even though there's ruin all around them. Paul went through a phase of painting sunflowers. He used to say they were absolutely extraordinary, different from any other flower, because they're as tall as a man, you look them in the face—or they look you in the face—and they move. Measurably, in the course of a single day, following the sun. And then they age in the same way as people. They develop a stoop, a sort of dowager's hump, and the seed heads fold in on themselves, like an old man's mouth without teeth.

Paul, Paul, bloody Paul. Just as I was getting thoroughly exasperated with myself, I felt a shadow falling across me.

Looked up and there he was. He was holding the notice with my new address on it. "I hope you're going to put that back," I said.

"Well," he said.

I wasn't going to help him out, but eventually he did manage to get going, all by himself. It was very sudden, he said. It really was rather a shock, he said. Was I sure I was doing the right thing? Had I really thought it through?

What I heard, loud and clear, was the one question he didn't ask: WHY? He didn't dare ask, because then I might have told him. And then the whole business about the girl would be dragged into the open and he's probably fooling himself it needn't be. Not now, and possibly not ever. I suppose I could have forced the issue, but really I couldn't be bothered.

He hung about. There was only the one chair, so after a while he sat in the grass at my feet, but that put him at a disadvantage so he stood up again, muttering something about if I wasn't happy I should have said. Meaning the cottage, I suppose. I did say; he wasn't listening. Anyway, it's not about the cottage. It was awful. Really, really awful. I was glad when he gave up and went away.

I just sat there, after he'd gone, looking at the ruin of our life together. Love affairs don't need much—you can manage the whole thing on moonlight and roses, if you have to. But a marriage needs things, routines, a framework, habits, and all of ours were ripped away. I could forgive him the girl—well, no, not yet, but one day perhaps. What I can't forgive, what I'm afraid I may never be able to forgive, is the look of relief on his face when all this was destroyed.

TWENTY-SEVEN

Neville walked as far as Russell Square before stopping to look back at the Ministry of Information: a brutal gray mass dominating the skyline. Then he selected a bench where he could sit with his back to it and began enjoying the last warmth of the sun as best he could through his heavy clothes. A few feet away, a pigeon crooned and preened, puffed out its neck feathers, gave its inane, throaty chuckle. He aimed a kick at the bird. "Why don't you do something useful? Piss off up there and shit on it?" The pigeon lifted off, flapped a few yards farther away, and settled contemptuously on the grass.

"Kicking pigeons now, are we?"

He spun round to see Elinor sitting on the grass. She was looking up at him, so amused, so, in a way, *accepting,* that he had to get up and go to her. Then, feeling he couldn't conduct even a brief conversation looking down on her like this, lowered himself onto the prickly grass. "Sorry."

"What for? Wasn't me you kicked."

"Language."

"Shouldn't worry, I don't suppose it understood."

All around, people were sitting or lying in couples or singly on the grass, the girls still in their summer dresses. The brilliant summer had given way to a golden and apparently endless autumn, almost as if the bombs that stopped the clocks had power to stop the seasons as well.

Elinor was stretched out, her eyes closed. It pleased him that she didn't feel the need to sit up, to make conversation. Slowly, he lay back himself, enjoying the warmth of the sun on his lids. Lying here like this, they had no past—or none that had the power to hurt them now—and, quite possibly, no future; but that didn't seem to matter. He knew from gossip at the depot that she was living alone. And he knew about Paul and Sandra. Some men would have seized the opportunity, but he'd always been held back by diffidence, the knowledge that he wasn't attractive. Long before the injury to his face, he'd felt that. Years of reconstructive surgery had merely confirmed what he already knew: that his place was in the dark, listening to the *tap-tap* of approaching feet, a muffled voice, a face he couldn't see, and didn't want to see.

After a while, though, he felt he ought to say something. "How's Paul?"

"Pretty well, I think. As far as I know . . ."

He pricked alert, listening not to the words, but to the tone. "It's just, I haven't seen him around much." This was a lie: he'd seen Paul "around' fairly frequently—and once or twice with Sandra.

"We're separated."

"Really?"

"Yes, he's having an affair."

"Actually, I—"

"You knew?" Immediately hostile.

"Somebody said something, but you know what it's like, gossip, I didn't pay much attention." He rolled over onto his elbow. "Do you know the girl?"

"I'm glad you said 'girl.' Every day of twenty-three."

"He's a fool."

"Most men wouldn't think so."

"I'm not most men."

Her face softened. "No, you're not, are you?"

He might, at this point, have told her that Sandra Jobling had left London, since she appeared not to know; but he chose not to. "Are you on duty tonight?"

"Yes, in fact . . ." She glanced at her watch. "I should probably be going."

But she made no move. She'd rolled over onto her stomach and was idly picking the grass. He was afraid to speak, afraid of disturbing the intimacy of the moment. After a minute or so, she turned onto her back again, raising one arm to shield her eyes from the light that seemed to become only more dazzling as the sun sank behind the trees.

A memory had begun nibbling at the corners of his mind. A year or two before the last war, smarting from one of Professor Tonks's more withering comments on his work, he'd walked as far as Russell Square, intending to calm down or, failing that, play truant, go to the British Museum instead. And there she was: Elinor Brooke, whom he passed every day in the corridors of the Slade and watched, covertly, during drawing sessions in the Antiques room, but whom—despite all the brash self-confidence of his public persona—he'd never yet summoned up the courage to approach.

Until that afternoon . . .

"Do you remember—?"

She smiled. "Warm lemonade."

"Oh God, yes." He'd forgotten the lemonade.

"There was a hut over there." She pointed behind her, but without turning her head.

So she did remember. He tried to pin down what he thought about that, but all thought was dissolved in warmth and light. He let his eyes close, aware all the time of how ridiculous he must look in his dark suit and polished shoes and his briefcase lying on the grass beside him. Lying side by side like this, they must look like an established couple, too tired, too jaded, to be bothered to touch each other, and yet so firmly bonded they couldn't bear to be more than an inch apart. In a word, married.

As always, when he was close to Elinor, memories of their student days drifted into his mind. He'd proposed to her, once, on a summer's day a long, long time ago, and this heat, the prickly grass, the tickle of sweat on his upper lip, reminded him forcefully of that day. Riding a bike, of all things, on his way to see the Doom in the local church—and a very fine painting it was too, though his pose as a Futurist had not permitted him to say so. And then, on the way back, he'd hit a bump in the road, soared over the handlebars and landed hard on the gravelly tarmac, cutting his hands and knee and sustaining quite a sharp blow to the head.

Tarrant, who'd been there, of course, waiting to grab Elinor for himself at the earliest opportunity, had gone for help, and he'd lain with his head in her lap. Briefly, when he struggled to sit up, the back of his head had touched her breasts—not entirely accidentally. And he'd asked her to marry him, and then when she refused, or rather laughed, he'd told her that being in love with her was like loving a mermaid. That must have hurt. Or perhaps not. Perhaps she'd just found him as ridiculous as he'd feared he was.

He didn't want to think about that day, but in this merciless, unseasonable heat, things resurfaced, like the spars of a submerged boat in a lake that was drying out. He saw Toby Brooke, in the conservatory, helping his friend Andrew revise for an anatomy exam. Toby, stripped to the waist, arms stretched out on either side, and painted onto his skin: ribs, lungs, liver, heart; all the internal organs. "Living anatomy," it was called. But standing there, in the sickly golden light of late afternoon, Toby had looked like a man turned inside out. It had disturbed him then in ways he'd never fully understood, and it disturbed him now. He felt a sudden chill, as if a shadow had fallen across his face, though when he opened his eyes there was nobody there, and the sky was the same ruthless blue it had been for months.

What an autumn it had been. What a year. He closed his eyes again and almost immediately something unexpected happened. He began to feel Elinor—not merely sense her presence; this was actual physical contact—all along the side that was closest to her. He raised his head and looked at her, needing to reassure himself that she had not, as in some libidinous dream, moved closer and was actually touching him. Of course she hadn't, one arm was still across her face, the other lying on the grass, an inch away from his own. He tried to think of something to say, to make her look at him, to dispel this strange hallucination. Could you hallucinate touch? Well, obviously, yes, since he'd just been doing it. And when he lay back and closed his eyes, the sensation came back. So, in the end, he simply surrendered to it, lying beside her on the grass, touching and not touching, soaking up the last of the sun.

TWENTY-EIGHT

The moment she turned the corner into Gower Street, Elinor stopped, for there, on the steps of her new home, was a familiar shape: Paul. No more than a silhouette in the darkness, but she'd have known him anywhere. He was dressed to go on duty, his shabby uniform recalling the long, black, obviously secondhand coat he'd worn at the Slade, always managing to look supremely elegant— in sharp contrast to Kit, who'd looked like a sack of potatoes in his expensive Savile Row suits. Paul hadn't even been aware of the contrast, which in Kit's eyes had rather added to the offense. The prince in Act Two, she'd called Paul once, teasing. All these memories, bobbing to the surface, merely sharpened her sense of betrayal.

He had propped a large parcel, wrapped in brown paper, against the railings, and was carrying another, much smaller, package under his arm. "I brought these."

The larger parcel had to be one of her lost paintings. She wanted to rip the paper off, find out which one, but she restrained herself. Confused now, for this obliged her to be grateful—he'd have gone to considerable trouble to get it and possibly some risk—she opened the door, and gestured to him to step inside.

She led the way upstairs. "A long haul, I'm afraid."

"You're on the top floor?" He waited until they'd finished their climb and she was opening the flat door. "Not very safe."

"I go to the shelter. Besides, it's cheap." She nodded at the parcel. "Which one?"

"Me, I'm afraid."

They looked at each other, and she turned away, unable to share the irony that, in other circumstances, would have had them both laughing. "Well, I look forward to that." She pulled the blackout curtains across and lit a lamp. "Sit down."

"There's two."

"Toby?"

"Yes. A bit damaged. Not too bad."

She couldn't bring herself to thank him.

"I think that's it, I don't think there's a lot left. A couple of parcels, you know, big brown envelopes with strong, coarse string round them, but I couldn't reach them. I'll have another go tomorrow."

It was imperative to thank him. "No, well, it's lovely to have these. Thank you."

The words stuck in her throat. An awkward silence fell. So far there'd been no mention of why they were here, in this strange room.

He cleared his throat. "So you decided you couldn't stand the cottage after all?" The cough was a nervous tic; he was inching his way forward.

"I need a London base."

Innocuous enough, on the surface, but "I need" was the language of separation and they both knew it. A few days ago this would have been a joint decision. He looked at the fireplace, at the empty grate. "I hear you've been commissioned."

"Yes, I went to see Clark."

"Congratulations."

"Who told you?"

"Neville."

"I don't know how he knew."

"He always knows; he's eaten up with jealousy."

He was inviting her to gang up against Kit, which at some points in the past she would have been very ready to do. But not anymore. "I saw you," she said. "With that girl."

"Ah."

After waiting a few seconds, she let out an incredulous laugh, only just not a yelp. "Is that it?"

"I don't see what else I can say."

"You could—oh, I don't know . . . *Explain?*"

"It just happened."

"It just happened?"

He spread his hands.

"Oh, I *see*. The war, the nasty bombs—everybody jumping into bed with everybody else. So you thought you had to jump too?"

"I'm not saying I'm proud of it."

"Hallelujah!"

Silence. His almost-unnaturally long, slim fingers were beating a tattoo on the arm of the chair.

"So what happens now?" she asked.

"What do you mean?"

"Well, are you going to live together? Do you want a divorce?"

He looked startled. "No, of course not, it's over. She's gone."

"Well, that's convenient."

"It didn't . . . Well, frankly, it wasn't all that important. Not to me."

"And you think that makes it better?"

He clearly didn't know what to say.

"Do you know, Paul, I'd actually rather you were breaking your heart over her. I wish you were in love with her; I wish you were suffering the torments of the damned, because then it would mean something. Better that than an itch in the groin you couldn't resist scratching."

The clock on the mantelpiece ticked, stitching the silence. The sound seemed to penetrate his brain, at last. "You bought a clock."

"Yes." She turned to look at it. "Which reminds me, I'm due on duty in a few minutes."

"Do you have anywhere you can paint?"

"Through there."

"North facing?"

She stood up. What did one say in these circumstances? It was hardly a normal parting: twelve hours from now one or other of them might be dead. She felt a tide of desolation sweep over her for the lostness of the one who would be left; never again to have the opportunity of saying what needed to be said. Well, here was the opportunity. Here. Now. And yet she couldn't speak.

He stood up. "There's no need to see me out."

She shook her head. Going down the stairs, they didn't speak at all. As she opened the front door onto the steps, she tried to think of something to say, but her mind had gone blank.

On the pavement he turned and looked at her. "Take care."

She nodded. "And you."

It wasn't much, but it would have to do.

TWENTY-NINE

The first call came just before one in the morning. Elinor had been lying on one of the sofas reading grubby, tattered magazines, unable to sleep, thinking about Paul, the look on his face, the way he'd walked off down the street. She'd known he'd stop at the corner and look back and she'd gone inside so he wouldn't see her standing there. A petty power-play, a means of hurting, of establishing control: she and Paul had never carried on like that, and now they did. Sad. Her mouth was dry and stale; she was too tired to think straight. It was almost a relief when the telephones started to ring.

She was working with Dana Kresberg tonight. She liked Dana, and was rather intrigued by her. As an American, Dana could so easily have sat out these nights very comfortably in the Savoy; she could have gone out onto the balcony after dinner, with a number of American journalists, watching the night's raid almost as if it were a firework display. And why not? This was not, after all, their war: or not yet. But Dana had chosen, instead, to become involved, to risk life and limb night after night, driving an ambulance through bombed and burning streets, and Elinor had never asked her why. Hatred of fascism? A love of adventure? Compassion for trapped and suffering people? An addiction to danger, perhaps? Everybody's motives were a great mixture, but, unlike Londoners, Dana didn't have the most basic motivation: defending your home. And that made her stand out in the team of drivers working out of the depot in Tottenham Court Road.

Dana's great advantage was that she was outside the English class system. Elinor watched, with some amusement, as Dana negotiated its various ravines and rapids with the assurance of a sleepwalker. She even got on with Derek James, whose years as a taxi driver had given him an encyclopedic knowledge of London's back streets, which was invaluable. But he had a chip on his shoulder. Well, it was more like a log, really. "Timber yard," said Kit, whose public-school accent made him the preferred butt of Derek's not-always-funny jokes. But Derek accepted Dana totally; was, in fact, almost mesmerized by her.

Tonight, though, Elinor and Dana were working together. Around about 12:45 a.m., their turn came. They grabbed their tin hats—very useful for shielding exposed wounds from plaster dust or putting out an incendiary, but almost certainly useless at protecting the brain from falling bricks—and pulled on the black greatcoats that reached to their ankles and impeded their movements much as a suit of cardboard armor might have done. It was Elinor's turn to drive and that pleased her. She and Dana each thought the other drove like a lunatic, and possibly they were both right. But then, perhaps, in these conditions there was no other way to drive. Oncoming vehicles were mere pinpricks of light, little, piggy, red eyes looming out of the night. Crashes were frequent in the early part of the evening, before burning fires illuminated the streets. Dana kept ringing the bell, its *clang-clang* adding to the baying and yapping of antiaircraft guns. Elinor crouched over the wheel, peering through the windscreen for new craters that had not yet been marked by blue warning lights. Dust sifted in through the open windows and settled on their shoulders. More seriously, it formed a film over the windscreen, blurring what little vision they had. But even in this darkness, Elinor recognized the familiar streets. She was driving along the route she'd walked three hours before, turning the corner, now, into Bedford Square.

"This is it," Dana said.

Elinor pulled up at the curb. They clambered down onto the road and started walking towards the scene of the incident. Two blue lights stood on the rubble-strewn pavement and the usual crowd had gathered. One house had been badly hit. The houses on either side were damaged, but they'd been empty, a warden told them. One belonged to an old couple who'd gone to stay with their married daughter in the country; the other to a middle-aged couple, but they definitely wouldn't be in there, he knew for a fact they always went to the shelter. "It's an old lady lives in that one. Two daughters and a—"

"Yes, I know," Elinor said.

It was Dorothea Stanhope's house. She knew the names of the younger women and the child, but in the stress of the moment they escaped her.

A handful of men was edging warily onto a scree of rubble. Nothing was visible of them but dark backs and bent shoulders; they were all hunched over as if that could protect them from falling ceilings. Elinor pushed to the front, trying to see what was going on. She noticed the mean, sneaky smell of domestic gas, mixed with the stench of high explosive. Paul said it was very like the stink of decomposing bodies on a battlefield, and she wondered what it did to him to smell that here. At home. In London. And then she thought: *Bugger*

Paul. Everybody was coughing and covering their mouths. That smell got into your lungs, irritating the mucous membranes of nose and mouth, and then there was the fine dust that repeated blasts sent swirling invisibly into the air.

One of the men on the scree raised his hand, calling for silence. Everybody stood and listened, they hardly seemed to be breathing. Nothing. They started to look at each other, shoulders beginning to slump, but then it came again. Somebody inside the ruined house, from under the collapsed floors and ceilings, was crying out: a thin, reedy wail; an old woman's voice, by the sound of it, although fear and weakness could make anybody sound old.

Work began again, with renewed vigor. Elinor and Dana ducked underneath the tape and stood on the opposite pavement from the wrecked house. Elinor looked at the bent backs of the men heaving away at the rubble; they were working more methodically now, loading buckets with bricks and lumps of fallen plaster, passing them down a chain. As one of them turned to hand a bucket on, she caught a glimpse of his face and recognized Kit. Somebody touched her arm. She turned and saw Violet, looking haggard, wisps of gray hair escaping from under her tin hat. The gutter was running with water from a burst main, turning plaster dust into a claggy paste that would set hard on every inch of exposed skin. "They're alive," Violet said. The tension of that knowledge, the need to work harder and faster, was in every face you saw. At intervals, the rescue-squad leader raised his hand and everybody stopped what they were doing and strained to listen. Violet was right: the frail voice under the rubble had been joined by other voices. One was crying: "My daughter, my baby, where is she?"—edging up into hysteria. They couldn't afford to let it affect them. The hand fell and they got back to work. The burst water main had turned the road into a slick of slimy mud. A rescue-squad worker, running up to help, slipped and fell.

Bombers went on droning overhead, bursts of orange light obliterating the stars. The men were sawing through a beam that had fallen across a mound of rubble and was impeding progress. Another voice started up inside—not the child's voice though—they hadn't heard the child. It was impossible to go on doing nothing. Elinor ran across the road and, clambering up the lower slope, began to talk to the women inside. She felt rather than saw Kit turn at the sound of her voice. She was telling them they'd be all right, they'd soon have them out, no need to worry, not long now . . . It was what you always said, what you had to say, though in the time she'd been standing there no visible progress had been made. But at least they were alive, or the women were. "My baby, my poor baby," the mother kept calling out, and the child's name: Libby? Lizzie? No, Livvy, *Livvy*, that was it, she remembered now: the little girl was called Olivia. "Livvy, are you there? Where are you, Livvy?" And then again: "My baby, my poor baby." On and on it went. Unbearable, you'd have said, except that they all bore it.

"All right, love, we're getting there," the rescue-squad leader called out. "Not long now."

Once the beam was out of the way, they were able to start tunneling into the rubble, but it was slow, arduous work since the tunnel had to be shored up and made safe every few yards or so. Elinor thought—she couldn't be sure—that the rescue workers had managed to pass bottles of water through a gap. If true, it might help the women go on a bit longer, but there was so much rubble to shift, tons of it, she didn't see how the old woman could possibly survive the night.

At one point, she and Dana were sent to answer another call. One incident led to another, through the long hours of darkness—she could never afterwards remember the precise sequence of events—though there were flashes of acute clarity. Her and Dana leaning against the ambulance, shoulders shaking, bent double, laughing till they whooped for breath. And the joke? They'd been asked to deliver four bodies to a mortuary, but when they got there—after rather a difficult journey—the attendant refused to take them: no death certificates. Off they went to the nearest hospital, where an exhausted doctor who'd been toiling all night in an overcrowded, badly lit basement flatly refused to stop work and sign death certificates for corpses that were nothing to do with him. Back to the mortuary. "Not without a death certificate," the angry little man insisted, trying to impose his own order on the chaos that was descending from the skies. "He's going to have a heart attack," Elinor said, as they left. "Oh I *do* hope so," Dana replied. In the end, they appealed for help from a couple of passing air-raid wardens and unloaded the bodies in an alley that ran between two department stores. There they lay, lined up on the cobbles, at a decent distance from the dustbins. There was nothing to cover them with, but Elinor and Dana closed their eyes, and the wardens did the best they could to straighten their remaining limbs.

As she turned to go, Elinor was half embarrassed, half grateful to see one of the wardens do what she couldn't do— cross himself and say a prayer.

Dana had stayed behind to thank the wardens. Elinor waited by the ambulance for her to come back, saw her shoulders shaking as she approached and reached out to comfort her, only to realize she was laughing. "What? *What?*" Elinor said. " 'Not without a death certificate.' Oh my God, that is so funny." Tears were streaming down her face, making rivulets in the beige dust.

By four in the morning, they were back outside the house in Bedford Square. Not long after their arrival, a bomb fell on the other side of the square and the buried women, hearing the crash and feeling the rubble above their heads begin to slide, screamed in shock and fear. Elinor half thought she'd cried out herself, only the bulge in her throat convinced her the cry was still trapped inside. A burst of flame from the fresh bomb site sent shadows fleeing across the square. A third rescue squad arrived, and then a fourth. Kit relinquished his place in the chain that was passing buckets of rubble from the tunnel to the pavement, and came and stood beside her. "Who's in there?" he asked. "Do you know?"

"Dorothea Stanhope. Do you remember, her husband was viceroy, no, he wasn't viceroy, something like that . . . Daughter, daughter-in-law. And a little girl, the granddaughter."

"How old?"

"Six."

He said nothing, merely turned to stare at the rubble and the bent, laboring backs. There was nothing they could do now except wait for the rescue squad to break through and start pulling people out. The old woman's cries were growing weaker, but the voices of the two younger women were still strong, and seemed—unless this was wishful thinking—to be getting louder. The chief rescue-squad leader held up his hand. "Careful. Slow down now."

Elinor craned forward, as the workers paused. For a long moment nobody moved, but then the teams began inching forward again. A hole had opened at the center of the rubble and the two halves of the beam had been used to reinforce the sides. Then came another long, familiar, shrieking descent.

The ground shook and a cataract of loose bricks and mortar cascaded down the sides of the slope. One of the rescue workers threw back his head and yelled, "FUCK YOU!" at the sky. Then he caught sight of Violet standing there. "Sorry," he said. "Didn't see you, love." "Oh, *please* don't apologize," Violet said, in her daughter-of-the-vicarage accent. "My sentiments *precisely.*"

The old woman's cries seemed to be getting louder again—either the rescue squad was getting closer or her own sense that help was at hand had renewed her strength. Perhaps, after all, she'd be the first one out. Suddenly, they all went quiet again. Men with sweat-streaked faces stopped and stared at each other, white eyes startling in their grimy faces. A child's head had appeared through a hole in the rubble. Nobody moved. For a long time, it seemed, nobody moved. Then the rescue-squad leader fell to his knees and, placing his hands on either side of the head, gently persuaded it to rotate, so that first one shoulder then the other and then, in a great rush, the whole body fell out of the hole. Still, no cry. People looked at each other, unable to accept the truth, but the body was small and floppy and it made no sound.

Dana, one hand across her mouth, ran to fetch a stretcher. Elinor followed to help. Only when they returned, did they see the dead child lying on the pavement. They knelt on either side of her and, not looking at each other, prepared to lift her onto the stretcher. Nobody spoke. From inside the ruined building, a voice cried out: "Livvy? My baby. Oh, my baby."

Neville looked down at the little body. "My daughter's that age." It sounded almost casual: the sort of remark you might make outside the school gates. Then, bending swiftly down, he gathered her into his arms and carried her to the ambulance.

The mother was brought out half an hour later, thickly coated in dust, bleeding from a deep cut to her head, but otherwise surprisingly uninjured. "My baby," she kept saying. "Where's my baby?" "Won't be long now, love," one of the rescue workers said. Elinor wrapped a blanket round her shoulders, thinking she and Dana should take her to hospital rather than let her travel in the back of Neville's ambulance with her dead child. But Elinor didn't know what to do. She didn't know what she would have wanted if this unimaginable pain had come to her. Neville took the decision for her. "You take the mother," he said. "I'll stay here." He gripped the woman's arm and helped her up the steps. "Come on, let's get you to hospital."

"But my daughter?"

"Don't you worry, love. They'll soon have her out."

Wrapped in a red blanket, too shocked to argue, she sat down on the bench. Dana climbed in beside her and put an arm round her shoulders.

At the last moment she started to struggle, trying to throw off the blanket and jump down into the road. "I want Livvy."

Dana restrained her. "I know, I know."

THE ALL CLEAR sounded as it started to get light. The dawn wind, tainted by the smell of high explosive, brought with it the assurance they were still alive. The rescue workers breathed deeply once or twice, then got back to work.

Elinor and Dana, returning from the hospital, stood shivering against the garden railings, taking in, for the first time, the full extent of the devastation. In this thin light it looked worse than anything they'd imagined in the dark, and yet both knew that in a few days, a week at most, they might walk along this terrace and hardly notice the gap.

A warden came up and stood beside them, watching the rescue workers still passing chains of buckets down the line. He was sucking something, a boiled sweet, perhaps, or else just his gums. "It's all very well saying Londoners can take it," he said. "But can they? How much more of this can anybody take?"

It was the forbidden question; neither of them answered it.

The old woman was brought out an hour later, garrulous with shock, but unhurt. Her daughter, injured but alive, was pulled out a few minutes later.

"Where's my granddaughter?" the old woman kept asking. She was still clutching her jewelry box, bright, acid-drop sunshine showing up the age spots on the backs of her hands. Dana tried to wrap a blanket round her thin shoulders, but she wasn't having any of that. "Where's my granddaughter?"

"She'll be all right," somebody said. "They've taken her to hospital."

Dorothea obviously didn't believe it. She stood looking from face to face. "I hope she didn't suffer."

Elinor said, "I think it would have been very quick."

The old woman looked at her and nodded. Then she turned to her daughter, held out her hand and together the two of them climbed into the ambulance. Elinor got into the driver's seat, checking with Dana that the two women were securely fastened in before bumping along the brick-strewn road in the direction of University College Hospital. There, she and Dana helped the two women into the entrance and handed them over to the porters, before walking out again into gritty sunshine and a song of birds.

Elinor stumbled as they walked back to the ambulance.

As she reached up to open the door, Dana pushed her gently to one side. "My turn," she said. "And I'll drop you off."

Standing on the pavement outside her new home, Elinor thought only about having a bath and falling into bed. Her skull seemed to have been rinsed in icy, bone-numbing water. She was incapable of thinking, or feeling, anything.

THIRTY

At some point he must have slept. He woke to find a cup of tea going cold on the table beside him and his tongue sticking to the roof of his mouth. For a moment, it was a normal day. He lay, gazing placidly at what little he could see of the ceiling, but then memories of the night before began to surface. Out of a vortex of darkness emerged the broken body of a small child lying on the pavement. He'd picked her up, yes, and carried her to the ambulance. Her mouth had fallen open to reveal the two adult teeth at the front, not quite through yet, still shorter than the baby teeth on either side. He remembered Anne at that stage: the "wobbly tooth" she'd insisted he feel half a dozen times a day, long before it was actually wobbly at all.

And then there was the gap, the all-important gap, the visit from the tooth fairy, Anne smiling, baring her teeth to show her friends. She'd been late losing her baby teeth. And for a long time afterwards, he'd noticed her running her tongue along the edge of the grown-up tooth, which was uneven, not smooth as adult teeth are after years of biting and grinding. That little girl, last night—Livvy, was it? Her two precious grown-up teeth would never be worn smooth.

He lay in bed in the darkened room and thought of Anne, whom he hadn't seen now for over a year. She sent him letters, of course, in the neat, joined-up writing she was so proud of, and drawings that were becoming more accurate and less imaginative all the time, but none of that made up for the lack of her physical presence. She used to get into bed with him in the mornings and her freshly baked smell made him ashamed of the sourness of his early-morning breath. "I'm smooth because I'm new," she said. "And you're wrinkly because you're old, but it doesn't matter, I still love you." All this in an American accent, which never failed to take him by surprise. Somehow, he'd always assumed she'd speak in the same way as her parents, but she didn't: she sounded exactly like the children she played with in kindergarten. He was smiling to himself, as he thought about the strangeness of it: his little American daughter.

Until last night, it hadn't occurred to him that he might die and never see her again. Now, suddenly, all that ungrounded confidence disappeared, swirled away like dirty water down a plughole, leaving only a gleaming white emptiness that was the certainty of his own death.

Get up. He was doing no good lying here. And it was late, oh my God, it was late.

Downstairs, in the kitchen, he made himself a pot of tea, swishing the first gulp of hot liquid round his mouth before spitting it out. No use, he could still feel grit between his teeth. The sun strengthened, casting his shadow behind him across the tiles. God, he was tired, he was never not tired, he couldn't remember what it was like not to be tired, and yet when he closed his eyes all he saw was the child lying on the dirty pavement. Some kind of pattern on her nightdress, he couldn't quite remember: pink bows, was it, or teddy bears? Rags twisted into her hair. Anne hated rags—but then next day you had ringlets, like Shirley Temple, and that was still the way little girls wanted to look. Only for Livvy there'd been no next day.

He wondered about Elinor, how she was managing to cope with it. And then he thought: *Why not go and see her?* After all, she was single now. And even if she hadn't been, they worked together; there was no reason he shouldn't go to see her in exactly the same way he might have arranged to meet one of the men for a drink. Yes, it was a good idea. He'd tidy himself up a bit and go.

AN HOUR LATER, he was standing outside Elinor's house. A shaft of sunlight, breaking through a gap in the terrace opposite, twinkled on the doorknocker. Across the road, an old man was setting off to walk his dog, a busy, bright-eyed terrier that stopped to sniff at every lamppost. Unexpectedly, Neville felt a spurt of exhilaration. At one point the previous night, while he was working on the scree, clawing at the bricks with his bare hands, a landslip had started. A lump of flying brick had struck him on the forehead. Nothing much, hardly worth bothering about, but it could have been. And now here was sunlight streaming through a gap in the terrace, a gap where no gap should have been. All over London, now, were little patches of illicit gold. Plants long stunted by deep shade sprouted new leaves, grew and changed shape in the unexpected light. Something lawless about all this: as there was about the interiors of houses, where a bomb ripped off the front or side of a building, leaving bedrooms, toilets, bathrooms recklessly exposed.

He rang the doorbell, wondering, now he was on the brink of seeing her, whether he was doing the right thing. She'd be asleep, almost certainly asleep, and not thank him for waking her, but then he heard her voice. Backing off a few paces, he looked up at the top of the house and there was Elinor, her head and bare shoulders framed in an open window.

"Kit." Her voice was blurry with sleep.

"I hope I didn't wake you?"

"No, don't worry, I should've been up long since. Is anything the matter?"

"No, I just thought we deserved some of this." He held up a bottle of whisky.

"What, at this hour?"

"It's nearly one o'clock."

"Good Lord, is it really?" She looked across the road where the old man with the dog was showing an interest. "Look, I'll come down."

She came to the door wearing a navy-blue silk wrap, her hair slightly damp and brushed straight back. "Come in. Mind the glass."

"When did this happen?"

"Last night. It's only the landing window. The landlady's supposed to be finding somebody to board it up. I'm just glad it's her problem, not mine."

"You must be freezing."

"No, not really. It's only cold at night and I'm not here then. Anyway, I think I'd rather be cold than live behind boarded-up windows."

He knew what she meant. Many of the rooms in his house—those he didn't use every day—had blackout curtains permanently drawn, and the darkness seemed to soak into the walls. He followed her upstairs, past the broken window that had a scurf of dead flies on the sill. The wrap glided over her skin as she moved, the silk a touch of prewar luxury incongruous among the splinters of broken glass that had been swept hastily to either side of the stairs.

Outside her door, she turned to face him. "Is Paul all right?"

"Yes; well, as far as I know." He was surprised she asked. How would he know? "I haven't seen him around for a while."

"I just thought you—"

She'd thought he was bringing bad news. "No, the last time I saw him he was with Sandra Jobling." No harm in reminding her of that. *Do you still love him?* he wanted to ask, as he followed her into the living room.

She turned to face him, pushing her hair out of her eyes. "I'd better get dressed."

"No, don't—" He meant: *Don't bother;* or at least he thought he did. But almost immediately, he realized the words were open to misinterpretation, and blushed. He was behaving like a schoolboy.

"No, it's time I was up."

He heard her moving around the bedroom, edged closer to the half-open door and caught, briefly, a glimpse of nakedness in the dressing-table mirror. Ashamed, he turned away.

A few minutes later she came back into the room, wearing slacks and a jumper. The plum-colored wool picked up the shadows underneath her eyes and emphasized them. She looked absolutely shattered.

"Well, can I get you a cup—? I suppose there's not much point offering you tea?"

"Not really," he said. "I've had tea. How did you sleep?"

"I got off all right, but then the traffic woke me and it took me a while to get back. And then of course I went deep."

"Yes, you do, don't you? If I let myself go back, I sleep through the alarm and everything."

He saw her noticing the cut on his forehead. "That looks nasty," she said.

"No, it's all right."

She leaned in closer. "You should probably have had that stitched."

"No, really, it's nothing." *In comparison with the rest*, he wanted to say, but it would've sounded self-pitying, not light, as he meant it to be. "It's just a bit of broken brick. I think they got most of it out."

She put a finger gently on the edge of the cut. "I don't think they did. Hang on, I'll get my tweezers."

She went into what he supposed was the bathroom. While she was out of the room, he prowled around restlessly, picking things up and putting them down. Being treated as an invalid was the last thing he needed . . .

She came back carrying a bowl of warm water, a wad of cotton wool and the tweezers. "Come across to the window."

Resigned, he sat on the arm of a chair. Out of the corner of his eye he could see the street three floors below, cars and people going past. This must be the window she'd looked out of a few minutes earlier, and he'd have been standing just there at the bottom of the steps. Looking down, he saw himself through her eyes. *Methinks I see thee, now thou art below, as one dead in the bottom of a tomb* . . . He shivered.

"Keep still."

"Yes, ma'am!"

Morbid nonsense. They were a long way from Verona and both of them too old for balcony scenes. And yet that sudden reversal of perspective, the foreshadowing of his own death, sharpened his desire—and his determination. As she bent over him, he felt the warmth of her body through the fine wool of her sweater, her breath on his face. She was frowning with concentration as she dabbed and tweaked, her upper teeth biting her bottom lip. It was incredibly erotic and yet, at the same time, impersonal, almost clinical. And there was something of childhood in it too. Children look at grazes on each other's knees with just that same intent, sexless curiosity. His cousin Blanche, on that holiday in Devon when he was five or six years old: *I'll show you mine if you show me yours.* Laughter bubbled in his throat.

"*Kit.*"

"Sorry."

Her leg between his thighs, her breasts level with his eyes. And then she straightened up. "There."

Brisk, bossy. Very much the nanny, the nurse, the mother. He wasn't having any of it. In one fluid, unconscious motion he stood up, grasped her thin shoulders and kissed her. She stiffened and tried to pull away, and of course he let her go at once, but for the merest sliver of a second her lips had softened under the pressure of his own.

"What was that about?" She sounded curious rather than affronted.

"You know . . ."

"No, I don't know."

"Yes, you do. I've always loved you."

She was shaking her head. "Kit, we've hardly been in touch for twenty years. And during that time—*No.*" She held up a hand to stop him speaking. "*During that time* you married my best friend and had a child with her. *For God's sake.*"

"I loved you the minute I saw you."

"You can't just turn the clock back like that, nobody can. The fact is, we're two middle-aged people who ought to know better."

"What about Paul knowing better? He could be living here with you now—if he wanted to—he *chooses* not to."

"No, he doesn't *choose* not to—he hasn't been invited."

"I'm sorry, I . . ."

"No, it's all right."

She looked so downcast he had to touch her again, but this time he simply placed the palm of his hand along the side of her face, more than half expecting her to pull away. Instead she let his hand lie there and covered it with her own. He lowered his head and kissed her again, a long, deep kiss. He was afraid of the moment when it would end. When, finally, they separated, he saw that she was working her tongue against her teeth to get rid of a piece of grit.

"Sorry," he said. "It gets everywhere."

She looked amused. "Oh, I hope not *every*where."

He'd never expected, or even hoped, to see that expression on her face. Heart thudding against his ribs, he let himself be led through the door into her bedroom. She pulled the covers back and, for some reason, plumped up the pillows to get rid of the hollow her sleeping head had left.

They were nervous now, both of them, gabbling, postponing the longed-for and feared moment. She went across to the window and pulled the blackout curtain across. A wind had got up and was blowing in gusts so the curtain, now sucked against the frame and now released, seemed to be gasping for breath. The bed seemed huge. She kicked off her shoes, then sat on the side, shuffling along to make room for him. He unlaced his cumbersome boots. Something about this nightly routine: undoing laces, setting the boots down, side by side—clump, and then another clump—peeling off his socks to reveal moist, white feet—all these actions, by their very domestic ordinariness, emphasized the enormity of his transgression. Elinor was married. Paul was his friend.

But then, her exploring hand found a space between his shirt buttons—her fingertips small, hot points on his cold skin—and then he was fumbling with her jumper, trying to tug it out of her slacks, and suddenly none of that mattered. "Elinor—"

A hand on his mouth. "Ssh, don't talk." She swung her legs onto the bed and pulled him down beside her.

LATER, HE POURED them both glasses of whisky, hers well diluted in deference to the hour. She lay on the pillow, looking up at him, her eyes in this half-light unreadable tunnels of darkness. He reached for his cigarettes and offered to light one for her, but she waved it away.

"Did you know this was going to happen?" She sounded faintly accusing.

"No, I just thought we deserved a drink after last night. That poor child."

They were silent a moment, thinking back. But that was yesterday and the pressure of their lives, the exhaustion, the nightly raids, meant they'd already started to move on. An apparent callousness very familiar to him from the last war, but he thought it would be new to her, and disturbing.

"Did you know about Paul?" he asked.

"And that girl? No. I think I was probably the last person to know."

"I wouldn't have told you."

"No, I know. Men stick together, don't they? The Boys' Brigade."

"That isn't why."

"Nobody told me; I saw them leaving his studio, having obviously both spent the night there. I just wish somebody *had* told me; it wouldn't have been so much of a shock. It's one of the worst things, knowing everybody knew except me." She pulled herself up until she was leaning against the headboard. "I think I will have that cigarette."

He lit it for her and handed it across. Her eyes closed as she inhaled. "You know what Paul said? He said it didn't matter. She wasn't important." A snort of derision. "Why do men think that makes it better? It doesn't; it makes it worse."

"Has it happened before? I mean, him—?"

"Once. We-ell, once *that I know about.* One of his students. He was going through a bad patch with his painting, and of course she thought everything he did was absolutely wonderful. Well, I think a lot of what Paul does is wonderful, but you see, I *know.* And he knows I know." She pulled a face. "Not the same, is it? Her admiration was—Oh, I don't know . . . reassuringly automatic."

"But you took him back?"

"He never left—she didn't matter either. The minute I found out, he dropped her. You know, the first time he asked me to marry him, I said no—"

"Yes, well, you were good at that."

"He said it was probably just as well because he wouldn't have been faithful." She shook her head. "I don't think I believed him. I don't *think* I did; I can't remember."

Neville was wondering what the last hour in bed had meant to her—if anything. A chance to get back at Paul? They seemed to have been talking about him ever since. "So, do you think you'll get back together again?"

"No." She looked steadily at him. "No."

He drew on his cigarette, creating a small red planet that hovered in the gloom. "Everybody's doing it, Elinor." He couldn't think why he'd said that. Why would he want to excuse Paul's behavior when her hurt and anger had been so delightfully convenient for him?

"Oh, don't worry, I know. It's like *A Midsummer Night's Dream,* isn't it, everybody getting mixed up, swapping partners?" She laughed. "Goering as Puck—now there's a thought. In tights."

"Only they woke up, didn't they?" He waited. "Is that what's going to happen, do you think? We wake up?"

"Who knows what's going to happen?"

She swung her legs to the side of the bed, leaned forward to reach for her wrap, and he thought—the artist's eye unexpectedly reasserting itself—that the human spine was one of the most remarkable sights on earth.

"When can I see you again?"

"I don't know. I'm going to the cottage this weekend, I might stay a few days—I really do need to get some work done."

"When you get back, then?"

A barely perceptible hesitation, then she nodded. He felt she was waiting for him to go. He'd just got to his feet and was reaching for his trousers when the doorbell rang, and rang again. She crossed to the window and pulled the blackout curtain to one side. "Oh my God, it's Paul."

His heart thumped. "You don't have to let him in."

"I'm afraid the nurses already have. They're on the ground floor, they let everybody in. I keep telling them." She turned to face him. "Look, you stay in here, I'll get rid of him."

"Can't you pretend you're not in?"

"I think he just saw me."

A minute later, he heard Paul's voice at the door of the flat. He started to get dressed, pulling on his trousers, snapping his braces into place, fumbling with socks and the laces of his boots, feeling all the time like a character in a farce. Elinor, who seemed to be talking to Paul in the living room now, sounded cool, confident, amused—not like anybody he'd ever met. Dressed, he sat on the side of the bed, his hands loosely clasped between his knees, feeling humiliated and resentful. Why was he being made to feel like a stage adulterer? It wasn't meant to be like this. The voices went on and on at a low murmur; he couldn't hear the words. Would Paul ever go? But he was beginning to feel slightly less alarmed. After all, there was no reason for Paul to come in here; all he had to do was keep quiet and wait. He tiptoed across and listened at the door: something about the house, photographs, a package Paul had rescued. But the voices were still very low, hardly more than whispers. They must be sitting side by side on the sofa. Well, why not? They were married, after all. He felt sad, old, fat, disillusioned—and very much alone.

At last, sounds of movement from the other side of the door. For one horrible moment, he thought he heard footsteps coming towards him. *They were.* He put his hands flat on the door, feeling Paul on the other side, inches away, but then Elinor said something, a floorboard creaked, and Paul moved away.

A few seconds later, Elinor's voice called "Good-bye" from the top of the stairs. Neville could breathe normally at last, though it took a while for his heart to slow down. He wiped his palms on the front of his trousers.

Elinor came into the room, pale but composed.

"What did he want?"

"Oh, nothing, he just brought me these." She was holding a brown envelope from which she pulled out a sheaf of photographs. The top one had been taken on a picnic, one of the annual outings the Slade had arranged for its students; he saw himself sitting beside Elinor, surrounded by faces he recognized, Henry Tonks's skeletal form visible in the back row. He had no memory of the occasion, but there they all were.

He wished he hadn't seen it. Elinor grimaced and put the

envelope down on her dressing table. "He keeps bringing me things; it's very good of him, really—it can't be easy—but . . . Oh, I don't know, sometimes I think he's returning our married life to me in installments." She smiled, as if to soften the bitterness. "I don't think we should go on drinking, do you? I'll put the kettle on."

While she was busy in the kitchen, he combed his hair, straightened his tie, looked around for something to do, something to postpone the moment when he would have to think. He noticed a couple of paintings stacked against the wall—presumably another of Paul's "installments." Kneeling down, he turned the nearer painting round to face him.

Paul. A full-length nude study; shocking, as nude portraits tend to be. How very much too thin he was, that was Neville's first reaction. The elongated arms and legs hardly seemed to belong with the slightly rounded, middle-aged belly and the scrotum's sweaty sag. Kit's gaze roamed all over the body before settling on the face, the eyes. He forgot, sometimes, how good Elinor was, but he was reminded of it now. Paul was here in the room. And had been all along, staring out of the canvas while they thrashed and heaved on the bed. Nonsense, of course. Absolute nonsense, of course he hadn't. But the sense of Paul's presence in the room with them remained. He couldn't talk himself out of it and it disturbed him so deeply and at so many different levels that in the end he just wanted to get away and be alone.

The door opened as he was turning the painting round to face the wall. Elinor came into the room. "Here you are." She handed him a cup. "Shall we sit through there?"

"Actually, I think I'd better be going."

"Are you all right?"

"Yes, I'm fine, I just think I . . ."

He didn't know what he just thought, but he and Elinor were of one mind. They both wanted him to leave. And when, a scant five minutes later, he did, the memory he carried with him down the stairs and out onto the street was not Elinor's naked body on the bed, but Paul's painted eyes staring out of a canvas. That, and the sense of him standing, silent, on the other side of the bedroom door.

❈ THIRTY-ONE

He'd have known the sound of Neville's breathing anywhere, even on the other side of a bedroom door: that unmistakable rasp. No, it couldn't have been anybody else.

But it seemed so improbable. He knew of course that they'd been great friends in their student days—perhaps even a bit more than that—but Neville's behavior after Toby's death had caused an inevitable breach. Never absolute—they'd met from time to time, but it had always been slightly awkward. In fact sometimes it was a struggle to get Elinor to be polite to him.

No, it made no sense. And yet there it was: the breathing. And he knew he hadn't imagined it.

THAT NIGHT, on duty, he walked up and down Gower Street as often as he could, always stopping to look at Elinor's windows. He knew she wouldn't be there—nobody with any sense stayed on the top floor of a house during a raid— but still he looked. He knew it wasn't his business. His own actions had made it not his business. But images of Elinor and Neville naked in a bed drifted about in front of him constantly, like floaters in his eye, distracting him from the outside world. And his imagination busied itself supplying the details . . . Creased and rumpled sheets, pillows tossed aside, clothes scattered over the floor . . . He kept reminding himself he had no right to be angry, but all the time his skin felt tighter. And tighter. Like a membrane stretched over a swelling boil.

When, late the following day, he encountered Neville again, it was at the National Gallery, at an exhibition of war artists' work. Paul hadn't wanted to go, but really he had no choice. Two of his recent paintings—the "vapid" ones, as Neville would undoubtedly have said—were on display. But he left it as late as he could to set off and arrived to find the gallery already crowded. Any event offering free drinks and nibbles attracted a crowd these days, though to be fair many of these people were hungry for culture as well. The gallery's paintings had been removed to safety and you were aware, somehow, of the blank walls and echoing emptiness all around. This one brightly lit room, lined with paintings and drawings, seemed to be floating like a bubble on a dark tide.

He got himself a glass of wine from a trestle table near the door and looked around. Clark's extravagantly domed forehead he recognized at once, and Henry Moore's stocky, no-nonsense, I-come-from-Yorkshire build and demeanor. Piper was here, and Featherstone, and—Oh my God, everybody. One quick circuit, he promised himself, a chat with Clark to make sure his presence had been noted, and then he would leave.

Laura Knight appeared in front of him. Good grief, what *was* she wearing? He liked Laura, he enjoyed her scurrilous views on agents and galleries and advisory committees—she had something of Neville's bite, but without his venom—so he stayed and talked to her, before moving on to Clark, who was so distracted by the pretty blonde topping up their glasses that he replied to Paul's remarks almost at random before setting off in blatant pursuit. It was all very much as usual.

He was just beginning to think he'd done enough and could go, when he saw Neville. He was on the other side of the room, standing well back from a painting—not, thank God, one of Paul's—and almost imperceptibly shaking his head. After a few minutes, he moved on. Paul retreated to a corner and watched his progress round the room, noticing how he created a ring of silence around him wherever he went. People were afraid of Neville. Everybody cringed before that vitriolic pen, though they all repeated—sometimes with glee—his contemptuous dismissals of other artists. They all took a vicarious pleasure in the pain inflicted, never quite knowing whether to hope that they themselves would be pilloried or ignored. Neville's reviews were long, prominent and *read*. So although pilloried was bad, arguably being ignored was worse.

Neville moved from painting to painting, pausing now and then to jot down notes or peer short-sightedly at some detail of a composition. He wasn't short-sighted: the whole thing was a performance. Now and then, somebody would come up to him, generally the artist whose work he was currently scrutinizing, but they invariably retreated after a few minutes' exposure to that basilisk stare. Oh, he was powerful, all right. Only Paul, who knew him better, probably, than anybody else in the room, understood that what would matter to Neville, at this moment, more than anything else, was that he hadn't a single painting on these walls.

Watching him, Paul felt something akin to hate: an intimate hatred, as physical as desire. Neville was at the other end of the gallery, much too far away for Paul to see the smear of shaving soap in the crease of his left ear, but see it he did. And he could smell him too: soap, shaving cream, cologne, whisky, tobacco; and under it all, the musky odor of his body.

Paul knew he was overreacting, *wildly* overreacting, but he couldn't seem to stop himself. Gradually, he began to work his way towards Neville, but he was always edging away, confirming what Paul had already begun to suspect: that Neville had seen him and was actively avoiding him. People were still arriving. It was becoming difficult to move around, let alone see the paintings, unless of course you were Neville and your reputation created its own space. As gently as possible, Paul threaded his way between the groups. He needed to confront Neville, to see his eyes as they came face-to-face, but then, just when he was almost within reach, a whole crowd of newcomers obscured his view, and, when he could see clearly again, Neville was gone.

Craning his neck, Paul checked to see if Neville was anywhere in the room, then caught sight of him standing in the hall. He was being detained, obviously against his will, by an angular young man, Clive Somebody-or-other, with a thrusting jaw and a reputation to make, not battle-scarred yet, not yet understanding what reason he had to be afraid. *Keep him talking,* Paul pleaded silently, pushing his way to the door, but by the time he'd got there Neville had disappeared.

He went outside and looked around. People were coming up the steps towards him and there was a queue of taxis at the curb. No Neville, though. But it was raining, and Paul couldn't remember if Neville had been wearing a coat, so he went inside to check the cloakroom. Not there either, but suddenly he saw him, saw somebody, a bulky figure slipping through the doors on the far side of the hall into the darkness of an empty gallery.

Paul followed him. No lights: probably the bulbs had

been removed. No paintings either. They'd been shared out to stately homes across the country or, some people said, stored at the bottom of mine shafts in Wales. He stood just inside the door, listening, and thought he caught the sound of footsteps in the next gallery, but the absence of paintings changed the acoustics and it was hard to locate the sound.

He began to walk across the unlit gallery, directing the thin beam of his blackout torch at the walls, where dust squares and rectangles delineated the shapes of vanished masterpieces. He felt the absence of the paintings as a positive force. A strange sensation—he couldn't put his finger on it. His footsteps echoed round the hall, but the echo was weirdly mismatched so that when he stopped—as he did frequently, to listen—there was always another step. Always one more step than there should have been, so he no longer knew whether he was pursuing or being pursued. The sound of his breathing slithered all over the gallery, little worms of sound chasing each other round the walls. And, abruptly, it was back: the vertigo that had plagued him, on and off, for most of the year. The darkness spun. He groped his way to the nearest wall and let himself slide down it.

At least, now, sitting with his back to the wall, he felt safe from falling. He directed his torch at a particular point on the floor and tried to focus on that, but the beam quivered with the beating of his heart. He trained the light onto his left hand, where there was a minute scar, a half-moon of whiter flesh, on the ball of his thumb, the memento of some childish scrape. He stared unblinkingly at it, and gradually the spinning stopped. After a while, he was able to stand and retrace his steps, the pencil beam wavering over the floor ahead of him.

He should have left it there, but he couldn't. He hadn't gone to the gallery searching for Neville, but the pursuit, once started, acquired a momentum of its own, beyond reason. He had no idea what he would say, or do, when they met, but he knew the meeting had to happen. It was—an odd word came to mind—"obligatory." The meeting had become obligatory.

Leaving the gallery, he took a taxi straight to Neville's house. The sirens sounded just as he was walking up the path, but he had no inclination to seek shelter. The bell clanged loud and deep, but brought no sound of footsteps coming to the door. He banged with his clenched fists, put his ear to the letter box and listened, but he had no sense of Neville, or anyone else, hearing the ringing or knocking and deciding not to answer. No, wherever Neville was, he hadn't come home. On duty? Well, yes, it was possible. In which case he'd be out all night. But he could be anywhere. He could be with Elinor now. In her flat.

That sent all the floaters into a manic dance: dented pillows, stained sheets, Neville's arse bobbing up and down between Elinor's spread thighs . . . For a moment, he thought he'd have to go there, but he managed to talk himself out of it. He'd no real reason to suppose Neville was there. Whereas, sooner or later, he would have to come home.

And so he settled down to wait. Total darkness, no moon, no stars, just searchlights on the heath and the roar of ack-ack guns. Perhaps it was a long time he waited, perhaps short, he had no sense of time passing. He might even have dropped off to sleep. Like everybody else, he was permanently exhausted; he could sleep anywhere. He probably had dropped off because he didn't hear the taxi draw up, or Neville's voice as he paid the driver; he didn't hear his footsteps coming up the drive, or his key turning in the lock. He heard his breathing, though.

Paul made no sound, didn't move or speak, but somehow Neville became aware of his presence.

"Tarrant?" Peering into the shadows. "What are you doing here?" He sounded nervous, even alarmed, but he disguised it well. "Come in."

Paul followed him inside. Neville slammed the door shut and then, for a moment, they simply stood together, in the darkness of the hall, Paul listening to Neville's labored breaths. Then Neville switched the light on. Chairs, table, hatstand, door, walls bristled into life.

"Come through."

Very much the jolly, welcoming host. Once in the drawing room, he took off his coat and threw it over the back of a chair. Underneath, he was wearing a dinner jacket.

"Good night?" Paul asked.

"Not bad. Well, you know, the Savoy . . ." Vaguely, he looked around. "Would you like a drink?"

"Whisky, if you've got it."

If he'd got it. Like asking Dracula if he had blood. Paul unbuttoned his coat and sat down, still feeling slightly dazed with sleep.

Neville had obviously been drinking, but he handed Paul a generous glass before pouring at least the equivalent for himself. "I must say, I can't stand the Savoy. All that standing on the balcony, watching the raids. It's ghoulish."

He was attempting to treat Paul's arrival on his doorstep as a normal social call, though it was past midnight and they'd never been in the habit of dropping in on each other unannounced. And yet it seemed, for a time, that the pretense would be maintained. Neither of them could think of anything else to do. So they talked about the Savoy. Paul was thinking how typical of Neville to say he hated the place, while spending, Paul suspected, quite a lot of time there. He'd had exactly the same love-hate relationship with the Café Royal in the last war.

At last the conversation dribbled into silence. Neville said: "Is anything the matter?"

"You tell me."

The clock ticked. Neville cleared his throat.

"Do you know," Paul said. "Just now, in the garden, I couldn't see a thing, but I knew it was you. Because I heard you breathing. You see, Neville, I'd know your breathing anywhere."

"Well, yes, I—"

"Even through a bedroom door."

"Ah."

Paul asked, on a note of dispassionate curiosity, as if he were only moderately interested in the answer: "What the hell do you think you're doing? Fucking my wife?"

"Well. Just that, I suppose."

If he'd been anywhere near Neville at that moment he'd have hit him, but Neville had retreated to the far side of the fireplace. And even in his present state of mind Paul thought he might have found it difficult to punch Neville in the face. Kicking him in the balls might feel good though.

"You don't deny it?"

"No, of course I don't, why should I? Aren't you forgetting something? *Sandra?*"

"Oh, don't worry, I know I've lost the high ground a bit."

"Totally, I'd say. You dump Elinor in the country—No-o, *listen.* You could perfectly well have found a flat and gone on living together—you *chose* not to."

"I wanted her to be safe."

"You wanted her out of the way."

"That's not quite true."

"Oh, of course it is. And why? So you could make a complete bloody fool of yourself sniffing round a girl young enough to be your daughter. Do you really think everybody isn't sniggering about it? Because, let's face it, you weren't particularly discreet, were you? Elinor's friends all knew before she did. The people she works with. How do you think that made her feel?"

"Oh, and you rushed round to console her? How very kind."

"I did, actually. Though not about you."

"How many times?"

"Do you know, I might be wrong—but I really don't think that's any of your business."

They stared at each other. There'd been several times already when Paul had felt like hitting Neville, but he hadn't done it. And now, somehow, they'd got past it. Though not into safer territory. It came to him that he had no idea at all how the night would end.

He said, sounding to his own ears rather pathetic, "I thought we were friends."

"Did you?"

None of this was true. So far neither of them had said a single true word. Somehow, he had to find the anger again, because at least that wasn't false. It was there, he could feel it, hear it almost, a drone at the back of his head. It was only when he saw Neville glance at the ceiling that he realized the droning was a real sound in the real world.

"They don't usually fly this low," Neville said. "The guns on the heath force them up."

This one was very low indeed. There was that awful drone, as intolerable as the sound of a dentist's drill, in the end so insistent he and Neville simply sat and listened. After a while, it seemed to go farther away, and they relaxed.

Neville looked at his empty glass. "Is she all right?"

"You mean you don't know?"

"I haven't seen her. She's at the cottage, I think. I thought you might have gone down there."

"No."

"So, anyway, Sandra's a thing of the past, is she?"

"Joined the Wrens."

"You ditched her."

"I didn't, actually, it was never meant to be permanent. She was engaged—sort of."

"Fair enough; you were married—sort of."

"You can talk."

"I'm divorced."

"So what do you think's going to happen now?"

"I don't know. I can tell you one thing though: if you force Elinor to choose between us, she'll choose herself."

"Well, obviously, it's her choice."

"No, I mean she'll choose her *self*. Don't you see?" Out of nowhere, an immense burst of anger: "IT'S WHAT SHE DOES!"

From somewhere uncomfortably close came the sound of a long, shrieking descent and the chandelier above their heads rocked and jangled.

"I see you still haven't got that bl-oo-dy th-in—"

The words elongated and vanished into air as the walls buckled and rushed towards them. Then, nothing.

SOMEWHERE NEARBY, a tap was dripping. He could feel random drops plopping onto his face and trickling down his neck. Something had fallen across his legs. He tried to bring his arms up to push whatever it was away, but they seemed to be trapped too. After a while, by arching his back and heaving himself off the floor, he managed to shift the weight a little. Another nightmare; he was fed up with them. The ones where you knew you were asleep, you knew you were dreaming, and you still couldn't wake up were the worst of the lot. This one was particularly vivid. He seemed to be in a kitchen. There were fragments of blue-and-white pottery scattered over the floor. He couldn't see much because his head was pinned down; he could only look sideways. *Dunstanburgh Castle at Sunset* was propped against a chair. Turner. Seeing it like that, it was very obviously a Turner. Why would anybody want to hang a Turner in a kitchen? The *steam* . . .

He couldn't make out where the light was coming from. Twisting his neck a painful inch to the right, he saw trees and branches wave. If he could only get out there . . . He tried wriggling his fingers, then his toes, and found he could move both. The pain, the pressure, was mainly in his chest. Something he couldn't even see was pinning him down. Flares blossomed and trembled. He was lying out in no-man's-land, waiting for the flares to die so he could scramble back into the lines. It made sense, more sense than lying squashed like a cockroach on the floor of a basement kitchen.

He heard a movement. Somebody knelt beside him, cutting off the draft of cool air.

"Are you all right?"

He forced himself to find words. "Yes, I think so."

With the sound of his own voice came a clearer sense of his situation. Not a nightmare, not no-man's-land, a real place, *now*. He was in Neville's house. They'd been talking, shouting, Neville had shouted something, but he couldn't remember what it was—or why they were in the kitchen.

"Can you move your feet?"

He tried again. "Yes."

"Well, that's a relief. I think there's a spade in the garden shed. We're going to have to dig you out. I could go and get it, I suppose."

"Wouldn't it be quicker to go for help?"

"Oh. No rush."

No rush?

And suddenly he was afraid. As if sensing his fear the voice went on: "Do you know, I could kill you now? Nobody would be any the wiser. I could pick up this brick—and why not? It's a perfectly good brick—and bash your head in."

He couldn't breathe. "Why would you want to do that?"

"Why not?"

"There's got to be a reason."

"No-o, don't think so. *Because I can.* How could anybody prove it hadn't just landed on your head? Of course I'd have to do it in one blow. Can't have the same brick landing twice." He giggled.

More than the words, the giggle terrified Paul, because it was not a sound Neville could ever possibly make. Arching his back, he tried again to lift whatever was pinning him down. Neville made no move to help, but neither did he leave—he seemed to be indifferent to his own safety. And there was real danger—the building could come down on top of them at any minute.

The words "I could kill you now" hung over them.

"Well, your decision," Paul said. "I suppose."

Paul closed his eyes and lay still. There was nothing he could do—and anything he said, anything at all, would feed Neville's rage just as everything fed the London fires. So he gazed sidelong across the floor at the scattered fragments of blue-and-white pottery, wondering where the real cockroaches were and thinking they'd probably survive. It wasn't looking too good for him.

Not that it mattered. And yet the need to understand remained. "Is this so you can have Elinor?"

Neville had switched his torch on and the beam was shining on the brick in his right hand. Paul tried again to heave the weight off his chest, but pain forced him to stop. Another bomb exploded, not nearby, at the end of the next street, perhaps, but still close enough to shift the balance in the rubble hanging over them. A hissing had started, water spraying from a burst pipe—or gas. "Whole bloody thing's coming down," Neville said, but dispassionately.

Paul tried to say something in reply, but his mouth was full of dust and, anyway, what was there to say? He closed his eyes and listened to Neville's labored breath.

A minute later, he became aware of a light moving across his face. Neville, shining the torch into his eyes, wanting him to respond, to plead. But when Paul opened his eyes the beam was moving haphazardly across the room, fluttering mothlike over collapsed walls and broken furniture. Footsteps clambering over bricks and rubble, and a voice: "Anybody in there?"

The neighborhood warden, his face a pale blur behind the torch. A long, still moment. Then Neville stood up. "Yes, there's somebody trapped, but I don't think you'll need a rescue squad. I think we can get him out between us."

He sounded brisk, ordinary. The torch shone full in Paul's face again, and he closed his eyes, but not before he'd seen Neville glance down at the brick in his hand, as if surprised to find it there, and toss it casually away.

❈ THIRTY-TWO

1 November 1940

A plane crashed here last week, on a hill about two miles outside the village. It's still there, the wreckage, they haven't started clearing it away. The fuselage is mottled black and gray, like one of those city moths, and there's ribbon tape all round it. Children wait till dark then slip under the tape, scavenge whatever they can find to take into school and show around the playground. Mrs. Murchison, whom I met this morning in the post office—I think she's quite lonely now with Rachel and the family away; she must be lonely if she stops and speaks to me—says one of the little horrors turned up at school with the pilot's thumb in his gym bag. "That's lads for you!" And then suddenly we were thinking of Kenny, and a silence fell.

A lowering sky today, scrawls of black cloud, wind rattling dry leaves around. I worked all morning and well into the afternoon. In London, the afternoons are always a dead time, but not here. Here—apart from walks and pauses to chop up vegetables for yet another nourishing stew—I work all day. Around about six, my eyes start burning with tiredness, and then it's blackout time, nothing to do but light the fire and settle down with a book, only I can't concentrate, I'm listening all the time for the nightly drone, for the window frames to start bumping, know-

ing all the time that any one of those bumps could be the end of somebody I love. I mean Paul, of course. Always Paul.

So why? That's the question I keep tiptoeing round. Because he betrayed me. And it was a betrayal. That girl, so young, so unmarked by life. Oh, and the one before too, the art student. People told me about her, and I'd feel my mouth twist into a little, wry, sophisticated smile—a sort of oh-well-you-know smile—which seemed to get stuck on my face for hours, getting heavier all the time until my cheeks sagged. That's why my periods went haywire. It was nothing to do with "the tears of a disappointed womb"—it was the strain of pretending, even to myself, that I didn't mind. When, in reality, I minded so much I wanted to scream.

So, yes, that's why.

Though it still leaves another question: Why Kit? Why him, of all people? Because he's the person who'd hurt Paul most? But that only makes sense if I tell Paul. Because Kit loved me when I was young and I want those years back? Sweep two world wars away? Oh, yes, why not? Easy: just jump into bed with your childhood sweetheart. We-ell, not childhood exactly, though we were very young. And not sweethearts either, not really, though he certainly wanted us to be. His head lying in my lap on that country lane all those years ago. The weight of it, the warmth. The way when he tried to get up he deliberately brushed the back of his head against my breasts and I wanted to laugh. I still do. Smile, anyway.

When he looks at me, Kit sees me. Or he sees that girl—and perhaps that's the same thing, or I want it to be. Paul doesn't. I don't think Paul's seen me for years.

2 November 1940

Today I walked miles along the riverbank. The painting, the one of the little girl on the pavement, is finished. At least, I think it's finished. I need to get right away, then go back and look at it with fresh eyes.

A blustery day, sunny spells, but mixed in with frequent heavy showers, one or two real downpours. Rooks whirling about above the bare elms like the scraps of burnt paper that drift down from London's incinerated offices.

I was trudging along, looking at my feet, thinking about the painting, my fingers still feeling the imprint of the brush, smelling of paint, probably daubed with it as well, but it hardly matters; I meet nobody on these walks. And then I glanced up and noticed a curious seething movement in the grass on the other side of a long field. I couldn't make out what it was: some reflection of the clouds, I thought at first, but then I realized the river was coming to meet me. It had burst its banks and flooded the low ground. I don't know what I felt—a kind of exhilaration, I suppose. It was so beautiful: fractured reflections of clouds dissolving and re-forming as the water advanced. And all at once a great spray-burst of seagulls wheeling about and settling on the water.

Now it's evening—every joint aches—but the painting is finished. And it's good—I'm almost sure it's good. Kenneth Clark's probably going to hate it. Bad for morale. Though, actually, if one of his aims is to persuade people to send their children to safety—or leave them there—you could hardly imagine a painting better calculated to get the message across. No message, though. I don't do messages. Anyway, it's done—and I'm not going to spend the rest of the evening double-guessing what Clark might say.

It's blowing a gale outside. The windows thump and for

once it's not a raid; the glass streams. I'm going to make carrot soup and light a fire.

3 November 1940

As I expected, I'm paying for that walk. I sat on the side of the bed this morning feeling like an old woman, bracing myself for the trip across the landing to the bathroom. I'm so stiff I can hardly move. Actually, though, it's quite a relief to have physical pain to contend with. Takes your mind off the other sort.

Because last night, too tired to read, I got Paul's envelopes out, intending to spend a pleasant, nostalgic hour sorting through old photographs. I thought I'd buy an album and stick them in. Oh, quite a cosy little evening I had planned! What I didn't know was that the envelopes contain letters as well as snaps. And the first letter to fall out was the one Toby wrote to me a day or two before he was killed.

It was a shock, seeing that familiar handwriting again after so many years. Neat, regular, forward-slanting ... You looked at Toby's handwriting and your first thought was: how easy it would be to read. Only when you looked more closely did you realize it was virtually indecipherable. A bit like Toby himself.

I started reading automatically, before I had time to prepare myself. And there he was, instantly, his voice, as clear and strong as if he'd been standing beside me in the room.

Elinor—I've had two goes at this already, so this is it, has to be, because we're moving forward soon and there'll be no time for writing after that. There's no way of saying this without sounding melodramatic, and I really don't think I am. In fact, I feel rather down-to-earth and matter-of-fact about it all. I don't think I would even mind very much, except I know it's going to be a shock to you—and I can't think of any way of softening the blow.

I won't be coming back this time. This isn't a premonition or anything like that. I can't even explain why. I used to think officers' letters weren't censored, but they are sometimes, not by the people here, but back at base. They do random checks or something, and I can't afford to risk that. I hate not being able to tell you. If you ever want to know more, I suggest you ask your friend Kit Neville—assuming he survives, and I'm sure he will. ~~He's been no friend to me~~. I know you'll take care of Mother as best you can. Father'll be all right, I think—he's got his work. And Rachel's got Tim and the boys. I don't know what to say to you. Remember

How easy it is to feel superior to the dead: we know so much more than they did. I didn't look after Mother. Father wasn't all right—he died of a heart attack in the back of a taxi on his way to work less than two years after Toby's death. He never even looked like "getting over it"—whatever that means.

Toby's last letter. Unfinished, not signed. Never sent. It survived only by accident because there was a hole in his tunic pocket and it had slipped through into the lining. And the sentence about Kit had been crossed out. As Paul said at the time: a crossed-out sentence in a letter never finished, never signed, never sent. What possible significance can you attach to that? But I did attach significance to it. And I was right.

But there's no point going over all that now. Now, the only word that matters is: "Remember."

But I didn't remember. If I'd remembered, I could never have gone to bed with Kit. I talk about Paul betraying me and

use it to justify a far worse betrayal. Because it wasn't Paul I betrayed—I don't owe Paul any more loyalty than he's shown me, and God knows, that's been little enough—no, it was Toby I betrayed.

I look at his photograph, the one of him in uniform when he first joined up. It's the one Featherstone used to do that awful portrait. He's young, so much younger than I am now, but it's not an unformed face, not by any means. There's great strength there, great determination, but no trust. I don't think I've ever seen a more guarded expression. I miss him.

Kit. I can't say, as Paul said about that girl—Sandra, whatever her name was—that it wasn't important. That it didn't matter. It was important. It does matter. But it can't go on. And I've no idea what I'm going to say to him. I do know one thing: I don't want to rake over the past, or try to explain why it's impossible. We'd only start arguing about things that can't be helped.

No. I think by far the easiest thing—well, easiest for me, and I hope for him—is just to let it slide. Not get in touch and— Well, I'd like to say: not see him again; but of course there's no hope of that. There'll be times when we're working the same shift, however hard I try to avoid it. I'll just have to be—cool, I suppose. And after all I might be imagining a problem where there isn't one. I mean, for all I know, he's regretting it every bit as much as me.

London again, tomorrow. So I suppose I'll soon know.

THIRTY-THREE

This was supposed to be a job interview, but it didn't feel like one. Half an hour into the meeting, wreaths of cigarette smoke hung stagnant on the air, swirling a little when a secretary came in with tea and biscuits, before settling into new patterns, rather like the marbled endpapers of books. A lot of people had been "interviewed for jobs" here: Neville could smell them. Essence of anxiety lingered on the air.

The questions focused mainly on his knowledge of German. The time he'd spent in Germany between the wars. His German wife. All the way back to his father's allegedly pro-Boer sympathies in the Boer War.

"He wasn't pro-Boer," Neville said. "He was anti–concentration camp, which at the time *we* were running. I think you can safely assume his sympathies with Hitler would have been zero."

His answers became increasingly acerbic as the questioning went on, though they produced no response beyond a brisk nod and occasionally a smile. And then the next question. "Why do you speak German so fluently?"

He'd have liked to say: *Because of the brilliant foreign-language teaching at Charterhouse,* but decided not to. "I had a German nursemaid when I was a child."

"Really?"

"Yes, really."

"Why?"

"How should I know? My mother didn't consult me about the domestic arrangements."

"So you were fluent before you met your wife?"

God, this was exasperating. "Look, I can translate German, I can do everything I'm required to do here. And yes, I can hold a conversation fairly easily. Parachute me into Berlin? No, I wouldn't last five minutes. But that isn't what this is about, is it?"

Dodsworth was tapping the papers in front of him into a neat pile. He looked up. "Nobody's accusing you of anything."

But Neville *felt* accused. On the way back to his office, he became increasingly angry. What right did Dodsworth, who'd been too young for the last war and seemed to be driving a desk in this one, have to question his loyalty? *Nobody's accusing you of anything.* Bollocks. It was an investigation, couldn't be anything else, and he found it insulting. He'd returned to England voluntarily and he'd volunteered to work in the fucking, bloody ministry. He wasn't one of the people who queued up for jobs here to get out of joining the army. No, he'd been entirely motivated by . . . insanity. Only insanity could account for somebody volunteering to work here.

But then, look at it from Dodsworth's point of view. If Neville was a German spy, what would he do? Get back to England as fast as possible and use his knowledge of German to secure a job at the Ministry of Information, where he'd have constant access to classified files. Perhaps he should just clear out. Go and live at the back of beyond somewhere and paint pretty little pictures of lakes and things. Get Dodsworth off his back, if nothing else.

He was passing Kenneth Clark's office. Never an easy moment. Still no letter, no invitation to tea and biscuits in the great man's office, though God knows that bloody little exhibition of his could have done with an infusion of talent. He'd almost made it to the other side of the landing when the door opened and Clark came out, accompanied by—oh my God—Nigel Featherstone. Now that really was scraping the barrel. Featherstone's "paintings"—and that was stretching the term till it sagged like a whore's knicker elastic—hung in every major public building in the country. You noticed them, if you noticed them at all, only to remark on how completely they blended into their surroundings—like frightfully well-chosen sofa cushions. Neville turned to face the wall, giving them plenty of time to get past because this was more than a brisk handshake and nice-to-see-you. As they walked towards the lift, Clark's hand rested momentarily between Featherstone's shoulder blades.

Neville found himself looking at Ullswater again. Was it one of Tarrant's? It had to be by somebody distinguished because it was positioned directly opposite Clark's door, though, looking at it again, Neville was inclined to acquit Tarrant. It pained him to admit it, but Tarrant was better than this. At the moment, any thought of Tarrant was painful. He was out of hospital—five or six cracked ribs, but apparently there's not a lot you can do about them, other than bind up the chest and wait for them to heal. Neville hadn't been to see him in hospital. It would have been awkward. His memories of that night were chaotic, but he remembered enough to know his behavior had been a bit odd. But of course he'd been in shock, and people in shock do and say the most extraordinary things.

Behind his back, he heard Clark and Featherstone laughing, then the lift doors rattled open. They exchanged a few more words—he was too far away to hear—and then, thank God, they were gone. He was free to move again.

Hilde looked up as he came into the room. Bertram's empty desk had been pushed against the wall, so they had slightly more space to move around. Bertram hadn't appeared for three weeks now. Was that significant? Probably not. Suddenly, he thought: *Perhaps there's an oubliette in the basement?* Somewhere they put people whom they want to forget? Perhaps Bertram and all kinds of other people were down there, still vainly protesting their innocence, as their long, white beards grew and grew until they reached the floor . . .

"I'm glad you find it amusing," Hilde said.

Oh God, he was supposed to be editing her draft translation of *Women Under the Nazis,* the latest pamphlet in the series they were working on together.

"Bowling along," he said, having not taken in a word. All those women under the Nazis. What a waste. Why couldn't at least one of them be under him? He glanced at the clock: *Oh God, another two hours of this. I'm going to leave,* he thought. *I really am going to leave.*

He was tempted to begin clearing his desk there and then. Well, why not? What was stopping him? He lifted his briefcase onto the desk and began filling it with odds and ends. There wasn't much: he hadn't been here long enough to accumulate a load of stuff. Hilde watched him without comment for a time, then, seeing him trying to stick some papers into a file that was slightly too small, came across and held it open for him. Then she cleared her throat in that way she had. "Have they asked you to leave?"

"Sacked me, you mean? No, quite the opposite, in fact. They've offered me a job." *Lies, all lies.*

"Here?"

"No, somewhere near Oxford."

"Will you take it?"

He paused in the act of taking his hat from the peg. "Do you know, I have absolutely no idea."

They shook hands. For some reason she blushed and on impulse he leaned forward and kissed her thin cheek.

Then he was off, down the corridor, past the Gents—no, on second thoughts, into the Gents. He splashed his face and hands—that hour in Dodsworth's room had made him feel dirty—then he glanced over his shoulder to check the cubicles were empty, twined his fingers round one of the chains that fastened the plastic nailbrushes to the wall, and pulled. He'd always loathed them. Tightening his grip, he pulled again and this time succeeded in wrenching it off the wall. It hurt like hell; the chain had actually left a weal on the side of his hand. But it was worth it. Then, raising his eyes, he confronted the stranger in the glass.

Would he have done it? The nailbrush rested in the palm of his hand, rough against the skin, rectangular, brick-shaped. Would he have killed Tarrant if that air-raid warden hadn't showed up and started flashing his torch? Ninety-nine percent of the time, his answer to this question was a resounding no, of course not, never in a million years. But, at other times, when he was fully absorbed in something that needed concentration, not thinking about Tarrant at all, he was aware of a belief taking shape in the shadows of his mind, not that he might have done it, *but that he had done it*. In dreams he relived those moments after the bomb fell, and woke knowing, not with satisfaction but with almost unbearable sorrow, that Tarrant was dead.

He looked down at the brush. A very nice little souvenir, he thought. He'd put it on the mantelpiece, he decided, and then remembered that he didn't have a mantelpiece. The house was boarded up; he was living at his club. A stultify-

278

ingly boring place, he was buggered if he was going back there, not until he'd anesthetized himself in the nearest bar.

Though, walking away from the building—for the last time, *the last time*—he thought he wouldn't go to the pub after all, he'd go to see Elinor, at least see if she was in. She was back in London—he knew that from Dana, who'd had lunch with her—but she hadn't been in touch. He sensed, ringing the bell, and ringing it again, that she was there, but not answering the door. It was starting to look as if their time together, which had meant so much to him, had meant little, or nothing, to her.

Drink. He walked away down the street and knew that he was being watched, that she was at the window behind him. Though he reminded himself sharply that he couldn't know; perhaps he was just being paranoid. God knows, there was enough paranoia about. He turned into the nearest pub; he thought he'd once had a drink with Tarrant in there, but couldn't be sure. There was nobody he knew at the bar. Almost, he missed his evenings with the terrapin, which was now, presumably, dead. Another link with the past broken. But then he wondered: how long did terrapins live? Perhaps his parents, for some extraordinary reason, had kept replacing the terrapin and not told him.

He knocked back the first whisky so fast his eyes watered—and that was saying a lot. Then he ordered the second straight away and sat morosely in a corner. Everything seemed to be conspiring against him. Dodsworth—that was unaccountable. Tarrant's success, his own . . . Well, "neglect" was hardly the right word, more like a bloody conspiracy. No wonder he couldn't paint. Everybody needs a context, an echo coming back to them—and he didn't have that. He seemed to be living in a vacuum, a glass tank that cut him off from the outside world. There was only Anne, really, to attach him to life. He lived and breathed in the memory of her. The way, when she was a tiny child, just a toddler, she used to come into his bed in the mornings, bouncing up and down, waving her favorite toy, a blue rabbit: *I love Babbit! I love Babbit!* It had been a small grief for him when, finally, she'd learned to say "rabbit."

Lost in his memories, he resurfaced to hear the sirens wailing. Several people immediately left, though he thought the pub had been emptying for the past hour. How many drinks had he had? There seemed to be an impressive array of glasses in front of him, unless of course he was seeing double. He got to his feet easily enough, but found it unexpectedly difficult to weave his way between the tables to the bar.

"Shame again."

Was that a fractional hesitation? He met the barman's eye.

"Right you are, sir."

By the time he left, he was . . . numb. Absolutely clear mentally, though: he did honestly believe there was such a thing as drinking yourself sober. The anger was still there, bubbling away under the surface, but he felt agreeably numbed as he stood swaying on the pavement, buffeted by waves of noise. He might have one last go at seeing Elinor. She wouldn't be in, of course. She'd have taken refuge in one of the shelters, but it was at least worth a try.

Several fires were blazing, the worst of them out of control. Black water lay around in puddles; he sloshed through them, finding it quite difficult to keep a straight line. A fireman was standing in the road holding on to a hose, his eyes glazed with the tedium of what he was doing. By far the worst job, the fire service: equal parts boredom and terror.

Elinor's house was completely blacked out, of course: no way of telling whether she was in or not, but he rang the doorbell anyway. Rather to his surprise it was answered immediately by a young woman wearing a nurse's cap and cape. She was going on duty and had come to the door almost by accident, but that didn't matter—he was in. He thought he might as well go up and see if Elinor was in. If not, fair enough, he'd just go back home, a friendly tap on the terrapin's tank and straight upstairs to bed. Only then he remembered that he couldn't do that. No terrapin, no tank, no home.

He knocked. No answer, as he'd expected, but then he heard a movement inside the room. "Elinor?"

A second later, the door opened. She was pulling her silk wrap together over her nightdress.

"You should be in a shelter," he said, accusingly.

"It's late, Kit. What do you want?"

"Just to talk. Please?"

"All right, but not long." She stepped back. "Have you been drinking?"

He slumped onto the sofa. " 'Course I've been bloody drinking, I've had that little pipsqueak Dodsworth on to me again." He couldn't remember whether he'd told her about Dodsworth—absolutely no idea. Told her again anyway. He was about to explain about Clark and Featherstone and Tarrant's—*possibly* Tarrant's—bloody boring landscape on the wall, and how utterly ludicrous it was that talentless Tarrant and fucking useless Featherstone should have been commissioned as war artists while he, Kit Neville, had been passed over—but he managed to stop himself in time. He was drunk, but not quite as drunk as that.

"I'm sorry about Dodsworth," she said. "It is awful."

He jabbed his index fingers at his face. "What right does he have to question my loyalty?"

She said, carefully, "Are you sure you're getting it right? You're sure it's *not* an interview?"

"I don't see how it can be, he keeps going over and over the same ground, doubling back, asking the same questions . . . No, it's got to be an interrogation—can't be anything else."

She had come across and sat on the sofa, but at the other end. Three feet of dark blue velvet lay between them. No-man's-land. Well, it had taken four fucking years to get across that, and he didn't have that kind of time.

"Elinor, can I stay the night?"

Deep breath. "No, Kit."

"Please?"

The sound of his own voice, pleading, released his anger. "Do you know, I haven't had a squeak out of you for . . . Oh, I don't know. Since you left, anyway."

"I've been thinking."

"Huh. Not your strong suit."

"What?" When he didn't reply, she said, "Kit, it's late and I'm tired."

"So that's it, then?"

"You know, that day, when it happened, we were neither of us in a particularly good state. I'm not blaming you, I'm not blaming anybody—I'm just saying I'm not *ready.* I think I need to be on my own for a while."

He didn't believe a word of this. In fact, he felt quite insulted; she was just spouting a load of *Ladies' Home Journal* tripe instead of coming right out and saying what she really felt. At the back of his mind was the fear that she found him as repulsive as he sometimes feared he was.

She wanted him to go—that, at least, was obvious—but he couldn't accept it. People had been saying no to him all his life, taking things away: his marriage, his daughter, his reputation, his house, his FACE, for Christ's sake! Well, no more. As she stood up, he lunged sideways, caught her round the wrist and pulled her down on top of him. She fell across his face. It was easy, so easy, to push the wrap aside, pull her nightdress off her shoulders; he was full of the scent of her, her voice in his ears sounding very far away on the other side of a red mist that rose and covered everything. They were on the floor, he didn't know how they'd got there, but his right knee was between her legs, didn't matter now what she did with her hands, she could flail away with her arms as much as she liked, once he'd got her legs apart his weight did the rest.

After a time, a long time it seemed, but it might have been only minutes, she rolled from under him. Ripped nightdress. White face. Scrabbling to get her wrap closed, she crawled onto the sofa. He should go, go now, before she started screaming. But she didn't seem to think screaming was the appropriate response. She was rocking herself backwards and forwards, but otherwise seemed remarkably composed.

He got up, turned away, fumbled with buttons, retreated to a chair, where he sat looking down at his hands. How big they were. "I seem to have become . . ." He was articulating the words very carefully. "A bit of a monster."

"Oh, Kit. You always were."

The clock on the mantelpiece ticked.

"I should go."

A brief, hard laugh, indicating, he supposed, agreement. She stood up and let him out.

On the landing, he stopped and looked back at her slim shape silhouetted against the light from the room behind her, then turned and went on, feeling his way down the dark staircase and out into the night.

THIRTY-FOUR

Afterwards, it was the horses she remembered, galloping towards them out of the orange-streaked darkness, their manes and tails on fire. One huge black shire horse with frantically rolling eyes came straight at them. Elinor wrenched the steering wheel violently to the left and, a few yards farther on, pulled into the curb. In the rear-view mirror, she saw the horses galloping away, their great, bright, battering hooves striking sparks from the road. She remembered a thud against the side of the ambulance and thought she might have caught one a glancing blow on the shoulder as it careered past.

She sat, breathing heavily, looking at her orange hands on the wheel. Even her skin didn't look like skin.

Beside her, in the co-driver's seat, Neville cleared his throat. "Would you like me to take over for a bit?"

"No, thank you," she said, with another glance in the rear-view mirror, preparing to move off. She might have taken that from Dana or Violet, but certainly not from him. "Actually, Kit, if you want to know what it feels like to have your testicles skewered and roasted over a slow fire *while you watch*, you could try saying that again."

"Fair enough."

She risked a sideways glance. His face in the light of the fires was an expressionless mask. Beaten bronze.

For so long she'd contrived to avoid working with Kit. But then, over the Christmas and New Year period, single people like Elinor—and, of course, Kit—had signed up for extra duties so that married people and parents could spend time with their families. Christmas Eve, Christmas Day, Boxing Day had all been quiet—she'd never played so many games of cards in her life—but the unofficial cease-fire was now unmistakably over. Hundreds, if not thousands, of incendiaries must have fallen that night and they were still clattering down. Yes, she'd had a moment of dismay when she'd looked at the duty roster and seen her name and Kit's bracketed together, but she could hardly protest.

As she turned into Gunpowder Court, incendiaries clattered onto the ambulance roof like giant hailstones, and when she looked out of the side window she saw dozens more fizzing and popping all along the pavement. A squad of heavy rescue workers were shouting and jostling each other, like footballers fighting for possession of the ball, as they competed to stamp them out. As she watched, the man nearest to her dived and put his helmet over one of the skittering devices. "Gotcha, y' little sod!"

Farther along the court, two fire engines were parked, taking up almost all the space. Half a dozen hoses snaked across the road, some gray and flaccid, but others very much alive—and she daren't risk driving over those because, for the fireman at the branch, that interruption in the water supply could be dangerous, and the sudden return of water pressure almost equally so. She'd seen firemen injured by a branch writhing and spinning out of control. So: the way ahead was blocked.

She looked at Kit. "You could try Wine Office Court," he said. "Try to get at it from the other side."

"Is there a way through?"

He shrugged. "They all lead into one another."

That was the trouble. They'd both have claimed to know London well, but neither of them was familiar with this particular area: the network of narrow alleys and courts off Fleet Street. Where was Derek when you needed him? Or any one of the other taxi drivers? Still, she wasn't going to give up. They couldn't. They'd been sent to a direct hit on a nurses' hostel and that meant, potentially, dozens of casualties. Unless, of course, they'd all been on duty, or in a shelter as they bloody well ought to have been, but you couldn't rely on that. Increasingly, exhausted people risked everything for the comfort and (spurious) safety of their own beds.

"All right, let's give it a go."

She reversed fifty yards or so, then pulled over near the entrance to Wine Office Court and stopped again.

They climbed stiffly down from the cab and walked across the narrow road. Elinor felt suddenly sick with tiredness, and cold; she was shivering inside her thick coat. Even the adrenaline rush of fear would have been welcome now, but she felt no fear; she felt nothing. Nothing, after the horses.

Just inside the entrance to the court was a fireman tending a pump, which roared and shook and pulsed gray water down its gray sides, deepening the pool of black water at his feet. He looked glazed, cold, wet, exhausted, bored, but he managed a wave. Kit tried to ask whether there was a way through, but he couldn't make himself heard. They were communicating with the huge pantomimic gestures of people guiding aeroplanes into their hangars. Turning to Elinor, Kit pointed to himself and then along the court, signing that he was going to see if he could find a way through. Elinor shook her head, and made a sharp, dismissive gesture with her hands indicating the court was too narrow. She meant for the ambulance.

Kit mouthed: *Stretcher.* She nodded: *Yes, that might be possible;* then pointed to her chest, meaning: *I'm coming too.* He shook his head, but she ignored him. They began walking along the court, keeping up a brisk pace because speed seemed to offer safety: a moving target, you felt, must be harder to hit. The road was black and gleaming wet, flooded for a stretch where a drain had been blocked by a great wad of charred and sodden newspaper. At first, the roar of the pump was enough to blot out all other noises, but then gradually, as they splashed through the black water, it started to fade, to be replaced by the crackle of burning brick and timber from the building straight ahead. Probably, the blazing building was a printing works or a newspaper office. Scraps of burnt paper whirled down from the glassless windows above their heads. Elinor could see flames and shadows leaping across the inside walls, making it look, unnervingly, as if there were people trapped inside. The two firemen looked dazed with boredom. They'd have been there hours, hands gripping ice-cold metal, doused from head to foot in ice-cold water. One man's lips were moving; she thought he might be trying to say something, but then realized he was singing.

The other man nodded, saw she was a woman, and grinned. "All right, love?"

She smiled, raising her hand, as she and Kit started to edge along the wall behind them. She felt heat from the blaze scorch her face and neck, though she was still shivering. The branch seemed to be producing a fine, cold spray that blew back into the firemen's faces and soaked everything. She was wet herself now, icy trickles running down under the collar of her coat. Normally, you wouldn't be allowed to get as close to a fire as this. All the other emergency services were supposed to hold back until the fire service declared an area safe, but there could be no question of declaring anywhere safe tonight. She'd just seen the pillars inside St. Bride's Church burning like torches. The whole City was on fire.

They walked as fast as they could away from the burning building, their shadows fleeing across the ground ahead of them. She felt like a mouse creeping along the floor of a great canyon, dwarfed by the four- or five-story buildings on either side. At the end of the court, they turned and looked back. The scene was fitfully lit by the flames leaping from the windows of the burning building, and it was unchanged. That solid-looking pole of white water the firemen were directing at the blaze seemed to be making no difference at all.

She looked at Kit.

"You could get a stretcher past." His voice was hoarse with shouting. "That's if we can get to the hostel."

To their right was another court which seemed at first to be empty, but then they saw two figures walking towards them: an elderly woman, in a pink candlewick dressing gown, and another, much younger, woman, who was hobbling along, grimacing with pain at every step. Elinor shone her torch. "Oh my God, Kit, look." The girl's feet were burned black. How on earth had she managed to walk this far?

"I'll take her," Kit said.

No point arguing: it was obvious the girl had to be carried and only Kit could do that. But Elinor was determined to go on and look for more survivors. If these two had got through, there were likely to be others. "You go with him too," Elinor said to the older woman.

"Oh, I don't think so, dear." A reedy, but authoritative, Edinburgh accent. "I'll be much more use back there."

Kit had lifted the girl and was looking at Elinor, obviously expecting her to follow, but she shook her head. He nodded, or she thought he did—the shadows leaping and flickering all around him made it difficult to be sure. But he turned, and his bulky, burdened shape disappeared rapidly into the murk.

THE GIRL WAS mercifully light; just as well too, because he was finding it difficult to keep his footing. Even in the few minutes since he'd last walked along here, the pool of black water around the blocked drain had deepened, and he was splodging through it. He hated leaving Elinor, but this girl was suffering from shock. The burns looked pretty bad; she needed to be in hospital as soon as possible. Which meant he'd have to drive her straight there, then come back for Elinor. He didn't like the idea. They should've stayed together, but Elinor was never going to come trotting meekly along behind him. He was level with the firemen now, and they shuffled forward a few paces to give him room.

The upper stories were still blazing, the flames inside leaping and dancing as tauntingly as ever, though the white pole of water was now being directed at another window. And there was a kind of clicking noise. He couldn't think at first where it was coming from, then realized it was the building. It was very like the sound a car makes on a hot day when you've just switched off the engine: the tick of cooling metal. But nothing round here was cooling. He wondered if the firemen had heard it—they must've done, but they were looking at each other and laughing, so evidently it was nothing to worry about. All the same, he tried to walk faster and was glad when the shaking and rattling of the pump drowned out the roar of the flames behind him.

As he emerged from the court, he saw another ambulance had drawn up at the curb. Bill Morris and Ian Jenkins came towards him.

"Would you mind taking her?" he asked. "She needs a doctor but I don't want to go and leave Elinor stranded."

He carried the girl the few yards to their ambulance, and saw her safely stowed inside, wrapped in a blanket, with Ian by her side. Bill said he'd try Bart's first. Apparently, they were still taking people in, though there was some talk of an evacuation. My God, it must be bad.

Neville watched the ambulance bump slowly away towards Fleet Street, then he went back and looked along Wine Office Court. The scene hadn't changed at all; the two firemen might have been carved in bronze. What to do? His first impulse was to follow Elinor, but then suppose she came back by another route and found him gone? If she could get through at all that was quite likely. He lit a cigarette. That was one good thing about tonight: there'd be no officious little pipsqueak of an air-raid warden shouting, "Put that bloody fag out!" Any leaking gas mains round here had long since exploded. He dragged deeply on the cigarette and then, rather belatedly, offered the packet to the fireman at the pump, who just shook his head and pointed to the cascading water. Poor bugger was drenched. And now, to make things worse, there seemed to be a wind getting up. He could feel it blowing along the court towards him, hot as a dog's breath on his face. At first, he was puzzled because there'd been no wind, no wind all day, and then the truth hit him: he was witnessing the birth of a firestorm.

That wind would carry sparks from building to building faster than a man could run. He was suddenly terribly afraid, and not ashamed of it either. A man who tells you he's not afraid of fire is either a fool or a liar. He lit another cigarette from the stub of the first. There was a strange smell, very sweet. He couldn't think what it was. If he'd had to guess, he'd have said: incense. It didn't smell like war. He thought it might be wood, centuries old, seasoned wood from burning churches. He thought he'd caught a whiff of it just now as they were driving past St. Bride's. He tried again to peer into the flame-lit darkness of the court. *Where was she?* The conviction that something terrible had happened to her was growing on him by the minute. He shouldn't have let her set off like that, with only the old woman as a guide, but then what else could he have done? Who'd ever made Elinor do anything she didn't want to do? And then the memory of that evening resurfaced, bobbed up like a turd in a sewer. He had—he'd made her do something she hadn't wanted to do. Oh, given enough time he knew he'd remember the events of that evening differently, smooth over the raw edges, but at the moment he couldn't bear it. At least, it goaded him into action. He'd leave the ambulance, he decided. Go and look for her.

He tried to speak to the fireman by the pump, so he'd be able to tell Elinor what had happened if she returned by another route, but he was signaling to the two men holding the branch. They'd backed away from the wall and seemed to be arguing about what to do. And then, with a great rush of relief, Neville saw her, standing at the other end of the court, waving to him. He started towards her. As the roar of the pump faded, he became aware of yet another sound coming from the burning building. Almost a groan. It sounded so human he thought somebody must be trapped. Was that what the firemen were arguing about? Trying to decide if it was safe to go in? But then he saw them look at each other, laughing, so he knew it was all right, and Elinor was still waving. Jumping up and down now, shouting, but he couldn't hear anything above the roar of flames. She'd been joined by a young man in army uniform, who looked vaguely familiar, but couldn't be, of course; it was just somebody Elinor had roped in to help carry the stretchers. Well, *good girl.* The more young, male muscle there was around, the better.

Whoever it was, he was waving too, or beckoning: *Come on, come on. Hey,* he wanted to say, *I'm coming as fast as I can,* but then, just as he drew level with the firemen, he heard the most stupendous crack, and the whole wall of the building bulged and loomed over him, hung motionless, and then, slowly it seemed, began to fall. He saw everything, in detail, without fear or emotion: the dark mass above him cutting slices out of the sky until only a sliver remained. He couldn't move; he couldn't speak. He heard silence, but then the roar came crashing back and red-hot bricks fell on his face and neck and dashed him to the ground. A cry struggled to his lips, but it was already too late—his mouth was full of dust. He thought: *I won't get to Elinor.* And then he forgot Elinor. What finally crushed his heart, as the avalanche of bricks and mortar engulfed him, was the knowledge that he would never see Anne again, he would never again see his daughter, in this world or any other.

THIRTY-FIVE

I n Bloomsbury, Paul was having a quiet night. He'd played a game of darts, flipped through yesterday's newspapers and then set out on patrol with Charlie. At the corner of Guilford Street, Charlie stopped to light a cigarette. Shaking the match, he gazed open-mouthed in the direction of the City. Billowing clouds of black smoke, showers of sparks whirled upwards, a broken skyline of buildings stark against furnace red. "By heck, they aren't half copping it."

Paul felt the first premonitory tweak of fear. Elinor could be in that. Would be, if she was on duty. Charlie threw away the match and they walked on, their footsteps echoing in the eerie silence. No guns now, no drone of bombers. The All Clear had sounded an hour ago, unusually early. "Don't worry," Brian had said. "They'll be back."

But they hadn't been. Not yet. And all the time, over the City, that extravagant, melodramatic, stage-sunset grew and spread, and, with it, Paul's fear.

Their patrol over, they decided to get a cup of tea and a pasty from the van in Malet Street. God only knew what was in the pasties—no substance previously known to mankind—but at least they were warm. Paul and Charlie joined the back of the queue, stamping their feet and blowing on their fingers in a vain attempt to keep warm. Three or four places ahead of them, a woman was talking about an ambulance driver who'd been injured. "Weren't there two of them?" another woman asked. And then a third voice: "Are you sure they were just injured? I heard they were dead."

Elbowing people aside, Paul seized her arm. "Who?" He was shaking her. *"Who?"*

She stared at him, her mouth a scarlet gash in the drained pallor of her face. He tried to calm down. "It's just, my wife's an ambulance driver." For some reason the word "wife" stuck in his throat; it sounded like the sort of thing somebody else would say, and that strangeness, the sudden unfamiliarity of the word, ratcheted up his fear.

"They didn't say. Just two ambulance drivers had been injured, one of them a woman, that's all I heard."

She was lying—he'd just heard her say they were dead. Of course, it might be another woman—Dana or Violet—but somehow, from the very first moment, he knew it was Elinor.

Tearing himself out of Charlie's restraining grip, he ran all the way to the depot in Tottenham Court Road and down two flights of stairs to the basement, which was deserted, except for three telephonists who fell silent as he entered. They looked nervously at each other. A middle-aged woman, who seemed to be the supervisor, came out of the office and stood in front of them. If he had any doubt, that dispelled it. He'd become somebody to be frightened of, as the bereaved always are.

"We can't be certain, we really don't know who it is."

He could tell from the way her gaze slithered down his face that she did. "Where?"

"Wine Office Court, but it's no use going there," she called after him. "They'll have taken them to Bart's."

She followed him into the corridor, shouting something about an ambulance in the yard, so he veered abruptly to the left, burst through the swing doors into the parking area at the back. Sure enough, there was an ambulance about to leave. He ran along beside it, banging with his clenched fist on the door. The vehicle slowed and an elderly man with pouches under his eyes peered down at him.

"Can you give me a lift? My wife works here. Elinor? They've taken her to Bart's."

To his own ears, he was gobbling, gabbling, not making any sense at all, but the man nodded. "Oh, yes, I know Elinor. Hop in." As Paul settled into the co-driver's seat, the man added, "I'm off to Bart's anyway. They're evacuating. We've all got to go."

The journey was a blur. Paul leaned forward, willing the driver to go faster, as they bumped slowly along, occasionally swerving to avoid craters in the road. With every mile, after the first, the orange glare grew until the sky was every bit as bright as noon. Everywhere, fires were raging, many of them out of control. Paul couldn't take it in, street after street burning. Only the details registered. Once, he looked down and saw a pigeon flapping about in the gutter with its wings on fire.

A hundred yards from the hospital entrance, the driver slowed to a crawl. Ambulances were queuing bumper to bumper all along the road. At first, Paul thought they might be delivering casualties, but then he saw that most of them were empty. They were here to evacuate the hospital. He reached for the door handle.

"Hang on," the driver said. "I'll try and get you a bit closer . . ."

"No, it's OK, I'll be all right." Paul jumped into the road and raised his hand. "Thanks, mate."

As he started running along the line of ambulances, the wind caught him, flattening his trousers against his legs.

Looking down the hill, he saw a wall of fire advancing on the hospital—he couldn't understand why it hadn't been evacuated already. The hot wind was snatching up bits of flaming debris and hurling them from one building to the next. At any moment, you felt, the hospital would be engulfed. Elinor. He had to find her and get her out, take her miles and miles away from here.

Inside the entrance, he stared wildly around him, until a passing nurse pointed towards the stairs. No lifts: the doors were all half open, frozen at the point the electricity had failed. He ran upstairs. No lights on the stairs, no lights in the corridor either, except for a couple of smoking oil lamps that signally failed to penetrate the gloom. He groped his way along, a hand on the wall. Nobody seemed to be trying to bring patients down, so evidently the evacuation hadn't started yet.

Bursting through swing doors onto a ward, he was dazzled by the sudden blaze of light. Emergency generator? His brain had time to form the thought, before he realized the truth. The staff had simply thrown open the blinds to let in the light of the blazing City. Doctors, nurses, even surgeons were working in the glare of the firestorm that was roaring up the hill towards them.

Paul ran from bed to bed, thinking: *No, this is wrong, it's all wrong, she can't be here.* These patients had all been admitted, and he knew there wouldn't have been time for that, but he couldn't get anybody to answer his questions, they were all so busy, so *intent,* but then at last he stopped a porter who told him, "You want to be downstairs, mate. Casualty's in the basement."

So he skidded down two flights of stairs, along another corridor, and burst into a huge room, lit by dozens of oil lamps whose coils of brown smoke hung heavy on the air.

Doors opened off to the left into smaller rooms; he could see beds, wheelchairs, tables, chairs, and torches held in gloved hands casting circles of light onto other gloved hands that were stitching wounds or applying dressings to burns.

Along one side of the main room, the injured were queuing for attention: white-faced, babbling, mute, shaking uncontrollably. The more seriously injured lay on trolleys in a corridor farther along, many still and silent, a few writhing with the pain of burns. One—an elderly woman with wispy gray hair and an open mouth—unmistakably dead.

He saw a warden he knew slightly near the back of the queue and asked him if he'd seen Elinor, but the man was too dazed to answer. Paul abandoned him, and began walking up the line, scanning every face, but there was no Elinor— and nobody else he knew to ask. At the head of the queue, he saw there was another smaller room: rows of benches crowded with people. He started walking along the rows, looking at face after face, panicked that when he saw her—*if* he saw her—he wouldn't recognize her. He kept seeing the old woman on the trolley: the open mouth, the staring eyes. Part of him was convinced the corpse was Elinor. It had been nothing like her, and yet he had to stop himself running back to make sure.

Still another room opened off this one. Here, three rows of benches faced a blank wall; people sat staring vacantly into space, waiting for somebody to come and claim them. He heard his voice calling "Elinor?" over and over again. Perhaps there was an echo, because the walls seemed to bounce the name back at him: *Elinor, Elinor.*

And then he saw her, sitting at the end of a bench, looking straight ahead. "Elinor?" She seemed to have trouble focusing on him. "It's me. Paul." He knelt down and reached for her hands, but she pulled them back. "Are you all right?"

The question seemed to plop into a deep well. She glanced from side to side and moistened her lips. "They say I can go."

Her face was gray; she had the hunched shoulders and anxious expression of smoke inhalation. She wasn't fit to be turned out. He looked round, angrily, but so many of the injuries he saw were worse than hers. And of course with an evacuation imminent they'd be clearing out anybody who could walk. "Come on," he said. "Let's get you home."

"Where's Kit?"

"Were you working with him?"

She nodded.

"He's fine. Queuing up outside, I think."

He was thinking he might beg a lift from the ambulance driver who'd brought him here, if he could find him, but in the event he didn't need to. A crowd of frustrated ambulance drivers had gathered outside the hospital entrance, and among them were Dana and Derek, who detached themselves from the group and came towards him. "Is she all right?" Dana asked.

"She's alive."

Until he heard himself say the word, he hadn't known it was true, and immediately he was flooded with relief, but he still had to get her home.

"Don't worry," Dana said. "We'll take you. If we can get out, that is."

Paul helped Elinor into the back of the ambulance, then turned to look at Dana, who was waiting to close the door. He mouthed: *Neville?* Dana shrugged, but Derek, who was standing a few feet behind her, shook his head.

It took a great deal of reversing, and not a little shouting, before they were able to get out of the queue. Paul tried to persuade Elinor to lie on the bunk, but she said she couldn't lie flat and so they sat, side by side, jolting and swaying as Dana swerved to avoid obstacles in the road. Lights flashed in the small windows and, once, there was a great clattering on the roof as more incendiaries fell—or perhaps it was just shrapnel from the ack-ack guns that seemed to have started up again, though Paul couldn't remember hearing the sirens.

Nearer home, the orange glow in the windows faded to black, and he was glad of it. Not long after, the jolting and bumping stopped. Footsteps sounded along the side of the ambulance, then Dana opened the door and pulled down the steps. Paul helped Elinor down onto the black, glistening pavement. She looked around her, then up to the windows of her flat. Dana kissed her good-bye, Derek slapped Paul on the shoulder, and then the two of them set off to rejoin the queue outside Bart's. Paul watched the red taillight diminishing into the dark, and the street seemed suddenly very quiet. The guns seemed to have stopped again, so probably it had been a false alarm.

Elinor was still looking up at the windows of her flat. There must have been times in the last few hours when she'd thought she wouldn't see it again. Her hands were so cut and bruised he had to fish the keys out of her pockets while she stood holding her arms away from her body, as helpless as a small child.

He thought she might find the stairs difficult and got behind her to push, but she snapped: "It's my *hands*, Paul. Not my *feet*." A brief glimpse of the old Elinor that came as an enormous relief.

Once inside the flat he settled her onto the sofa, then went into the kitchen and filled the kettle for tea. He kept glancing through the open door. She was sitting hunched forward, though more upright perhaps than she had been in the hospital. Her hands were held straight out in front of her. When the kettle boiled, he added a generous dollop of brandy to the tea, and carried the mug through to her.

As she drank, he looked at her more closely. She had several cuts to her forehead, though none very deep. Her hands were worse than her face. He fetched a pillow and blankets from the bed, thinking, as he pulled the counterpane back, that he caught a whiff of Neville, but he couldn't be sure and anyway it hardly mattered now. She snuggled into the blanket, but still wouldn't lie down. She was sitting right on the edge of the sofa, trying now and then to flex her spine, but still with her shoulders rounded.

He kept assessing her, noticing symptoms in a completely detached way. At the same time, he was terrified of losing her, though he knew it wasn't a rational fear. Most of this was shock. At times her eyes went completely blank. Somewhere in the depths of his mind, a thought was forming: that this helplessness of hers might be his opportunity. She needed him now; she'd have to take him back. Only then he looked up and caught her watching him. *Not so fast.* So she came and went: one moment, totally alert; the next, blank and limp.

"What happened?" he asked during one of her more alert spells. He knew she'd have to get it into words, probably tell the story over and over again, until its sting was drawn, but all he got back was a shrug. Too soon. So they sat in silence by the bluish light of the little popping gas fire until he thought he saw her eyelids start to droop. Then, just as she seemed about to drop off, she started awake again. "There were horses," she said. "Galloping towards us. Their manes were on fire."

Dray horses, they'd be. Probably shire horses, and they were huge. A brewery stables must have caught fire.

For a long time, it seemed that was all she was going to

say. He warmed up a tin of soup, but she didn't drink much of it. Her breathing seemed to be getting easier, though, and her color was definitely better. It might even be possible to get her to bed.

"I kept waving at him: *Go back, go back.*" She pushed her hands repeatedly against the air, and the movement brought on a fit of coughing. When it was over, she went on: "I could see the firemen were pulling out, but he didn't seem to understand, he just kept coming, and then the wall came down and all I could see was smoke and . . ."

Silence, for a time. Did she know? Feeling his way forward, he asked: "Did you see him again?"

She shook her head. Then, obviously afraid of the answer, she asked, "Did Derek say anything?"

"No."

"I hope he's all right."

Injecting scorn into his voice, he said: " 'Course he's all right! You know Neville—he'll outlive God."

She seemed willing to accept that, for the time being at least. He took the bowl and spoon from her. "You know, I think you'd be better off in bed."

"Yes, I think I would."

Leaning on his arm, she hobbled into the bedroom and sat on the side of the bed, while he knelt to take off her boots. She was shivering again, with shock or cold, so he got her under the blankets as fast as he could. It took several arrangements of all four pillows to get her comfortably propped up. "I'll be next door if you need anything." He hesitated. "You will call me, won't you . . . ?"

She nodded, without opening her eyes.

He went back into the living room, rolled up his overcoat to use as a pillow and stretched out on the sofa. It was too short for him, and lumpy besides—he doubted if he'd get much sleep. He closed his eyes, and saw shire horses galloping towards him with their manes on fire, as if the impossible had happened and the membrane dividing his brain from hers had become permeable. What lovers are supposed to want—except they weren't lovers anymore.

Perhaps he'd nodded off, because it seemed only a second later that he felt a jogging at his elbow, and opened his eyes to find her bending over him.

"Oh for God's sake, Paul, you can't possibly sleep like that. Come on, get into bed . . . We are *married,* after all."

That *"married"* was pure, unadulterated acid. Nevertheless, he got up and followed her.

Lying beside her on the bed he thought perhaps she'd drifted off to sleep, but then she said, "I keep seeing him walk towards me, you know that walk he has—and then that awful sound. It was like the building was screaming." She turned her head and looked at him. "*Why* didn't he go back?""

A long silence. He thought, hoped, she'd finished. So they lay, side by side, not speaking, not even looking at each other, while the long hours of darkness passed. He remembered the old couple on the bed, lying there as if they were stretched out on a tomb, with the silence spreading out around, while outside the fires raged and the bombs fell. How he'd pulled back the counterpane and found them holding hands. Elinor's breathing was quieter now. Something of the tension had gone from her shoulders and neck. He closed his eyes and tried to relax. Perhaps he slept. Finally, towards dawn, he became aware that he was awake, and so was she. "I've been thinking," he said. "I might get a little dog."

"*What?*"

"Just a thought."

He got out of bed and pulled the blackout curtains back. Sparrows were chirruping and fluttering in the gutters, there were footsteps and voices in the street below, a hum of traffic. Glancing back at the bed, he saw that Elinor was lying with one arm across her face. He waited a moment, hoping she'd take it away and look at him, but she didn't. Then he pushed the windows open, as wide as they would go, letting in the clear, cold air of a new day.

THIRTY-SIX

Ever since the raids ended, she'd been recording the progress of the ruins. If she'd ever thought about ruins at all, before the destruction of her house, she'd have said they were static, unchanging, or if they did change, it would be the work of centuries, decades at least, of wind and rain and scouring ice. But these ruins changed week by week, even day by day. And so, every morning, she set out to draw them; she scribbled notes as well in the margins of the drawings, diary entries, or sometimes just lists, mainly lists of the flowers and plants she found growing in the gardens of wrecked houses, but also, increasingly, out of the walls of the derelict buildings themselves. There seemed to be no crack so narrow, no fissure so apparently barren, it couldn't support the life of some weed or other. She even, as the days lengthened, became attached to particular plants: a clump of bright red flowers growing out of a sagging gutter, too high up to be identified, but bobbing about on the slight breeze, like the flowers in a mad woman's hat. And then, a few doors down—although now there were no doors—a great pool of forget-me-nots caught in the hollow of a wall. *Remember*

These ruins were all close to home; gaps in terraces she'd known intimately as a student, walking every day to and from the Slade. There were far more impressive ruins surrounding St. Paul's, most of those created in a single night: the night Kit Neville died. Her grief for Kit was unexpectedly sharp and deep, and she wasn't ready to revisit the courts and alleys they'd walked down together on the night he died.

In good weather, she stayed out all day, filling one sketchbook after another, though she had no idea where this project might be leading, if indeed it was leading anywhere. It was some time now since she'd done a big painting. There'd been the dead child on the pavement, and another ambitious project after that: children queuing outside Warren Street Underground station to claim their family's place on the platforms. Clark hadn't liked either. "It's not the quality of the work, it's . . ." And his voice had trailed away into silence.

Every afternoon, around about five o'clock, she packed up and went home, sometimes stopping at one of the barrows at the corner of Store Street to buy vegetables for dinner. There wasn't much choice, but the cauliflowers and carrots were usually all right. And the apples, though wizened and rather small, hardly bigger than crab apples, were good enough for apple pie. Tonight, she was cooking for two, which these days was quite a pleasant experience. Paul was coming to supper. They saw each other regularly, met for drinks or tea and buns, even went on outings to Kew Gardens or Richmond Park, often accompanied by that wretched little dog he'd bought, a brown-and-white Jack Russell terrier, rather unimaginatively called Jack—not even Russell, which might have been marginally better. She knew Paul would have liked more than occasional outings with her. He'd more than once hinted they should start thinking about living together again, but she'd grown to value her independence. Living alone is a skill, and she seemed to have reacquired it. She actually enjoyed having nobody but herself to consult. And yes, of course there were times when loneliness crept up and bit her on the backside, but she had plenty of teeth—and she was learning to bite back.

The barrow boys—always "boys" though some of them were old men—were mainly market gardeners from Kent. She'd got to know a few of them, though these, today, were new. Two men, one elderly, the other middle-aged—their profiles so similar they could only be father and son—and a ginger-haired boy, white-faced and gangly, with surprisingly big, raw hands. She watched him weighing potatoes, dropping one very small one into the pan to make up the weight. Then he poured them into a paper bag, twisting it briskly to produce two nice, neat ears, and handed it across to the customer. As he did so, he half turned towards her, and she saw that it was Kenny.

It couldn't be.

But it was.

At last it was her turn to be served. She asked for a cabbage and a pound of apples. "Oh, and carrots," she said, all the time staring at him, thinking: *No.* He'd grown, my God, he'd grown, and the shape of his face had changed, but he was at the age when boys do change—sometimes almost beyond recognition. He hadn't noticed her yet. He was so busy scooping and weighing and pouring into bags and then giving the bags that final, expert twist. You could see the pride he took in his own skills. There he was: doing a proper job, earning money. In his own estimation, at least: a man among men.

When she came to pay, he looked her in the face for the first time, and suddenly blushed, shedding, in the process, several months of growth.

"Hello, Kenny."

What to say next? *We thought you were dead?* Well, why not—it was true. Glancing over his shoulder—evidently chatting to the customers was not encouraged—he said, "Me mam couldn't stick it in there, she couldn't breathe, she got herself into a right old panic, we had to come out . . ."

She whispered, "Do you know how many people died?"

"Yes, I heard."

"So what did you do?"

"Walked all the way to me nanna's in Bermondsey. Then she got bombed and we got on the back of a lorry and went to Kent." He kept looking over his shoulder. "And I got this job."

"You're busy." She handed the money over. "I'm glad you're all right."

"Glad" wasn't the word. She could have burst out singing.

At the corner, she stopped and looked back, watching him move on to the next customer, and the next. Then, smiling, she turned into Gower Street and began walking home, burdened by drawing pads and pencil cases and shopping bags, but still quickening her pace until she was almost running. She couldn't wait to get home and tell Paul.

ABOUT THE AUTHOR

Pat Barker is most recently the author of *Toby's Room* and *Life Class*, as well as the highly acclaimed Regeneration Trilogy: *Regeneration; The Eye in the Door*, winner of the Guardian Fiction Prize; and *The Ghost Road*, winner of the Booker Prize. She lives in the north of England.